beware

that

girl

ALSO BY TERESA TOTEN

The Unlikely Hero of Room 13B

beware that girl

TERESA TOTEN

EMBER

Text copyright © 2016 by Teresa Toten
Cover art copyright © 2018 by Javier Retales Botijero/Getty Images

All rights reserved. Published in the United States by Ember, an imprint of Random House Children's Books, a division of Penguin Random House LLC, New York. Originally published in hardcover in the United States by Delacorte Press, an imprint of Random House Children's Books, New York, and simultaneously in hardcover by Doubleday Canada, an imprint of Penguin Random House Canada Limited, Toronto, in 2016.

Ember and the E colophon are registered trademarks of Penguin Random House LLC.

Visit us on the Web! GetUnderlined.com

Educators and librarians, for a variety of teaching tools, visit us at RHTeachersLibrarians.com

The Library of Congress has cataloged the hardcover edition of this work as follows:
Name: Toten, Teresa, author.
Title: Beware that girl / Teresa Toten.
Description: New York : Delacorte Press, [2016] | Summary: When a scholarship girl and a wealthy classmate become friends, their bond is tested when a handsome young teacher separately influences the girls in order to further his less-than-admirable interests.
Identifiers: LCCN 2015028074 | ISBN 978-0-553-50790-4 (hc) | ISBN 978-0-553-50791-1 (glb) | ISBN 978-0-553-50792-8 (ebook)
Subjects: | CYAC: Friendship—Fiction. | Secrets—Fiction. | Mental Illness—Fiction. | Psychopaths—Fiction. | Teacher-student relationships—Fiction.
Classification: LCC PZ7.T6458 Be 2016 | DDC [Fic]—dc23

ISBN 978-0-553-50793-5 (trade pbk.)

Printed in the United States of America
10 9 8 7 6 5 4 3 2 1
First Ember Edition 2018

Random House Children's Books supports the First Amendment and celebrates the right to read.

For Ken, again and always

"Will you walk into my parlour?" said the Spider to the Fly.

—MARY HOWITT

beware
that
girl

KATE AND OLIVIA

Neither girl moved. The young blonde on the bed didn't move because she couldn't, and the blonde in the chair didn't because, well, it seemed that she couldn't either.

Two doctors, a nurse and an orderly barged in, disturbing their silence. They lifted the body in the bed using a sheet, changed the bedding, checked her pulse and heart rate, tapped, touched and shone lights into unseeing eyes. This time they removed the long cylindrical tube that had been taped to the girl's mouth. The withdrawal of the tube was ugly.

The body seized, arced and then spasmed.

When they left, the girl in the chair resumed her vigil numbed by the reek of ammonia and latex. The doctors never told her anything, so she'd stopped asking. The bedridden girl was attached to a tangled mess of tubes and wires. They led from her battered body to several monitors and a single pole that branched out like a steel tree blooming with bags of IV fluid. Things beeped and hummed on a random timetable that neither girl heard. In the forty-eight hours since their arrival, the girl in the chair rarely broke

1

her vigil to stretch, sleep or go to the bathroom. Her normally perfect blond hair clung to her scalp, greased darker now with sweat, mud and dried blood.

She sat spellbound by the monitors, by the ever-changing colored dots, the indecipherable graphs and especially the wavy green line. The green line was important. She didn't waver, not in all those hours—not until Detective Akimoto cleared his throat in the doorway. She struggled to meet his eyes.

"I'm sorry, but I'm going to need you to step outside for a moment."

The girl turned to her friend, whose mouth was red and angry from where the tape had been ripped away.

The detective flipped open a small black notepad.

He clicked his pen several times.

"Now, please."

Other men were outside, milling about the corridor. Cops.

"We have a few questions about your friend, and also about a . . . Mr. Marcus Redkin."

Mark.

She rose slowly. The room swayed in the effort. "Yes, sir." She stole one more glance at the wavy green line.

The girl on the bed was no longer inert, not entirely. But no one saw. Words fell out of her mouth, silently slipping off the sheets and onto the ground.

But no one heard.

THURSDAY, SEPTEMBER 17

KATE

I'm not a pathological liar and I don't lie for fun. I only lie because I have to. Thing is, I've always lied, because I've always had to. I'm comfortable with the weight of my lies. So I'm good. That's all there is to it. Well, that and I want a better life. Wait, that's a lie. I want a *big* life.

And another thing—dogs and little kids love me, so there goes that lame old saying. Demented rich girls love me too. I am *that* friend, the how-did-I-live-without-you friend. The you-are-such-a-riot friend. The friend with the shoulders that are soggy from your tears. I am the lifeline friend, and lifelines come with a price. But I digress. Love that word, *digress*. It's snotty and not as easy to work into a sentence as you'd think.

I'd been watching her for days.

The first few days were all about the hunt, about not walking into walls. There was that familiar head-spinning hell of where to go, who was who, don't make an ass of yourself at the new school,

3

etc., etc. But I can focus like nobody else. A handful of girls were examined and dismissed. Too regular, too normal, too together or (the true kiss of death) not genuinely loaded, even though they seemed to have all the trappings. I know the difference. Before coming here, I spent most of high school out west in the very best private girls' schools. I was the scholarship kid, the boarder. The girl you convinced your parents to bring home for weekends, for holidays. I've had plenty of practice.

See, I know how whack these girls are behind their armor of Range Rovers and Louboutins. There had to be *someone*. My meal ticket was in this senior class somewhere.

And then, at the beginning of week two, there she was—all born blonde and rich and just messed up enough. Beautiful, no cliques and reeking of Lexapro or Paxil or something. Mind you, that could apply to half the school. But this girl was like an extra. There was definitely something. Olivia Michelle Sumner: if that doesn't spell money, I don't know what does. She was head-to-toe Barneys and Bloomies, preppy with a price. The rest of the girls gave her a wide berth even as they squealed, "Welcome back, Olivia!" "You're back!" "Great to see you! Hey, wow!" But they weren't her people. That was clear. Olivia kind of glided around on remote control. There was a story there. Excellent. Olivia Sumner and I shared only one class, AP English, but that's all it takes.

Watch me now.

Pay close attention.

Survival of the fittest, baby.

4

FRIDAY, SEPTEMBER 18

OLIVIA

Olivia cradled the phone, shaking her head. "No, Dad, it was fine. More than fine, *really*. Just like you said." She paced the length of the sunken living room. When that was no longer calming, she stepped up into the dining room, circling the stainless steel table, then veered through the library and eventually invaded all four bedrooms one by one. Olivia stayed out of the kitchen. Anka was throwing pots around and cursing the Cuisinart. "The whole week was a nonevent, just like we thought. It was the right decision not to transfer out."

She found herself back in the living room. "No, the teachers didn't make an obvious fuss, but they let me know they were there for me in the very best Waverly fashion." Olivia hovered over more than sat on the mohair chaise before getting up and pacing again.

"Well, as I suspected, AP English is going to be intense because I got Ms. Hornbeck again. Thank God I've already read the Albee play and the Cormac McCarthy. But I may need a tutor to keep me in solid merit-scholar range, okay?" Where was that Cormac McCarthy book? She drifted to her room, forgot why she went there and drifted out again.

"No, I can sleepwalk through math and physics, you know that." Now she was in her father's bedroom. Sleek burled oaks and flannels in varying hues of gray and taupe embraced her. She let them. Olivia loved his room. The soft buttery gold of the LED art lights glowed against the Modigliani and Caravaggio sketches. The art rested quietly against walls covered with charcoal fabric that warmed the room, making it feel safe, making it feel like her father. "No, nowhere. I'm buried in work already. It'll take me all weekend to dig myself out. Yeah." She nodded. "Just a little rusty."

The rest of the penthouse featured impenetrable modern Brazilian art juxtaposed with ancient Chinese sculptures. It looked as if it was curated, which of course it was. Wife number two. But here, in his haven, was the closest her father came to the traditional, and to himself.

"No, just every other Wednesday now. I told you that yesterday." She stifled a groan. "Yeah, still five fifteen. Look, it was Dr. Tamblyn's suggestion. He's super positive." Olivia glimpsed herself in his mirror and turned away. "Of course I am. Check with Dr. Tamblyn whenever you want. I won't ever go off the meds again. Lesson learned, big-time." She gripped the phone so tightly that it dug a groove in the palm of her hand. "I promise, *never*. Can we stop? I'm good, we're good. Besides, Anka is here and she's a hawk. Hey, you just tie up all those big international deals so that we can keep the lights on in this place." She was smiling, but Olivia could feel the weight of his worry pressing against her.

"Well, you know"—she sat on and then got up off the manicured bed—"they were fine." What time was it? Her stomach began to foam. No longer soothed by the Modigliani and all that gray flannel, Olivia was on the move again. Back to the living room, back to the floor-to-ceiling windows stretching the length of the penthouse. She became mesmerized by the art outside the windows, the whole expanse of Central Park and the beckoning lights from the Dakota. Having New York at her feet cushioned her soul.

"I don't really know the girls, Dad. Remember, they were juniors last year, a full year younger, and last year, well, was last year. But they've been fine." Have they? There must be gossip. Did it matter? "Come on, it's Waverly, Dad. Anyone who's anyone has their shrink on speed dial." The sky had slipped out of its silky purple dress into a basic black. "I'm sure I'll find a friend. And if not, it's only a year, right?"

She liked the inky-black sky best, always had. It was soothing. "No, I didn't mean that. Of course I'll find friends. Hey, do you have to stay in Chicago before you head out to Singapore?" She had to stay focused. "On Sunday? That's great, Dad! Does Anka know? Okay, I'll tell her. No, I'd rather just go to our bistro. I'll call."

Olivia walked back to the chaise. "Is seven thirty okay?" The foam in her stomach bubbled. She had once described the foam as a pink thing, a mixture of warm blood and spit. "Yes. No, that'll be great, Dad. Can't wait." Dr. Tamblyn had said the medication would eventually take care of that too. He'd also said that she had to be religious about taking it exactly on time.

"Sure. Stop—you know I'll be fine. I love you too." Olivia put the phone down. She sat on the chaise with her full weight this time.

And waited.

"Olivia? You off za phone wit Mr. Sumner?" Anka strode in, wiping her hands on her apron. The housekeeper had a formidable collection of aprons. "Is not your time for za medications tablet? Is six thirty o'clock. Should be at six o'clock, no? You want me to get your waters? Olivia?"

She was going to have to talk to Anka about backing off. Olivia knew the schedule.

Instead, she nodded, sighed and then waited to *feel* something. Anything.

MONDAY, SEPTEMBER 21

KATE

I pretty much live in a sewer.

Making the leap from sewer to the prize of Yale is starting to shake my focus, and believe me, that's saying something.

I deserve better. Way better.

I'm this year's Waverly Scholar, and that baby comes with a decent stipend. I also put in mornings at the school admin office *and* I'm working my ass off at the market with two ten-hour shifts every weekend—*and* still this rathole is the best I can do. My home for the past few months has been a converted storage room in the basement of Chen's Chinese Market and Apothecary. I'm broke. Grooming costs are a killer, even in Chinatown; hair, makeup, nails—it adds up. Don't get me started on accessories. Thank God for uniforms.

Waverly, of course, doesn't know about Chen's. They think I'm living with my nonexistent aunt. I was a boarder at all the other private schools, but Waverly doesn't have boarders. What it does have is the best record in the country of getting its students into their first-choice college picks. Thing is, they had to be assured that my accommodation was locked down before I got the package. I needed an address. Hence the sewer. Like I said, I only lie when I have to, and I have to a lot.

I haven't unpacked. I won't. This is *temporary*. Besides, I'm freaked that the slime that's weeping down the walls will marry up with the stink of the decaying cabbage and infect my brand-new secondhand uniforms. I've got an iron bed topped with shredded Spider-Man bedding, a small round table, one aluminum chair, a decent mirror, a TV tray that I use as a night table, a sink scarred by rust and a floor cabinet with a Coleman-like stove propped on it. I've lived in worse, like those times in between foster nightmares and boarding, but it's harder now. I know what's out there and I want some.

Alarmingly, Mrs. Chen does not appear to like me. I don't like not being liked. It makes me nervous. Being liked is the biggest arrow in my quiver. Exhibit A in the "not liked" column is that despite the fact I am strictly "front of the house" material, Mrs. Chen usually has me in the alley unloading the bok choy and mango shipments. My charm offensive landed with a thud on Mrs. Chen's tiny slippered feet, and Mr. Chen seems to live in fear of her. So I take my cues from him and stick to hauling boxes, prepping and pricing the veg, and staying invisible. I know I'm not the first student to partake of the Chens' indentured-dungeon opportunity, but it's a sure bet that I'm their first Waverly student *and* their first white chick—or *gweilo*, as I've heard them call me. I think it means "ghost girl" or "foreigner" or something. Either is perfect. On the bright side, I eat really well, although it's mainly vegetables and fruit. I've become pretty handy with a wok, and my skin has never looked better.

I'd kill for a steak.

In comparison, the Waverly office gig is like a day at Canyon Ranch. Waverly's classrooms and lecture theaters are wireless and outfitted with the latest Smart Boards and apps, but their filing system is right out of Hogwarts. They brought in a consultant last year, and I'm helping with the grunt work of transitioning all their paper archives onto servers braced by clouds. They need me.

And I need access to that system.

I'm always the first one in, at 6:55 a.m. Mr. Jefferson, Waverly's building services manager—or head janitor, in other words—opens up for me. Even Ms. Draper, the registrar and Olympic-caliber workaholic, doesn't get in until 7:05. My likeability quotient is through the roof with her and pretty well everyone else in Admin, including the head, Ms. Goodlace; Mr. Rolph, head of the Upper School; Ms. Kelly, head of the Lower School; Dr. Kruger, the guidance teacher/school shrink; and most important, the administrative assistants, Miss Shwepper and Mrs. Colson. Every school has a Miss Shwepper or a Mrs. Colson. Both ladies are older than God, and they hold the real keys to power because they know where all the bodies are buried. Student crap and staff crap, it's all color-coded and kept safe under their over-processed hair.

Waverly's staff and directors are still awaiting the much-anticipated arrival of some hotshot cyber-savvy fund-raiser to be the head of advancement. But Mr. Rolph will have to swim alone in Waverly's estrogen pool a while longer, because Mr. Mark Redkin was immediately swept into a northeast conference on the future of independent school endowments.

When Draper charged in today, she doubled back toward me. "You're showing admirable initiative, Kate. You've beat me in every day so far." She perched on the edge of Shwepper's desk, which I used as a staging area for my files. Draper had a whippet-lean body that hardened her looks some. She'd missed the memo on picking "face or figure after forty." I dissected her scent. The top note

11

was Jo Malone's Orange Blossom. The whole school was into Jo Malone. They might as well have issued it along with the eggplant jackets and gray pleated skirts. Under the Orange Blossom was a hint of expensive shampoo, the kind you buy at the Vidal Sassoon salon. Sharp architectural haircuts to match her sharp architectural suits. You could cut yourself on the woman. Struggling under those scents was a hint of black coffee, a breath mint and the unmistakable stink of Camels. My old man smoked Camels.

Our registrar was a secret smoker.

Draper seemed to be waiting for me to speak. I hadn't acknowledged the compliment. That was sloppy.

"Just trying to make myself indispensable here, ma'am."

"And you've accomplished that in record time, my dear. This office is going kicking and screaming into the modern world with your help. And when Mr. Redkin gets here . . ." She paused, lost herself for a second. "Well, I just want you to know that we're pleased."

I tried blushing. It usually worked.

"Thank you, ma'am."

Draper nodded before striding into her office, which contained the all-important registrar's computer. That's where I was headed tomorrow. I had to get here by 6:30 a.m. Everything I needed to know would be in that computer. Somebody at Waverly could use a roommate to fill her existential void. Hopefully, that somebody was Olivia Sumner. I could see it straight ahead. The good life. A clear path to the prize.

Nothing gets in my way.

TUESDAY, SEPTEMBER 22

KATE

6:34 AM

The near-comatose computer was taking forever to sputter to life. I knew that Miss Shwepper and Mrs. Colson were attached to their museum pieces, patiently waiting for the whole digital fad to blow over, but what was Draper doing with this behemoth? The entire front office looked like it was being prepped for a 1993 Microsoft commercial.

Okay, okay, come to Mama. Come on. All right! Waverly student records ... Finally! The script rolled in on lazy paragraphs, but there they were. The student records were organized alphabetically according to graduating year. What would mine contain? No time. *Okay, okay.* I hadn't even turned the lights on for fear that Mr. Jefferson might come to check. Every creak in the old oak floors caused my stomach to pitch. I typed in "Olivia Michelle Sumner" and held my breath while the screen took its customary three to five years to load. Who works like this? With this? *Loading, loading ...*

Got ya!

It was a standard bare-bones registration, but it also had a one-page report appended.

STUDENT RECORDS PROFILE
SOCIAL WORK REPORT

STUDENT'S NAME:	**Olivia Michelle Sumner**
STUDENT NUMBER:	**624501**
DOB:	*2 September 1997*
GENDER:	*Female*
SCHOOL:	*The Waverly School*
FATHER:	*Mr. Geoffrey Sumner*
MOTHER:	*Mrs. Elizabeth Sumner*
	(née Whitaker)—Deceased
PRESENT AT MEETING:	*Dr. Virginia Kruger,*
	Dr. Russell Tamblyn,
	Mr. Geoffrey Sumner

BACKGROUND INFORMATION: *Student spent ten weeks as an inpatient and six as an outpatient at Houston Medical.*

ASSESSMENT OF CURRENT FUNCTIONING: *The presenting psychological issues are fully resolved as per the readmittance policy and according to Houston's assessment documents, provided by Dr. Tamblyn.*

GOAL/INTERVENTION: *None required.*

SUMMARY AND RECOMMENDATIONS: *Dr. Tamblyn and Mr. Sumner requested that the student's Readmittance and Assessment Summary remain sealed. All applications for the release of confidential information would as of this date be*

denied. Dr. Armstrong concurred and assured Mr. Sumner that
Ms. Goodlace, Head of School, also concurred.

Dr. E. Armstrong   4 September

Sealed? What was sealed? That had to be good. Hmm, mother deceased . . . I got lost in that one until I realized it was 6:46 and I had to start the laborious process of logging out. Okay, so there was good stuff there, although I didn't know what exactly. Olivia was hospitalized? Why? I mean, that in itself wasn't remarkable. Anorexia and substance abuse were the go-to issues at private schools, but anxiety disorders and depression were fast closing in on the top spots. Was it one of those? Something else?

I was safely lugging out boxes of file folders to presort when I heard Ms. Goodlace's unmistakable footsteps. I didn't have to turn around. The head of school had a solid, serious footfall like the seriously solid person she was. All she wore day in and day out were two-inch Stuart Weitzman pumps that had to be older than I was. But the thing was, they were different each day. I notice things like that. Goodlace must have stockpiled like a hundred pairs when they were in vogue fifty years ago and had them in heavy rotation ever since. It was early for her. Draper wasn't even here yet.

"Good morning, Kate. My, you're in early."

"I could say the same about you, ma'am."

"Touché." She almost smiled, but she looked too preoccupied to see it through. "Our much-heralded director of advancement is finally arriving, and I want to get a jump on my notes for our meeting at nine. Our board, and certainly this office, is"—she cleared her throat—"greatly anticipating his arrival."

"Well, fund-raising is the lifeblood of a school like this. I learned that at all my other schools."

"Did you? Yes, yes, it is." She paused. "And I am sure Mr. Redkin will be a tremendous asset. So you know why *I'm* here. Why are *you* here so early?"

"There's a lot to do, even in the presort. The file cabinets are a bit of a mess. Actually, the files are kind of unbelievable." I glared at the boxes for effect.

"Kate, you're the Waverly Scholar, not the Waverly slave." She joined me in box glaring. "I can't have people concerned about your welfare, after all."

"I think we both know that no one would be all that concerned, ma'am."

"Not true, Kate. Not true," she said as she walked away. "I would be concerned."

Goodlace was as decent as these types come, so who knows, maybe she did give a fart. But it wasn't enough. I knew from before. I needed way more to get through the year, to get to where I was going. I needed an Olivia to care.

"Yes, ma'am. Thank you, ma'am," I said to her back.

MONDAY, SEPTEMBER 28

OLIVIA

It looked as if the contents of Olivia's closet had barfed on her bed. Five maroon school jackets—ranging from extremely fitted to boyfriend-style and from sparkly new to charmingly distressed— wrestled with eleven crisply laundered white shirts that hailed from Barneys rather than the school tuck shop. Struggling under that pile were four short to very short gray flannel kilts with mandatory silver kilt pins from Tiffany's, as well as a rat's nest of maroon-and-gray-striped school ties. There was a small mountain of tights in various hues and textures, all unopened and likely to remain that way. A senior wouldn't be caught dead in tights in the middle of a blizzard, let alone on a fall day. Seniors wore kneesocks with the elastic appropriately stretched out, making it imperative to keep yanking them up. There were uniforms within uniforms—always had been and always would be.

Olivia scrunched up one of the pristine shirts and sat on it for good measure as she slipped on her baggy kneesocks. Those steps complete, she tucked the freshly wrinkled shirt into her second-shortest skirt and reached for her most fitted jacket. It was her third pass at the complete outfit and it was the correct one, the right blend of caring and not giving a damn.

This is how the routine had always played out. After a full thirty-five minutes under a searing shower, she would sort through and discard the contents of her closet with an ever-increasing burden of urgency. With a choice finally made, Olivia would race back into her bathroom suite to begin the thirty-seven-minute routine of hair and makeup, emerging dewy and seemingly fresh-faced. With moments to spare, she'd gulp down her morning meds with the green smoothie that Anka had whipped up. Breakfast over, the housekeeper would shuffle to Olivia's room to begin the process of re-engorging the closet, while Olivia shoved her feet into one-size-too-small, just-so-scuffed Doc Martens and grabbed her black Prada backpack. She was "perfect." Not that it mattered. It's just the way things were done.

Before she left, Olivia always called out: "Okay, I'm off. Later, Anka! You have a great day!" And Anka, buried deep in the walk-in closet, always called back: "Good luck, Miss Olivia. God blessing you all za day." Neither heard the other's actual words, but both were certain that they had been wished a day of miracles.

Waverly was a handsome old stone mansion just up the street on Fifth. Olivia always used that walking time to prepare herself. This year, she even prayed a couple of times. That was new. Prayer was not any part of the cognitive behavioral therapy that had been doled out at the Houston hospital last year, but it was big with her roommate, Jackie, who was in for near-crippling OCD and cutting. Jackie maintained that it helped the "traps" in her head, and besides, what could it hurt? Concluding that the logic was sound, Olivia took up occasional praying with indifferent enthusiasm.

She glided through the heavily carved Waverly doors, past her locker and straight to Ms. Hornbeck's AP English. Olivia nodded, smiled and "heyed" at all the correct girls. She even feigned interest when Madison Benner panted hysterically about the dreamy new director of advancement. "Wait 'til you see him! OH, MY GOD! And I mean it. No one that hot has walked through these halls in a hundred years!"

"So I keep hearing. Can't wait to get a peek!" Olivia delivered this with dripping envy, which she was sure was the emotion called for. A small victory, but worth noting.

She steeled herself for AP English and Sylvia Plath. Olivia didn't "get" Plath, but she knew she should and that just made the abstruseness of her poetry all the more galling. They were going to dissect "Lady Lazarus." She could speak to it analytically, but that was never enough for Hornbeck, who wanted her students to engage with the material on some gut-wrenching emotional level.

Olivia would have to hire help, and soon.

"Fasten your seat belt for another mental car wreck."

It was the scholarship kid, new from out west or somewhere. Olivia had already noticed how the other seniors had been weighing, judging and, in the end, vying for her. The girl started rummaging in her bag—last year's Chloé, but still a Chloé. She was supposed to be some kind of genius, noticeable even in a school choking on them.

"You think? If it is, it's beyond my mental capacity," said Olivia. "Me and Plath are an epic nonstarter."

The scholarship kid had excellent hair. A Bergdorf Blonde, like most of the school, but it was styled all loose and beachy-like—a bit messy, a bit stiff. Superb. Olivia got annoyed all over again about Plath.

The scholarship kid rolled her eyes in sympathy. She was pretty even in the eye rolling.

"Plath is a way easy ride for me. Maybe you have to be crazy to really get her."

She knew how to wear her blazer too. Secondhand maybe, but boyfriend-style. The girls were still milling about the seats near the back of the small lecture room.

"My name is Olivia."

"I know." The scholarship girl smiled. "I remember from our first class. You're kind of noticeable." She turned toward Olivia. "I'm Kate."

"So, Kate . . . poetry—Plath, you really get her?"

"Sure." Kate shrugged. "I did my entrance essay on Plath, and apparently it was enough to get me into this place. It's physics that's going to get me tossed out."

And right then, Olivia, who had not made an impulsive decision since her return to Waverly, decided it was time to do just that. There was no weighing and measuring of outcomes, no deliberating about implications and consequences. "Physics?" she said. "Physics is a breeze. I have a feeling we can work something out."

Olivia sat and patted the seat next to her.

FRIDAY, OCTOBER 2

KATE

Step one, contact—total success. Step two, meeting in the library re: AP Physics—even better. It was a bit of a challenge to pretend to be unable to follow Olivia. There's a fine line between slight confusion and hopeless stupidity, a shorter road than you'd think. I'd made Olivia feel like she was an award-winning tutor by the end of the session. She asked me over to her place on Sunday night so I could return the favor with "Lady Lazarus." So big win all around. Atta girl.

Yet.

I couldn't hold on to "Atta girl." I was sitting in the dark on the Spider-Man sheets on my cot, trying to think about other things—about Olivia, about the prize, about, well, just about anything else. White-knuckling it. Impending change does that to me. A lot of stuff does that to me. It just happens. I don't want to get sucked back, but back I go, over and over again. I could hear the rain pinging off the sheet-metal roof on the back shed. I should study. I should touch up my nails. I should . . . but I couldn't't. I pushed it away, but it pushed back—the evidence, the memory. See, I was a liar even then, even when I was ten.

The peeling wood-framed windows were eight feet tall. They had that old wavy kind of glass that was useless against the cold but made the sunshine extra pretty. Class hadn't even started and already chalk dust was swirling and somersaulting in long skinny beams of captured sun. I got hypnotized by stuff like that. Not this time, though. This time I stood at attention in front of the teacher's desk. Chalk, erasers, a box of HB pencils and paper clips were in the first drawer on the left. A strap was all by itself in the second one, and a Bible and pink crystal rosary beads were in the bottom.

"But see, the thing is . . . the nuns are always the worst!" I shifted from one foot to the other. "No offense or anything."

"None taken." Sister Rose smiled. "And just why is that, Katie?"

"Well, you know, they . . . you all make such a big deal about it, especially, especially on the Friday before Father's Day. Everyone feels all sorry for me and gives me these fake sad looks."

This would have been enough for Mrs. Cotter, my grade four teacher back at St. David's. Sister raised one pretty eyebrow.

"But lying is a sin, Katie."

Sister Rose was tougher than she looked.

"But, Sister, it isn't a lie. Not really. All I'm asking is that I be allowed to do what I do every year. You said it was real touching and everything when I told you about it a while ago. Remember?"

Sister nodded.

"I still make my Father's Day card, just like the rest of the class. Then, after school, I walk over to Prospect Park, which used to be Dad's favorite, and then, then I bury the card in the flower bed in the corner. And then I wish him a happy Father's Day!" I gave her the smile I'd been practicing since 6:20 a.m.

Sister raised her eyebrow again.

"After I've prayed for the deliverance of his immortal soul."

I checked the clock: 8:25. The bell would ring at 8:30.

"So all I'm saying—I mean, asking—is that since this is a new school for me, couldn't we please, just this once, not tell the whole class that poor Katie's father is dead? And, and then make everyone count their blessings by saying fifteen rosary rounds at recess? I don't want them to feel sorry for me, and I really don't want them to hate my guts because of the stupid rosary rounds. No offense. Sorry, Sister."

"None taken, Katie." She patted my hand.

Sister Rose had soft, cool hands all the time, no matter what. All nuns have soft, cool hands. It's like a holy thing.

"So you see? We're not lying, not really. Not even with that 'by omission' thing, because it's not like anyone's asking. See? We just don't have to advertise it."

Sister Rose looked down at her hands. Her lashes seemed to shade half her face.

"And, and . . . I've been praying on it for weeks—real hard, like—and, well, and I bet that Jesus would be okay with all of this."

Sister bit her lower lip and frowned. She did this whenever she was trying to stop herself from laughing.

"You are impossible, Katie."

"That's what my mom says, Sister."

She shook her head.

I had her.

The bell rang.

"Okay, Katie," she sighed. "We won't make an announcement about your deceased father. No rosary novenas." She put her soft, cool hand on mine again. "This will be our little secret, Katie. Not a lie, a secret."

You had to hand it to me.

I was good.

We got to the card-making right after religious studies. Mary-Catherine and I worked on ours together. Mary-Catherine had a deeply superior artistic soul. Just like me. So we'd been best friends since practically my first week at St. Raymond's. Mary-Catherine knew about it all. Well, except for the part where I really wanted Mr. Sutherland—Mary-Catherine's father—to be my father.

Sometimes I wanted it so much I felt sick.

He was such a nice dad.

Mr. Sutherland was an important businessman. He had four different suits and a dark brown briefcase with worn handles. He worked in an office with a door in one of those big towers on Wall Street. His office was on the thirty-fourth floor! When school was over, Mary-Catherine and I were going to meet him in his personal office and then we were going to go out for lunch.

He said.

Mr. Sutherland called me "slugger" because I was on the Christie Pirates softball team. I was deeply artistic and athletic. It's a rare combination, Mr. Sutherland said. Sometimes, when he got home early, he would get the three of us big tall glasses of Coca-Cola with lots of ice and then ask us about school or our friends or just stuff. He asked me too, not just Mary-Catherine.

I hated Coca-Cola.

But I drank it right down and I always said, "Thanks, Mr. Sutherland!" And he always winked at me and said, "Well, you're welcome, slugger."

Anyway, Mary-Catherine and I were hands down making the most fancy cards in the whole class. Father Bob said that God is in the details. Our stuff was always bursting with God. My card said "You Are My Hero" on the front and "Happy Father's Day to the BEST Dad in the World" over a pop-up striped tie on the inside.

I headed straight to the park after school.

I looked all sad.

You never know. Sister Rose could go right by in the school van or something.

There was a spot of bare earth behind the orangey roses and just in front of the yellow bushes. I dug a hole with my ruler, then I folded up my card and buried it. I made a sign of the cross. Not a little fast one in the middle of your chest but a big one—just in case.

I prayed.

Not for my father.

For Mary-Catherine's.

I prayed that God in his infinite wisdom would figure out how to make Mr. Sutherland my father. And that he would do this without hurting Mrs. Sutherland, who's nice enough, or Mary-Catherine, who's my very best friend, or my mother, who has been hurt bad already. Thank you very much. Amen.

I prayed a lot when I was ten. I have not prayed since.

SUNDAY, OCTOBER 4

OLIVIA

It was going to be an A-list party, and that would have mattered to Olivia before, sort of. But not now. Suze Sheardown and Emily Wong were throwing a birthday bash for Alejandra Morena, whose parents were in Colombia. All the best kids from Waverly and Rigby, Waverly's brother school, would be there. Alejandra was harmless and sweet in that "which one is she again?" way. A total yawn, in other words. But that wasn't why Olivia's answer was no.

Been there, done that, directed the movie. Olivia sighed, swallowed a pill and started wandering through the penthouse. She had lobbied hard for a redo of grade twelve at Waverly rather than somewhere else. As he did with almost everything, her father had smoothed the way and reentry was a nonissue. Why *had* she been so hell-bent on returning? She couldn't remember. It didn't matter. Olivia kept her distance, but when she had to, she mimicked the pitch-perfect giggling and the squeals of fake shock, fake outrage and fake sympathy—all the hallmarks of any good girls' private school. It was easy.

What threw Olivia was how much older she felt than the other girls. Sure, some of them were already eighteen, but when she was gliding through Waverly's halls, Olivia felt like she was forty. This further dampened any desire to hit the party circuit. What drowned it completely was the lack of a posse. Olivia didn't have a crew anymore. Her former best friends, Anita, Gwen and Jessica, were away at college. Oh sure, they sent flowers like clockwork, and they still texted and messaged on occasion, but on Facebook, so . . . you know. She could hardly walk into a party alone. Olivia needed at least one pal. You didn't need a phalanx in grade twelve—a phalanx was for grade ten. One would do, one awesome person, and Olivia was pretty sure that she had found her in Kate. Together, they would make proper entrances at a couple of select parties.

She checked her watch, which was actually her father's Rolex. Apparently, wearing men's watches was still a thing this year. Olivia was the one who'd started that trend last fall. Her father had an extensive collection, but he only wore the Cartier that Olivia's mother had bought him. Kate never wore a watch. Other than that, she was right on or just ahead of trend. A good sign. That she did so while appearing not to care was an even better one.

A month into school and Kate had not settled into any one clique, although most of them were visibly bidding for her. Street smart, book smart and beautiful were good cards, but being poor *and* mysterious was catnip to the inbred denizens of Waverly. Kate moved from class to class, unfailingly polite, occasionally funny and seemingly oblivious to their offerings. But she *was* coming here in an hour, and Olivia was pleased. Perhaps it was because she sensed that Kate was also "too old" for her age. Something had aged her. They had that in common.

It was all working out.

Still, to make doubly sure, she headed off to her room to her makeshift altar at 6:50. She lit a lavender-scented candle and propped up the gold crucifix that Anka had given her. Pretty much everything Olivia knew about God and the Bible was learned in disjointed snatches from her Houston roommate, Anka and the Christian Television Station ("CTS, Television You Can Believe In!"). As a result, Presbyterian merged with Baptist and mingled in a confused soup with Catholic. Olivia wasn't entirely committed to the praying, but she still enjoyed the candle-lighting part.

The door chimed. She heard Anka shuffle off to get it. Olivia blew out the candle, checked her smile in the mirror and went to greet her new best friend.

SUNDAY, OCTOBER 4

KATE

I took the subway. I hate the subway. Public transportation makes me feel poor. If I had the option I'd walk to school, but the Upper East Side is almost two hours from Chinatown. Two hours and two different planets. I sometimes did it on the way home. On the bad days. Olivia's place was just a few blocks south of the school. Nice.

A doorman who looked like he'd stepped out of a *New Yorker* cartoon greeted me. "My name is Aftab" was dressed in full Upper East Side regalia: hat, gold braiding, brass buttons—it doesn't get better. "Miss Sumner is expecting you, Miss O'Brien." Aftab raced around his desk to the elevator and pressed a button marked PH. Was I supposed to tip him? "Thank you, sir," I said to the closing doors.

My body pulsed in time with the door chimes. It was the penthouse, for God's sake! A Middle European–type opened the door. She looked relieved to see me. "Goot evening, hello! I am Anka." She flashed a gold tooth on her upper-left incisor as she smiled. "Please to coming in." Anka had a big pudding of a body topped off by a bullet-shaped head. This rather extravagant presentation was further intensified by badly dyed jet-black hair that was swept up into a beehive. The hair seemed to hover above her like an exclamation point.

I liked her immediately.

Olivia appeared out of nowhere and Anka disappeared into nowhere. I remained pinned to the marble vestibule. "Come in, come in!" She tucked my arm into hers. "Have you eaten?"

I hadn't. There was no time between my shift ending and getting ready. "Yeah."

"Well, I'm afraid you'll have to indulge Anka nonetheless. She's prepared enough snacks for the Polish army." She leaned in closer. "It's like a litmus test. Anka's pretty well had it with my vegan/bulimic/disordered-eating/gluten-free/lactose-intolerant friends."

"Can't say I blame her."

"Oh, me too! What a bore, don't you think?" Olivia squeezed my arm and pulled me through the hallway into a space that seemed to hover above Central Park.

"Wow."

My eyes slid across plump built-in sofas in a sunken living room framed by discreet stone and primitive woods. And the art! It was like walking around MoMA. The marble flooring in the vestibule gave way to slate and to soft grays and caramels on all the seating. Sparkling glass and warm yellow halogens mirrored the silent lights across the park.

"It's like a poem."

Olivia looked at the room as if she'd never seen it before. "My dad is just going to love you!"

"How big is this place?"

"I don't know." Olivia shrugged. "There's four bedrooms, Dad's library, the kitchen and pantry, three . . . no, three and a half bathrooms." She seemed to be sorting out the floor plan in her head. "And Anka's suite, of course. That's it."

God, I could move in and no one would even notice. "And here I thought the elevator couldn't be topped."

"You're too funny."

"Defense mechanism. It's what I do," I said. "Disarm with charm. Don't say I didn't warn you."

"Duly warned. Speaking of charm, have you caught sight of the new megawatt moneyman? You work in the office, right?"

"The director of advancement? No. So far, I'm in and out before he gets in. But I can tell you it's like a sexual tsunami hit the place. Draper's changed her cologne, and both Colson and Shwepper have sprung for new shades of lipstick that they are very diligent about reapplying."

"Ha! That's rich." Did she smile? Olivia Sumner wasn't a big smiler. "Come on, we're going to command and control, aka Anka's kitchen."

The kitchen, in contrast to the living room, was a gleaming white-on-white-on-white. It was wrapped in the same Carrara marble that was in the vestibule. Marble on the walls, counters and floor. Even the kitchen table had a marble top. It should have felt antiseptic, but instead it was inviting. Olivia's laptop, books and notepad were at the far end of the table, but set in the middle was a platter piled with cut salami, pâté, cheeses and baguettes. My stomach growled. I'd so had it with stir-fried bok choy and rapini.

"How was your weekend?" I asked. "Nonstop parties?"

Olivia paused in front of a coffee-making contraption. "Not my scene," she said, shrugging. "At least not anymore. You?"

"Not on my priority list, to tell you the truth."

I watched her take that in.

"Coffee? Espresso? Cappuccino? Name your poison," she said.

"I'd sell my soul for a double espresso." I walked over to her laptop. "Is Plath open on this?" She nodded while reaching for the tiny cups and saucers. "Okay." I flipped it open. "I'll talk while you play barista."

"That's why I'm wining and dining you. Hey, I'm a double espresso girl myself."

"Wow." Of course she was. I could spot the type at fifty paces. "Okay, so 'Lady Lazarus': brutal, autobiographical, very theatrical. Listen . . ."

Dying
Is an art. . . .

"Oh," she said. "I wasn't expecting you to start there." Olivia piled meat, cheeses and dips onto a plate and placed it in front of me. "Like everybody knows she was all suicide obsessed and everything but I thought where she talks about the lamp shade was cool. You know, that weird line about her skin being as 'bright as a Nazi lamp shade'?" She scrolled through the poem.

"So, I dug into that one." Olivia leaned toward me on the counter. "My big find there was that we know Plath had made at least one suicide attempt, maybe two, by the time she wrote 'Lady Lazarus,' but did you know that there were rumors the Nazis made lamp shades out of human skin? She was going from her horror to theirs. I know I nailed that part."

"Yeah, sure," I agreed. "That's correct and analytical, but it won't hit the personal response that Hornbeck's looking for. She wants your blood."

Olivia groaned as she handed me the espresso. Her sweater sleeve rode up her arm just enough to reveal a very faint scar. There was a lot I had to learn about this girl. She saw me catch it and pulled down her sleeve.

"Relax, I didn't try to off myself, and more to the point, *that* wouldn't be my style."

I nodded. "Cutter?"

"Not with any enthusiasm," she sighed. "I quickly discovered that I have a rabid and fairly hysterical fear of scars. It was a sleepover. You know, grade ten? It's the same everywhere. Everybody was doing it."

God, rich chicks were nuts. "What would be *your* style? If you . . ."

"I'd jump." She said it without a second's hesitation. I thought about the floor-to-ceiling windows framing the city at her feet. One of them was a door leading to the balcony, leading to . . .

"There. That's your response to Hornbeck. Go from there." I took a sip of my espresso and watched everything come together on her face.

"Right, I get it, I get it. That's the entry. Me into Plath. You are a genius!" Olivia sat down beside me and began piling up cheese and bread for herself. "How about you? How would you, you know . . ."

"I wouldn't. Besides, it wouldn't matter." I looked her square in her lovely rich face. "I can't be killed."

TUESDAY, OCTOBER 6

KATE

Dr. Kruger riffled through a few papers and checked her screen. "Well, Kate, not surprisingly, your academic work has been stellar. Nothing less than a 3.9 in any assignment across the board." She turned to me. "We were concerned that the office work might prove to be too taxing. It has, you know, for other Waverly Scholars."

Amateurs. "No, not at all," I assured her.

The office work was the least of my problems. Mrs. Chen had extended my weekends to eleven-hour shifts, plus two hours every Thursday. But then, out of nowhere, she'd started shoving aluminum containers of food at me every Sunday night. "Extra," she barked each time. The containers were enough for four dinners. I was both grateful and confused. I was pretty sure she still didn't like me, but hey, I needed the protein and the "extra" always contained chicken, pork or fish. My lunch at school consisted of a piece of fruit, which of course went entirely without comment from Olivia and the diet-obsessed world of the Waverly dining hall.

"Be that as it may, our Achilles' heel is after-school activities. You know that all the universities—and especially Yale—eyeball extra-curriculars hard. Even with stratospheric marks, we don't want to drop the ball here." She frowned at the screen. "You captained your basketball and lacrosse teams at St. Mary's, *and* you were on the debating team."

"With respect, ma'am, I was a boarder at all my other schools. The situation with my aunt, well, it's a long commute by public transit."

"Of course, of course." Dr. Kruger frowned. "It would be a con-siderable burden, especially on top of the work hours here." She turned back to the computer and scrolled. "There has to be some-thing we can offer that would sound impressive but would take minimal involvement and minimal time."

"You find it, ma'am, and I'll do it."

"I'll keep looking. Leave it with me."

Kruger wanted me to succeed—needed me to—not just because it would look good on the school but because she had invested herself deeply in me, in my story. I'd made sure of that.

My eyes traveled to the bookshelf. I always checked it out, and she always noticed. She was fairly sharp, as far as shrinks go.

"Ah, yes, I finally got the new *Diagnostic and Statistical Manual of Mental Disorders*. Interested?"

"The DSM-5?" Over the years, I'd come to rely on the old DSM-IV, looking up things, symptoms, wanting to get a handle on shrink-speak. This one might come in handy too. I could figure out what was up with Olivia, because there was something. "Maybe. I was kind of thinking about doing something psychological for my exit thesis."

"Hmm." She liked that idea. "Well, if you decide to, you can borrow it whenever you need it." She turned off her screen. "I think we're good for this month."

"Thanks. Thanks a lot, Dr. Kruger."

"It's my job, Kate. One of the nicer bits." She waved me off, and then said, "Before you go, it looks as if you're doing well with the other girls, but looks can be deceiving and entering a new school in senior year is—"

I was already standing. "You can chill on that front. It's good, and I think I've maybe even found a real friend. Olivia Sumner."

"Olivia." Dr. Kruger nodded to herself. "Olivia's a wonderful girl. Good for the both of you!" She got up to walk me to the door just as someone knocked.

A man—and I mean a truly *male* representation of his species— strode in. It had to be him, the brand-new director of advancement. I don't know how to describe it, but the guy was *such* a guy. That must be it. He wasn't like a movie star or anything, not really, but God, he exuded raw masculinity. And then he smiled. And then I really got what the fuss was about.

"Oh. Forgive me, Ginny, I . . ."

"No, Mark, we were just finishing." Her hand fluttered to her chest. Dr. Kruger *fluttered.* "Kate O'Brien, I don't think you've met our new director, Mark Redkin. Kate is our Waverly Scholar this year." Kruger was fairly beaming at this point.

I held out my hand. "Pleasure, sir."

"Well, I am honored." He shook my hand. "You're the one stuck inputting the archive files, so you've probably heard that I'm here to shake up fund-raising in the same way. Bring it up to speed with the times and the technology. At least that's what the board of directors is praying for." Big, blinding smile. Okay, really good smile.

"I came in to run something by you, Ginny. I was toying with the idea of starting up a student advancement arm to keep us current and to keep the parents more involved and dialed in."

"That's a splendid idea, Mark!"

"And now that I've met her"—he turned to me—"I'd like to have our Waverly Scholar front and center, not just for the committee but for foundation dinners, board meetings. They'll take one look at you and wallets will fall open!"

"Mark!"

"Sorry, I get carried away. But let's say we strike a small student advancement committee. You could head it, Miss O'Brien. Not onerous—a few ideas, a couple of meetings, and you'd have 'Chair of Student Advancement' on your resume. What do you think?"

Wow. Like, was he listening at the door?

"Kate?" Kruger was still beaming. "It would fit the bill perfectly."

"I . I'd be honored."

"Great. I'll be in touch with the details."

And that's how it is sometimes. Things just start.

THURSDAY, OCTOBER 8

KATE AND OLIVIA

The girls moved as if they were choreographed, each with a phone in her hand but on a separate stage. Olivia was bathed in light, Kate in dark. One stage was spacious and elegant, the other cramped and damp. But this dance, like all their other conversations, drew them closer. Becoming friends was a kind of courtship. A ritual of presenting your best self to the other. Each knew not to push too much, too fast. In their conversations, the girls reached for all their similarities willfully ignoring the differences. They'd got into the habit of having long phone conversations.

"I love that you hate texting!" said Olivia. "It's such a bore. You're held captive to multiple idiots 24/7. I refuse to play."

"Totally with you," echoed Kate. "Not only that, but those words stay on your phone forever, you know. Digital stuff comes back and bites you in the butt."

"Yeah," said Olivia. "My dad drills that into me nonstop." It was true. It was also true that all devices were removed from patients in Houston and discouraged in therapy afterward. *Houston.* "Hey, look, you've been real cool about not pressing on why I'm redoing senior year."

"No sweat. I figure you'll tell me when you're ready." Fully alert now, Kate focused hard on Olivia's tone, the pitch of her voice.

"Thanks, that means a lot. I don't really want to wade into it, but you should know that I got sick and ended up in the hospital for a few months. Can we maybe leave it at that for now?"

"Absolutely. 'Nuff said. So how did you do on the last Plath poem?"

Olivia exhaled. "Thanks to you, I aced it—3.8! How about the physics lab?"

"A 4.0! Look out, Yale, here I come!"

"Yale?" Olivia plopped on her bed. "Really? Yale, is it?"

"Yale is everything, Olivia. It's the prize, the only thing that matters. I promised my mom as she was . . . before she . . . uh, passed . . . Can we table that for later too?"

"Sure! But, Kate, this is perfect! *I'm* going to Yale. I mean, if I don't flame out. All our people—well, my mother's people—are Elis. My parents met there."

Kate stopped breathing. Was there a God mucking around somewhere after all? "I don't even care about safeties, Olivia. It's Yale or nothing."

"You'll get there. We're a force!" This was good. Olivia rearranged all her pillows, destroying Anka's perfect tableau. Talking to Kate was better than taking an Ativan.

"That we are." Kate eased herself onto the bed. She had to do it just so or the springs would scream in protest, a sound that scraped her bone marrow. "I'm handing in the next lab tomorrow."

"Great. Want to meet for breakfast and I'll run through it with you?"

"I wish, but I work, remember?"

"Right, sorry. I forgot. But hey, my dad is going to be in town this weekend. How about you come over? I'd love for you to meet him."

The clammy damp of the basement invaded all the soft surfaces. The sheets and pillows felt perpetually wet. "Can't do that either."

"Oh." Olivia's stomach bubbled up. What? It was going so well. She popped off the bed and reached for her best breezy tone. "Anything up?"

"No. Yes. Look." Kate had prepared for this. She had a plan. Kate *always* had a plan. It's just that now, steeped in this sewer, she had trouble focusing. Still, she decided to go for it. She had primed Olivia, but it had to be played just so. "Look," she repeated. "You have to keep this to yourself. It would get me tossed. It's a secret. I have secrets, Olivia."

"You can trust me, Kate. God knows I've got a couple myself." Her breathing slowed, but the bubbling hung on for the ride.

"I work all weekend too."

"But . . ."

"Yeah, and it's strictly verboten with the scholarship. It's supposed to be, like, seven hours max per week at the office, but I also work at this Chinese market. Two eleven-hour shifts on the weekend, and Thursday nights now that the fall veg are in."

"That's ridiculous, it's awful." Yet Olivia's body unclenched. "But your aunt . . . sorry, it's kind of an open secret that you live with your aunt."

Kate smiled. She was the one who had unpacked that particular secret. "My aunt is a greedy bitch who hates my guts." Well, it was true as far as it went and wherever she was. "She makes me pay rent, and if the school finds out, I'm done."

"Craziness! How can you possibly work so many hours there,

then at the school, then study? How can you have a life? How can you possibly prep for Yale?"

Kate sighed into the receiver. "It is what it is, you know? I can't . . . I don't want to talk about it. Cool?"

"Sure, yeah." How could Kate get the marks she was getting? How could she even get through the day? It dawned on Olivia in that moment that she knew less than nothing about her new friend. They seemed to talk about everything except anything personal. "Fine, then. Dinner with my dad on Saturday night. I'll make it as late as you need. I'll make reservations at Le Cirque. You'll love it." Then she caught herself. "If you're maybe . . . like, if you need a dress I have a million."

"Thanks, but I'm good. Well, if you promise to pretend you've never seen it before, that is, every time you see it again. It's a sweet little Kate Spade. I got it in Chinatown. My hair person has this, uh, connection."

"I promise to drool every time I see it. Will eight be late enough for you?"

"Eight is perfect." Kate would be ready to chew off her right arm by eight. "Just perfect."

"Good, so I'll see you in English, then. Langston Hughes." She groaned.

"Piece of cake, I promise."

"If you say so. Later." Still riding on relief, Olivia smoothed out the duvet and plumped up her pillows. Everything felt right.

Kate got up, letting the bed scream at will. It was ten feet from one end of the basement room to the other. The table got in the way as she paced, so she shoved it against the wall, causing layers of cement skin to crumble off. She resumed pacing, hugging herself against the chill and the dust.

"Well done, Katie. Well done."

SATURDAY, OCTOBER 10

OLIVIA

The restaurant devoured reality and replaced it with its own version. The moment you set foot in Le Cirque, life became sculpted and spun. Le Cirque was a perfect rearrangement of what *was*. It's why Olivia loved it. Her father preferred the minuscule bistro with its ancient waiters around the corner on Madison, but she knew he loved to indulge her.

Of course, there was a fuss. There usually was whenever she went out with her dad. Managers and chefs appeared out of thin air to greet them and ask about their health, his travels. Olivia was relieved that they had arrived before Kate. This kind of thing could be intimidating. They were swept to their favorite table by the window. Benjamin poured ice water and proffered menus. He knew not to ask about bottled water. Mr. Geoffrey Sumner was an energetic proponent of tap water.

"Can a proud old man comment on how gorgeous his daughter is?"

"Yes, of course, Dad, but you've already said it three times." Olivia opened the menu. "Methinks it might be time to consider starting up a new wife search."

Mr. Sumner groaned. "Three is more than enough, baby. I've sworn off marriage. I just miss you. All this crazy nonstop travel and I feel—"

Olivia found herself chafing under the weight of her father's concern. She reached across the table to touch his arm.

"I'm fine. I mean it. I should be at college this year, and you couldn't hover around me on campus. You practically blew off a whole year when . . . Look, I officially absolve you of all travel guilt." Did he wince? "Besides, Anka is on me like a Navy SEAL on steroids. Dad, no one could have done more for me than you. It's all fine. It would have been okay even when I thought I was going to be a bit lonely. But now that I've found—" She glanced up. "There she is!" She waved to her friend as the maître d' escorted Kate from his station to their table. Kate was glowing.

Mr. Sumner rose, buttoned his suit jacket and extended his hand in a movement so fluid that the component parts were invisible. "Welcome, Kate, I've heard so much about you. Thank you for coming."

"Thank you for inviting me, Mr. Sumner." Kate reached for his hand. Was she blushing?

"Please call me Geoff."

"I'll try, sir, but I can't promise. All my other schools were very strict Catholic institutions." She blushed again. "'One does not refer to one's betters by their Christian names, young lady!'"

Mr. Sumner smiled as he pulled out Kate's chair. "Well, do your best. I couldn't possibly think of myself as anyone's better."

"Oh, Dad," Olivia groaned. "That is so not true!"

"Harrumph." But he was still smiling. "Kids today."

Olivia turned to her friend. "I'm crazy about that dress! Kate Spade?" She winked.

"Why, thank you. It's yours whenever you want to borrow it."

Benjamin was back in a flash for drink orders. Mr. Sumner fortified himself with a single malt neat as the girls fussed with the menu. Olivia ran through her favorites, discreetly guiding Kate, who didn't actually appear to need much guiding.

Mr. Sumner had the saddle of lamb. Both girls ordered the organic dry-aged rib eye, which proudly proclaimed the name of the farm it hailed from. Olivia's father ordered a glass of Amarone from his reserved stock.

"And even though the ladies are going for steak, a half bottle of white, a nicer Chablis. Will that do, ladies?"

"That's perfect, Dad. Thanks." Olivia turned to Kate, who seemed caught off guard. "It's okay. Dad knows we all drink. He's been pretty European in his approach to the reality. And except for a couple of blips, I've tried to be pretty responsible in return."

Mr. Sumner nodded in acknowledgment. Benjamin poured a splash of white wine into Olivia's glass, then the red into Mr. Sumner's. This was followed by a pantomime of glass swishing, aroma sniffing and taste testing.

"So, Kate"—he raised his newly filled glass—"my daughter swears that you're a genius, and that you're single-handedly getting her through AP English and probably AP History, if I know my Olivia."

"And SAT prep too!" said Olivia between sips.

"No, sir, it's not like that at all. Olivia can handle anything thrown at her, and she got me clear on physics. It's just that English and standardized tests come easy to me, and I did AP History while I was a junior."

"See? I rest my case!" Olivia clinked her glass to Kate's.

"Well, that is formidable," Mr. Sumner agreed and then directed his attention back to his guest. "So, Miss O'Brien, tell me, where are you from? Who are your people?"

"Dad!" Olivia turned to Kate. "Forgive him—he's a lawyer. He can't help himself."

Kate picked up her napkin, folded it in half and placed it on her lap. "Well, sir, Olivia probably told you that I'm living with my aunt."

Her father didn't respond, waiting for the rest.

"And, well, I've lived a lot of places, I guess." She took a sip of her wine, as did Olivia. Olivia let the crispness of the wine settle her. It let her *hear* what her friend was saying. "I grew up here—well, Staten Island and Brooklyn until the end of grade five—then we moved out west, lived in a few places, even Canada. One move for every school year. I was the 'scholarship kid' in all of them."

Olivia was rapt, imagining her friend, packing up and starting all over again, year in and year out. All those schools, always the new kid. How grueling, and yet she felt a granular envy. What would it be like to—

"And your parents?"

"Both deceased, sir."

Olivia gasped. "Sorry, I . . . sorry." She quickly took another sip of wine. She knew about the mother because Kate had mentioned it, and there were rumors about her being orphaned. But Olivia knew that there were crazy rumors swirling about her too, so she hadn't pried. Besides, they had so much else to talk about: life, judgment calls, the ideal man, the pathetic nature of the other seniors, even poetry.

She should have asked.

"It's okay, really. It was . . . an accident. When I was thirteen." Now Kate took a sip of wine and exhaled. "All the schools since, since that time, have been boarding schools."

45

Olivia's father put down his glass. "Oh, my dear girl. How insensitive of me."

"No, no, please. It was more than four years ago. A lifetime." She took another sip. "I suppose it's not common knowledge exactly, but it's not a secret either."

Not a secret? "I have secrets, Olivia," Kate had said. There were more?

"You probably know that we lost Olivia's mother quite some time ago."

"Yes, sir." Kate blushed. "Well, one of the girls mentioned it early on. Maybe it was one of the reasons we were drawn to each other."

Olivia reached over and squeezed her hand.

Their appetizers arrived. Benjamin busied himself with a monster pepper mill. Olivia's next sip was the one that was just enough to make the lights bedazzle the room. Her father was handsomer and her friend tragically lovelier. She stopped drinking then.

When Benjamin disappeared, Mr. Sumner smiled at Kate. "You're clearly a remarkable young woman to get here with all that you've gone through."

"No, not so much." Kate shrugged. "Tragedies happen. There's no going back. And I had a ton of people in my corner. You have no idea how many committed teachers, guidance counselors and social workers lifted me up and got me to all those schools—and to here, I guess."

Olivia turned to the window, to the shadows of the pedestrians outside. It sounded, what, practiced? But then again, she couldn't begin to imagine how many times Kate had been called upon to recite that story. Her admiration for her friend grew.

"You see, sir, I have always depended on the kindness of strangers."

Olivia's father lifted his glass. "Tennessee Williams."

"A *Streetcar Named Desire*." Kate smiled.

Olivia settled into her chair. They liked each other. Thank God.

Leaving all things tragic by the main course, the threesome concentrated on Mr. Sumner's stories about his work in Rio de Janeiro and Singapore over the past few weeks. Olivia's father was a senior partner at Brookefield, Holden and Sumner, a law firm with a substantial international arm. But there had been precious little "international" last year for him. After he had entertained them with his best Brazil stories, the girls launched into a giggling précis of the senior class.

"Even lamer than last year?" ventured her father.

"Children!" They both said at once, clinking their glasses.

Kate excused herself to the ladies' room when the dessert menus arrived. Olivia watched her wind gracefully through the tables, chairs and expansive diners who had indulged in a glass or two too many.

Mr. Sumner opened the menu and sighed. "I suppose I order the dessert and you two eat it?"

Olivia put her hand over his. "I told you, didn't I? Isn't she great?"

He placed his hand over hers. "Yes, you did, baby. You were right—she's charming." He glanced back at the menu. "I'll have some port, but I'm guessing that I have to order the rhubarb–sour cream thing, right?"

"That's exactly right," Olivia agreed. "Kate and I both love rhubarb best, and double espressos too."

"Hmm, yes." He smiled at his daughter. "Two unlikely peas in a pod. What are the odds? But I'm glad you've found each other."

"Oh, me too, Dad. You have no idea."

MONDAY, OCTOBER 12

KATE

I had to walk back to Chinatown. I'd just blown $4.35 on a double espresso at Starbucks with the girls and I didn't have enough money for the subway. For days, I'd hinted to Olivia that we had to look like we were connecting with our cohort. When that didn't work, I mentioned that Admin was watching me re: "healthy social interaction." This interested Olivia but didn't spring her into action. Finally, I had to explain just how much I needed the Student Advancement Committee on my application for Yale. That got her. But it was way more work than I was used to.

At least the Starbucks meeting went okay. Olivia had summoned Serena Shaw, Morgan Singer and Claire Wu. According to her, they were the least offensive and infantile of our crop.

We spent the whole time talking about how smokin' hot Mark Redkin was. Okay, a couple of minutes were devoted to the Student Advancement Committee, but the rest was on who spotted him when and where, and what he was wearing at the time. The whole school was on Redkin alert.

"Hey, this is like a movie I caught on TCM last summer," said Claire. "*The Beguiled.*"

"Yeah, I saw part of that once," Morgan said, nodding. Morgan and Claire were besties. Serena generally rolled on her own, but since her dad owned half of London, she had serious cred. That and a wicked accent.

"It's about this injured Civil War soldier who holes up in an all-girls boarding school in Louisiana and everyone goes batshit with desire. Clint Eastwood."

"Ew!" Olivia made a face.

"No, no, no!" The girls protested as one. "This was Clint Eastwood from, like, fifty years ago. Ladies, he was smoking!"

We were a little tentative around one another, still wary, but we were moving in the right direction. It was good, all good. But I got lost in thought as I ambled down Park Ave to Chinatown. This was never good. I was spinning around the fact that I still lived in the sewer, that I still broke my nails hauling veg and that Mrs. Chen was still impervious to my charm. The Mrs. Chen thing pissed me off way more than it should have. It didn't matter that she didn't like me, except that it did. I tried telling myself that it was a culture thing, but man, she lit right up whenever she saw the bakery boy. The guy always wore dark jeans and a black T-shirt, like he'd just stepped out of the nineties. That really bugged me. He saluted whenever he swaggered by the market, and she pretty much beamed at him as she waved back. When I made the mistake of asking her who he was, she just grunted "Bakery" at me.

So bakery boy was annoying. Hell, my whole situation was annoying.

Thinking is good when it's in service of the plan, but thinking for thinking's sake is a mistake. Hot tar seeps in. By the time I got to Union Square, I had to sit. I was ruminating. I get stupid when

I ruminate and start gulping memories. Like the day I buried my father's card in the park.

Mom and I lived on top of the ALWAYS OPEN hardware, electronics and variety store that was closed on Sundays, Mondays and Tuesdays. It was my favorite place of all our places. You'd never know it from the sidewalk, but a lot of those apartments over stores are really nice. Ours sure was. We were happy. We each had our own bedroom. There was a kitchen in the back, a dinette and a massive living room that looked right onto the street. Our apartment was loaded with charm and personality. Mr. Sutherland said so.

Mom was in the hallway before I even got my key out of the door. Why was she home so early?

"Katie, honey?"

I couldn't really see her in the soupy darkness of the hallway, but I could tell she was still in her white dental assistant uniform.

"Hi, Mom. How come you're . . . ?"

"I have great news, honey."

She was using her chipped china voice, all high and cracked.

There was a crash, then rattling in the kitchen. I stepped toward her. My heart hurt.

"Yes, that's right, honey." Her eyes widened, but her tone didn't change. "Your father's home. Let's go into the living room."

Daddy? He found us?

Mom grabbed me by the arm and mouthed, "He's a little drunk."

The whole left side of her face was pink and mottled.

A little drunk was bad. Very drunk was better, because he'd miss you two out of three times. Passed out was best.

My father lumbered in.

Mom whispered, "I'm sorry, honey. I told him too much." She said it so fast and low, I wasn't sure what I'd heard.

"Katie! Hey, look at you, huh?" He wasn't weaving, hardly.
Just a little drunk.

"How's my baby, huh? Give your old man a hug."

He yanked me to him. I could take the reek of cigarettes and even his sweat. It was the dark, syrupy smell of rye and Coke that made me gag.

My father started to chuckle. "I'm here for the big Father's Day picnic at St. Raymond's on Sunday. Whaddya say to that, huh?"

My stomach filled up with ice cubes.

"Your daddy can't wait to meet all your new friends and your new teacher," he slurred. "So you landed a real live nun this time?"

"Stephen, don't."

"Sister Rosie or something, right?"

He grabbed me tighter.

"Stephen, please."

I decided not to breathe. That's how you die. From not breathing. I wondered how long it was going to take.

He chuckled again, except it sounded more like gurgling. "S'okay, sweet cheeks. Your mom told me about your whole scam." He let go of me, then thought better of it and grabbed me by the back of my hair.

"So I'm dead, huh?"

She told? No, Mom, not again.

"Stephen!" Her face was already starting to swell.

He reached over to the side table and picked up his glass with his left hand, still hanging on to my hair with his right.

"You little con." He pulled my head from side to side. "You got the best of both worlds. You get a load of sympathy from your Holy Roller nun, and the rest of the class doesn't know. So if I'm ever spotted with you, no one thinks anything of it."

He took a swig of his drink.

"Bloody brilliant." Rye and Coke oozed out of every pore.

"You're a chip off the old block." He yanked my head back. My father was eleven feet tall.

51

"Ow, Daddy. Ow!"

He looked down at me. "I'm proud of you, sweetie. Ten years old and lying to a nun. What balls!"

"No, it wasn't . . ." My eyes welled up. "It was like this special secret or . . ."

"You mean a lie, Katie. You're mine. Don't tell me you didn't feel a thrill when she bought it."

Oh, God.

"Fruit don't fall far from the tree. You're just like me, through and through."

Like him? No! It wasn't like that. He made it dirty. I just didn't want Sister Rose to know about him, about this. It's bad when they know. And maybe it was kind of smart to convince her to keep "our secret" from the rest of the class, just in case. But that wasn't all of it. I was hazy about how my secret lies got started. The details somersaulted over each other just like the classroom chalk dust. Maybe I thought . . . maybe I believed that if I told the holy sister Daddy was dead . . . that somehow God would make it true.

I wanted him dead.

I was worse than him.

I sat on the bench for hours staring at the truth. Then I stood up and walked to Chinatown.

OLIVIA

The afternoon sky looked bruised and tender, the aftermath of the day's violent storms. Her father's twice-delayed flight was now scheduled to depart at 7:15 p.m. Olivia tore away from the windows and turned to her father's well-worn Dunhill briefcase and overnight bag, standing like sentinels in the vestibule. She could hear the ebb and flow of last-minute instructions between her father and Anka, but their voices were too far away for her to make out the words. Olivia was calm. She had doubled up on the Ativan.

The intercom lit up twice and Olivia walked over to press it. Message received.

"Dad, the car's here!"

Her father strode into the foyer and folded Olivia into his arms. She inhaled the soothing flannel and his spicy scent.

"It may be a long stretch this time, baby girl."

"It's okay, Dad. I'll be fine, I promise. We'll Skype."

He groaned.

"Okay, we'll *talk* every day."

"It's São Paulo for five days, then to Singapore for the Braxom deposition, and then back to São Paolo and Rio. Remember, Tilde can track me down at any given moment."

Olivia nodded. Tilde was her father's "office Anka."

"Dad, I've got all the times zones memorized, and I'll hardly be lonely if—"

"Promise me you'll think long and hard about that. Consider every eventuality. I agree it *sounds* ideal, and it would certainly make me worry a little less, but—"

"Hey, it was you who said it would be the perfect arrangement for all concerned." Olivia inhaled and counted to three. "Kate's a good influence on me. She's already got me involved in this Student Advancement Committee thing. We've picked the other girls and everything." She parroted Kate's pitch. "It's a visible and healthy social interaction with my peers in a common cause. What more could you want?"

"Yes, yes." He smiled. "And it would make me feel better to have her here, but"—he held her arms—"it's just that Kate doesn't know about any of—"

"But she does! I told her I was hospitalized last year. Look, Kate's razor-sharp, Dad. I'm sure she's figured out that it wasn't for tonsillitis. Half the school has figured that out, and they're all just pretending to ignore it. It's what we do. We've already lost one of the seniors to an extended stay, and it's only October. It's a private girls' school. It happens."

"But you're—"

"Feeling great. I haven't had a single issue, not a whisper. No altered realities, not for a nanosecond. The meds work. They always did. I just won't go off them this time."

He raised an eyebrow.

God, she was tired of constantly reassuring him. "Or ever. Not until I get the all clear, *if* I get the all clear."

"Well, Dr. Tamblyn does seem very impressed."

She looked squarely at her father. "Is it Anka? Is Anka . . . ?"

"Delighted. She likes Kate." As if to underscore that point, banging pots sounded in the kitchen. Among her many attributes, the housekeeper possessed a sonar-like hearing that would be the envy of any North American bat.

"Think on it long and hard, that's all I'm saying."

"Of course, Dad. I won't be impulsive."

The intercom flashed twice again. They both sighed.

Her father embraced her once more. They told each other to be careful and safe, and said that they loved each other. Olivia walked him to the elevator bank carrying his briefcase. They embraced again, awkwardly, quickly, because the elevator doors started to close.

"Love you, Dad!"

"Just give it more thought."

"I promise!"

Olivia watched the console as the elevator descended from PH 1 to 50, 41, 33, 26, 25, 24 . . . she reached for her phone . . . 4, 3, 2 . . . and when it hit the ground floor, she hit the speed dial.

"Hey! What's up?"

"Hey yourself. Look, Kate, don't say anything for a minute, just listen. I have a massive idea. It's *brilliant!* It is *so* perfect." Olivia could not stop smiling. "How about you move in with me?"

SATURDAY, OCTOBER 24

KATE

I'm OUTTA HERE! See ya! Am I good or what? So long, weeping bat cave—hello, good life. Next year this time, I'll be at Yale. Mission complete. And in the meantime, I get the life I deserve.

Except . . .

Small thing, but still a thing. When I gave Mrs. Chen a week's notice, I felt . . . I don't know, dead sad for a second. The damp was making my brain spongy. I mean, that grizzled old chicken hated my guts.

But she took me in, no questions asked, and she was honest in her own way. Straight up.

Not too many people are.

Including me.

The week whizzed by on fast-forward. I handed in three essays and a physics lab. I also charted out how I'd reorganized the Apothecary section for Mrs. Chen so she wouldn't screw it all up the moment I left. Then I tried to convey how she should lead with her most colorful and exotic fruits. Not sure how that went down.

We had two meetings of the Student Advancement Committee. The girls were growing on me despite myself. The first meeting was with Mr. Redkin, and he "suggested" position titles. Even though I had the least cred, I was formally named chair. More shocking still, the girls seemed happy for me. Redkin had somehow made each of them feel like they'd just been crowned prom queen as he doled out the rest of the titles. He was good. I can always recognize a fellow traveler.

Olivia was going to be the secretary, Serena the alumni liaison, Morgan the communications liaison and Claire the PTA liaison. One of our "jobs" was to keep in touch with our counterparts on the board of directors. We were going to be trotted out at the next board meeting. The rest of our duties sounded vaguely glamorous and a bit fuzzy, which in no way gave us pause.

The second meeting was held in our "office" at Starbucks, where we christened ourselves the Waverly Wonders. It had a perfect ring to it. That accomplished, we circled back to our main agenda item: Mark Redkin.

"Like, I didn't know men like that existed in the real world," said Claire, shaking her head. "How old do you think he is?"

"Old," offered Olivia. "He's the director of advancement, guys. He's got to be at least thirty."

"Thirty-four," I said. "Which is still young for a director's position." They all turned to me.

"What? I work in the office, remember?"

"Thirty-four! That would be like making out with your dad! But . . ." Morgan paused. "I'd make an exception for the exceptional Mr. Redkin."

"Morgan!" Claire tossed a coffee stirrer at her.

"You and every hormone-high girl at school." Olivia was laughing. She didn't laugh much.

It was good to see.

"Have you caught how Jody and her crew of tools hyperventilate when they even walk by the office?" Somehow this, like everything Serena said, sounded elegant rather than disparaging. "Did you hear about yesterday? He took off his jacket and climbed a ladder to help Mr. Jefferson remove the ceiling fan in the second-floor hallway. I swear girls fainted. Ladies, the school is throbbing."

"Yup." I nodded. "It's that seriously male thing he puts out—that and, I'll grant you, a high-voltage smile. Let's face it, the man is in a candy store at Waverly."

"And you, Madam Chair, are his favorite lollipop." Serena patted my thigh. "But fair warning—I'm going for him."

Did the others tense just a little?

"Hey, he's all yours." I drained my coffee. "Remember, I've moved around a lot. Guys like that . . . they'll use anything they've got, and at the moment it's us. Redkin has got to prove himself fast. He has to raise big money. You'd all know better than me, but apparently Waverly goes through advancement directors like tissues."

Serena rolled her eyes.

"I don't blame him," I said quickly. "Look at us! We're a publicist's dream. Me, the Waverly Scholar, and the much-vaunted Olivia Sumner, who can trace her old-girl lineage to her great-grandmother. And we're two burning blondes, if I do say so myself."

Olivia crossed her legs. "Crudely put, but impeccably argued."

"Then we have the gorgeous South Asian from London. Hell, Serena, whenever you open your mouth, I want to sleep with you."

Serena winked at me.

"Claire looks like she just stepped off a Hong Kong movie set

58

to get her makeup retouched," I continued. "And Morgan Singer, despite her name, has this too-hot-for-words Latina vibe going."

"Yeah, that's my mom's side," Morgan agreed.

"We look like *Vogue*'s 'Beauty Around the World' edition, and we handed ourselves to him on a platter to loosen purse strings. That's what this is, ladies, and don't you forget it. We are *his* wonders."

"You mean his Waverly Wonders. All right, all right, Madam Killjoy." Olivia raised her hands in mock surrender. "We have been duly warned."

They all nodded. All except Serena, who'd leapt up to get another cappuccino.

The bat cave was steaming by the time I got back, even though it had been unseasonably dry for days. I was packing up my two little suitcases and backpack when Mrs. Chen appeared in the doorway. The woman never knocked. I always thought she was trying to catch me at something. She was holding an aluminum container that was bigger than she was.

"Pork," she said.

"Oh, wow, Mrs. Chen. Thank you so much." It was enough for a week. "And thanks, you know, for everything." Rather than disappearing with a grunt as was her usual habit, she stood rooted in the doorway.

I took the container from her and placed it on my little table. How was I going to get all this over to Olivia's in a cab? And what was Anka going to do with it?

"Mrs. Chen?" She didn't look happy, but then she never did.

"You good worker. Good girl. You trouble?"

It took me a moment to realize she was asking, not accusing.

"Trouble?"

And then it dawned on me. Mrs. Chen had probably housed a billion students of questionable status in this very basement. Who else would live here? And even if the student was a *gweilo* in a fancy uniform, that student had to be in trouble—and had to be leaving because she was in even more trouble. I honestly don't know what came over me. I was at her in three steps, hugging that fierce little coat-hanger body. Much to my shock, she hugged back.

"No, no, Mrs. Chen!" I finally let go. "It's good. This is a good thing. No trouble." I shook my head and smiled at the same time, probably confusing the hell out of her. "Remember I told you, I'm moving in with my best friend. Very rich, very good for me." And yet . . . "It's all very, very good for Kate."

"Ha." She looked doubtful.

"I'll bring her here. We'll shop in your market. But, Mrs. Chen, please never, never say that I lived here, okay? I'm crazy happy, really."

"Ha." I could tell she wasn't buying it. Mrs. Chen rifled through a pocket in her apron. That apron was a thing of wonder. It was threadbare but immaculate, despite the fact that the woman hauled around massive boxes of seeping veg that would make a stevedore weep. She retrieved a small card. It had a name that was printed in Mandarin and then crossed out, with "Kevin Chang 212-555-6310" written above the crossed-out part.

"Uh . . ." I could hear a commotion above the stairs. Mr. Chen calling down. The taxi must be here.

"For trouble, you call." Mrs. Chen tapped the card vigorously. "Big trouble only." She seemed to be straining for a concept, for words. "Bad emergency trouble. He fix. Ha."

"Yes, yes, I understand." But of course I didn't. I had a sense from the beginning that the Chens were connected to some powerful stuff that tunneled deep into the bowels of Chinatown. Enough late-night visits from gentlemen who did not appear to be interested in purchasing after-hours mangoes gave me that clue. But this guy? What was he going to do for me? Besides, what kind of deep, dark *fixer* is named Kevin, for God's sake?

"I tell taxi, ha."

And with that, Mrs. Chen disappeared up the stairs, her slippered feet slapping against the damp cement steps. No good-bye, and certainly no more hugs. Her quota had clearly been breached with the one. I was disappointed. The stupid card was still in my hand. Ridiculous. I was going to the very top of the world, the lap of luxury, safe at last. I crumpled up the card, ready to toss it. I slid it into my backpack and then picked up the larger suitcase and my purse, but before I reached for my small suitcase and the pork, I uncrumpled the card and stuffed it into my bra.

What could it hurt? I knew how quickly the world could fall apart. Survival at any cost. Always.

SATURDAY, OCTOBER 24

OLIVIA

Olivia tried to see the room through Kate's eyes and failed. Her friend was uncharacteristically silent and still clutching a rather bizarre aluminum container.

"Is it okay?" asked Olivia. "We can change anything you like. They're Pratesi sheets, but if you prefer Frette, I understand. I have Frette in my room and would totally get it if you . . ." She should have taken an Ativan before Kate arrived.

"Olivia, I was sleeping on polyester Spider-Man sheets that Walmart would be embarrassed to stock." She walked around the room slowly. "*And* paying rent for the privilege. By the way, this is for . . . uh, Anka. I'll just put it on the floor until I collect my wits, okay?"

"That's your bathroom behind that far door."

"*My* bathroom?" Kate opened the door and fell against it.

"It's only ever been used as a guest suite and, well, we haven't had a guest in years." Olivia took in anew the cream-on-cream of it all—the bed linens, the wall color, the furniture itself. It was boring. She'd hate it. "We can get some posters or artwork to kick it up."

"Jesus, Olivia! That I get to call something like this home . . ."

The relief was immediate. "You like it?" All of Olivia's unmedicated anxiety spiders were swept away, or at the very least, they scurried deeper into the crooks of her mind.

"Like it? *Really?*" Kate plopped onto the bed and popped right back up again, smoothing out the duvet.

"Sit down—or better yet, lie down, goof. Mess it up. It's *your* bed, your room."

Kate lay down obediently while Olivia went to some double doors, opening them wide.

"This is your closet. There's all kinds of storage in here for shoes, drawers for your folded items and jewelry, and so on. There's a full-length mirror behind this door, and don't worry about the mirrored bureau. My dad had it antiqued because the guests used to freak out about leaving fingerprints all over it." Olivia plopped onto the bed beside Kate. "You sure you like it?"

"Shut up or I'm going to cry."

"I'm so glad."

The two girls stared at the ceiling for a time.

"And your dad's okay with all this?"

"He's major relieved, and I mean it. The poor guy is bent out of shape with guilt about being away for weeks at a time when . . . well, he's thrilled."

Kate sat up and rearranged the wall of pillows. "You know, for two newly minted best friends . . ." She turned to Olivia and seemed to wait for confirmation.

Something flickered within Olivia. "Besties? Yeah, absolutely."

"Okay, so as two best friends who are now roommates, we kind of know squat about each other."

"I know." Olivia rolled onto her side. "I feel awful for not asking about, well, the whole . . . I'm gutted about your parents, about what you must have gone through. I honestly don't know how you can be you. I mean it."

Kate turned back to the ceiling. "It was a long time ago. The past is the past. You've got to keep it there or else it'll flail you alive." She hugged herself. "Only look forward, Olivia. Right now and tomorrow. The rest is horseshit."

Olivia burst out laughing.

"What?" Kate sat up, looking alarmed. "What did I say?"

"No, no," Olivia managed to stammer before she erupted again.

"Olivia Sumner, are you mocking my simple self?"

"*No!*" Olivia wiped the tears from her eyes. "If you had any idea how much my father has blown on clinics and shrinks in the past year alone . . . The rest is horseshit! You've earned your keep with just that one. Wait 'til I tell my shrink! Come on." Olivia slapped Kate's thigh. "I'm smelling something delicious. Is that pork in that aluminum thing? It's making me crazy. Anka has Saturday afternoons and most Sundays off. Let's dig in."

Kate trailed after Olivia, lugging the container to the kitchen.

"So you're seeing a therapist? I know from shrinks—they threw a busload at me. I hope you like yours more than I did mine."

"Shrinks, plural?" Olivia turned around. "I guess that makes sense given all you've been through, but I haven't heard any rumors. You've kept it all airtight. Unlike me."

"Well, I wasn't here, for starters." Kate placed the pork on the counter. "Do you, uh, want to know about your rumors?"

Olivia tightened. There was no chance that anyone would know the real deal. No chance. "Sure," she said, shrugging. "I mean, I was a bit of a party queen before I started to unravel, so I can imagine."

"Yeah, there's a bit about that. Mostly it's standard-issue." Kate settled herself onto a stool while Olivia doled out the moo shoo pork. "There was supposedly a guy, a mystery boy. Or there were drugs—overdose, maybe. Or you had a meltdown or anxiety-disorder stuff, and hence the self-medicating and hence the hospitalization. Nothing's stuck. Nothing's touched your reputation. If anything, you have a shiny sheen of mystery about you now. I'd let you know otherwise. Give you a heads-up, you know?"

"Yeah, Waverly has always liked a little mystery." Olivia felt neither relieved nor annoyed. She could work with this. "Huh. They're pretty good guesses."

"Oh?" Kate didn't make eye contact as she was handed her plate.

"Yup." Olivia nodded. "There was a boy. I lost my head, like, completely. He was public school, wrong and rough. In the beginning, I thought he was so cool, so real, you know? We all did—my friends at the time, I mean. We thought that about public school kids. The other girls dabbled in the public pool too, but they—"

"Got out clean," finished Kate.

"Something like that." Olivia stopped then. Her voice was flat. She could hear it. She corrected. "Not me, though." Still too flat. She went for a smile. She knew for a fact that a smile often altered her tone. "I'd be lying if I didn't admit it was a thrill. Up until then, I was a good little perfectionist with rolling anxiety issues, like seventy-three percent of our student body. Vibrating but high-functioning."

"I'm familiar with the breed." Kate dug in to her food.

"So mandatory meltdown with mandatory R & R in a Houston hospital. They got that part right."

Kate reached for her arm. "I'm sorry, Olivia. That blows. If I'd been around, I would have hurt him bad."

Olivia considered that for a moment. "Uh, what you said, about keeping an eye on the rumors, giving me a heads-up . . . you'd do that?"

"In a heartbeat. Hey, you may not have noticed, but you're my only best friend. You already know stuff about me that's not out there. I'm living *here*, Olivia. If someone wants to get to you, they go through me first."

"I believe you," she whispered. And she did. The believing felt good.

"And more important, the past . . ."

"Is horseshit!" they said in unison.

"Glass of wine?" Olivia was already heading to the wine cabinet.

"Sure."

"So, Kate, my girl, I'm obviously damaged romantic goods. How about you?"

Kate raised her newly poured glass. "Pure as the driven snow. Boys mess with your mind, trip up *the plan*. I don't trust a single one of them."

They clinked glasses.

"Me either. Too late, but hey, better late than never." Olivia sighed into her glass. "I mean, I trust my dad, obviously. He's solid. So *my* game plan is only older men from here on in. Real men." Until that moment, Olivia hadn't even realized she had a game plan. Kate was a clarifying influence. Kate *was* better for her than Dr. Tamblyn.

"I get where you're coming from." Kate eyed the aluminum container. "We arm ourselves according to past wounds."

"There you go again—so speaks the poet-philosopher."

Kate helped herself to more moo shoo. "Thing is, we shouldn't live like cloistered nuns either. You have a thing or two to prove to the rumor mill, and I have to look like I'm enjoying 'healthy social interaction.'"

Olivia rolled her eyes.

"We've got to pitch up to at least a couple of the better parties," said Kate.

Olivia knew she had to make appearances. It was one of the bonuses of having Kate by her side—image. Image was important, although she couldn't put her finger on exactly why anymore.

"Hey, I get it. It's not my scene either. I'm talking a couple of parties each term, max. It'll make your shrink happy, it'll make your dad happy and it'll keep Kruger off my back during my monthly check-in."

Olivia studied her friend. "You're right, again." And she was. Everything would be fine with Kate in her corner. "We're good for each other. I knew it from that first moment in English class. I knew we'd be good for each other."

Kate raised her glass. "Here's to us."

MONDAY, OCTOBER 26

KATE

I tried reviewing my situation with a clear head, but couldn't. I grinned all the way to school. Hey, I now lived in a kingdom high above the clouds. My subject (Olivia) adored me, as did my servants, Anka the housekeeper and Aftab the doorman. I mean, holy hell, I am *Miss* Kate. Plus, plus, plus it took me less than ten minutes to walk to school. Seven minutes from *my* penthouse door to the Waverly admin office.

I was impressed with myself.

What next? I wanted a dog. Whenever things got good for even a minute, I'd want a dog. Of course, when things went to ratshit, I'd *really* want a dog, but let's not go there. I just wanted a dog, is all. A dog would be nice. A dog would love me and need me totally, no questions asked. What would that feel like? Got to get a dog, *would* get a dog. Too soon? No, I had the skill set to make Olivia want a dog. Child's play. It could be my next thing.

As I turned on the lights in the office, I warmed to the idea of telling Dr. Kruger about my new status. No, I should hold off until my monthly check-in, when we were all settled and got our groove on. I'd tell her about the move, the Waverly Wonders, the party we'd have gone to by then. What a list.

I even smiled at the file folders towering on Miss Shwepper's desk. They'd breed over the weekends.

Speaking of files, there was stuff that was obviously missing from Olivia's. The serious juice would probably be on paper, and those files lived in Kruger's office. That's where my story was stowed. I knew from checking myself out that the registration student file didn't have any of it, which was refreshing. Every school I had ever attended had promised complete privacy. Total bull. But at Waverly, even relevant staff members didn't know the whole deal. My story appeared to be locked in a secret silo. That's what Dr. Kruger had promised. I didn't believe her then.

I believed her now.

Still, my next play had to be the files. I had to break into Kruger's cabinet. I needed better intel on Olivia in order to bind her close and guarantee my sweet ride all the way to Yale. As it was, the girl was way too . . . calm. Or flat or something. I was the only person who could make her smile a real smile, the kind that reaches your eyes. I liked being able to do that. I'll grant you she was good at the fake ones. But I needed even more to help cement me into sisterhood. That was the plan, but any good plan must allow for contingencies. A plan A needs a plan B, and a C, and in worst-case scenarios, a D.

I was busy inputting when I heard laughter down the hall. Almost eight o'clock, a bit late for our registrar's arrival, but in she waltzed with Mr. Redkin trailing behind. They could have met in the parking lot . . .

"Ah, my favorite Waverly Wonder." Mr. Redkin tapped my file tower. He usually didn't get in until nine.

How did he know what we were calling ourselves?

"Good morning, Kate!" Draper was beaming. Draper was not a beamer.

"Morning, Ms. Draper, Mr. Redkin."

He followed Draper into her office. "About that matter we were discussing . . ." He closed the door. I still heard them laughing.

All righty, then. *So that's your game?* Nicely played. It had taken me weeks to figure out that Draper was the real wheel in the school, not any of the heads, including Ms. Goodlace. Draper could trace her lineage straight to the founder of Waverly. She was in tight with every single board member who mattered, including the new chair, Mrs. Pearson. She knew the families that mattered, because she came from a family that mattered.

And Redkin had scoped all that out in a minute and a half.

Again I say, nicely played.

The rest of the staff dribbled in, asking about each other's weekends. Miss Shwepper waved me down as I started to pack up. "You can stay there, kid," she said, winking. Shwepper was always winking at me. I'd decided to take it as a gesture of affection. "Mrs. Colson is off sick today, so I'm going to use her desk."

Mr. Rolph lingered by my pile for a moment to encourage me to think about my thesis topic. I assured him that I was on it hard and was considering some psychological angle. "Excellent, Kate. There's been a significant uptick of mental illness plaguing the modern school system, and yet it's under-researched on the thesis front. It would be a fine topic to weave into your university interviews."

"Yes, sir."

"And of course, we have the finest resource right here at the school with Dr. Kruger." He glanced at her office door.

"Just what I was thinking, sir."

"Excellent, excellent." He tapped my pile and drifted away to his office. Damn, now I was committed. I didn't like being cornered like that. Committed before I'd had a chance to think through every aspect of a commitment. Still, I *had* been toying with the idea.

I was so lost in thesis thought that I crashed into Mr. Redkin with my arm full of files. He reached out and steadied the pile before a single paper had a chance to escape.

"Sorry, sir."

"Please don't *sir* me, Kate."

Redkin had great hair. You had to give him that, on top of the other stuff. It was blond and wavy, just a little long, just a little unruly. It was the kind of hair that made you think surfer or rock climber rather than administrator. It was the kind of hair you wanted to touch.

"I've been meaning to get a word. I just mentioned it to Ms. Draper, and she thinks it's a great idea."

"Sir? Sorry, Mr. Redkin."

"Mark."

"Mark," I repeated.

"I'd like to arrange a photo shoot with the Waverly Wonders. I want you girls to feature prominently in any promotional or advancement material we send out. Ms. Draper agrees that it would be an excellent investment."

"The Wonders would *love* that! Wait until I tell Olivia. We'll call a meeting."

"Good. I'd like to get on that right after the board meeting. After everyone has met you girls, seen you." He wore a wheat-colored jacket that complemented his hair. But I swear you didn't notice any of that when he smiled. You just saw the smile. And he knew it.

"Sounds cool," I agreed. "I'll alert the Wonders right away."

"Thank you, Kate." He opened the door to the storage room, where all the general file cabinets still lived. As he held the door open, he put his hand on the small of my back. It was a nothing gesture. Gentlemanly. Forgettable.

But my stomach rolled over.

No. One. Touches. Me. That's the rule.

And Mark Redkin just broke it.

I want a dog, damn it.

FRIDAY, OCTOBER 30

OLIVIA

Olivia was dialing down on the Ativan and the Lexapro. It didn't help as much as she thought it would. She still felt removed from herself. It had to be the other meds, but no dial-downs were possible there. Never again. Olivia didn't "share" any of this with Dr. Tamblyn. Her psychiatrist wasn't nearly as pumped about the whole Kate-moving-in thing as he should have been.

"At first blush it seems a rather *impulsive* decision, and we must always be alert for that. You've been exceedingly careful in your actions over the past few months." Dr. Tamblyn paused and tented his fingers, classic old-school shrink. "I do concede, however, that it may also be an indicator of growing confidence. Perhaps a positive signal."

What an old lady he was. But she'd been going to Tamblyn since forever, and he was so pleasingly pliable. So Olivia kept the dial-downs to herself. He would have rained on that party too. "Party," she sighed. The Wonders had agreed to go to Claudette

Zimmerman's tomorrow. Claudette was a mouth-breather, as was her older sister before her, but the Zimmermans knew how to throw a party. The Wonders had made a group decision to attend in head-to-toe knockoffs for a laugh. At least that part would be amusing.

Kate said that she had them covered. "Leave it to me, kemosabe. Tell Anka no dinner tonight. We're heading to Chinatown."

That evening, Olivia and Kate scoured the stalls like pros, which meant that Kate whipped Olivia in and out of vendors at lightning speed. She grabbed Olivia's hand at the very first stall. "Never the stuff in the front," she insisted, pulling her straight to the owner in the back. "Greetings, Kumar!" Then Kate drew him in and whispered, "We need two Rodartes, size 4."

Kumar looked stricken. "Party frocks, right? I have fabulous Cavallis."

"Ooooooh!" said Olivia.

"Wrong vibe." And with that, Kate dragged her out of that store and into a dozen others.

"Is, uh, are these things legal?" Olivia was stroking a Hermès bag.

Kate shrugged. "Not so much. Some of it falls off the back of a truck, but most of these are knockoffs. People gotta get by however they get by. Let it go, Olivia."

And she did. Her friend was a pit bull. Olivia had sensed that about Kate from the start, admired it, was intrigued by it. The girl was a class A survivor. Olivia needed to be around such fierce will. She would listen, learn, observe. And one day, the pupil would surpass the master.

Chinatown was total chaos on Friday night. The streets would have done Hong Kong proud. They were rendered nearly immobile with swarming shoppers, hawkers, mothers with babies, old men with bundle buggies and shady-looking sharp guys. Everybody smoked. Music blared and pulsed out of the stalls and stores. All the screeching, cackling and guttural noises scraped Olivia's ears. Twinkle lights, bare lightbulbs, lanterns and neon store signs assaulted her eyes, while the competing aromas of Peking duck, dried fish and rotting fruit threatened her nostrils.

She loved it!

Olivia loved the buzz gathering deep inside her, and she remembered just how much she had loved *feeling* that way, before. It was Kate's doing.

"Hey, roomie," she called. "I'm going to fall over unless we eat soon. We've got the dresses. Me hungry now!"

Her friend was deep into the vendor's stall, heading toward the back door. "Cho has the best fake Jimmy Choos in Chinatown." Kate beckoned to her. "Shoes, then food. Promise."

In keeping with the illogic of the neighborhood, they ended up in the "Very Best Chinese Restaurant in the City," which you had to be a secret agent to find. There was no signage whatsoever. They entered through a deserted little mall and took an elevator to the third floor. The elevator doors opened directly onto a massive banquet hall that was swathed in gold drapery and red braiding à la 1986. The place was teeming with locals—kids, babies, grandparents and all manner of extended families. Kate seemed to be on friendly terms with a maître d' who did not speak a word of English. The girls ate like emperors for $11.99. It was the best meal of Olivia's life. Her father would have loved it. But where were they? If Kate left her in this rabbit's warren, she'd never find her way back. She couldn't remember seeing any taxis.

"So"—Kate raised her green tea—"brilliant?" It had become their code for "Did I nail it?"

Olivia raised her cup too. "Mega brilliant, and our secret, right?"

"To the first of many."

They clinked teacups.

"Come on." Kate started gathering up their considerable stash of bags and boxes. "One more place. We should bring Anka some mangoes."

It seemed like Kate was scanning the street on the way.

"What are you looking for?"

"Nothing." Kate shook her head. "There used to be this guy from a bakery . . . nothing."

Olivia frowned at the store that Kate was pulling her toward. *Here?* The signage proudly declared that it was Chen's Chinese Market and Apothecary in both English and Chinese script. Even though it was after ten p.m., it was still crammed with shoppers. Clearly oblivious to her friend's hesitation, Kate threaded them deep into the store.

"Mrs. Chen? Mrs. Chen?" Kate waved at someone. "There she is!" A wretched-looking little woman in a blindingly white apron started toward them. A near smile shifted into hostile suspicion as soon as she spied Olivia. She examined her as if trying to place her. Kate then surprised Olivia by hugging the creature. "Mrs. Chen, this is my best friend in the world, Olivia Sumner. Olivia, this was my . . . uh, my boss. I worked here. This is the place!"

The best Olivia could manage was a "Wow, hey."

"Olivia is like a sister to me, Mrs. Chen."

"I'm pleased to meet you, Mrs. Chen."

"Ha." The old woman grimaced. Olivia took an instant dislike to her.

It seemed to be mutual.

"I'm living with Olivia uptown, near the school. It's wonderful. I'm very happy now. Very."

Kate seemed to be looking for applause that she clearly was not going to get from this dried-up twig. Olivia was tired. The whirl of the night had caught up to her. The bags were heavy and her arms ached. It was time to go.

"We need to buy some mangoes, Mrs. Chen, for Olivia's house-keeper."

"Ha." The woman barked something, and in the midst of that throng, a box of Alphonso mangoes appeared out of nowhere and was thrust into Kate's already-too-full arms. "Present." Then she narrowed her eyes at Olivia.

Not dislike, Olivia hated this woman.

"Kate"—Mrs. Chen leaned into her—"that girl . . ."

The din from the crowd was so loud that Olivia didn't hear the rest, but she did hear Kate's sunny reply: "She's a very, very good friend to me, Mrs. Chen."

Mrs. Chen grunted. "You still got number?"

Kate frowned and then nodded. The old woman turned and left without so much as a good-bye.

Kate flashed Olivia a "what are ya gonna do?" smile. "Don't mind her," she said. "For months I thought she hated my guts. It's just her way."

Olivia thought she was smiling, but she couldn't be sure. She got sloppy when she was tired. She'd sometimes think she had her "outside" expression on and then she'd catch a glimpse of herself, stunned to see a lovely blond girl looking like she was dead inside. She put down her parcels and rummaged through her purse.

"Okay, partner," said Kate. "Time to move up and out. I'll get us to the main drag and we'll hail a cab. I'm wiped."

"Me too!" agreed Olivia.

Kate started heading for the street, and Olivia turned back in time to catch Mrs. Chen watching her.

"Brilliant night, roomie?" Kate called back to her.

Olivia nodded. "Beyond brilliant!" And then she dry-swallowed an Ativan.

SATURDAY, OCTOBER 31

KATE

Claudette had all the personality of a bag of hair, but she knew how to stage a party, I'll give her that. It was like an anti-Halloween party. Pretty much everyone was dressed to the nines. She'd also built a nice two-to-one ratio of private to public boys. This pissed off the Rigby and St. Joseph guys hugely, but it made them work harder. Genius, really.

We Wonders arrived together in Olivia's car service. Everyone squealed as soon as we opened the door, mainly because no one had seen Olivia at a party in almost a year, but also because the sharp-eyed but dull-witted Claudette immediately screamed, "Superb knockoffs!" We posed hard, working our polyester like Lagerfeld was in the house.

What can I say? We made an entrance.

Before we scattered to conquer various parts of the scene, Olivia grabbed my arm. "Two things. First, note that Claudette is wearing brand-new Louboutins. It's her downfall. She tries *waaay* too hard. Second, don't leave me hanging, okay? I'm rusty."

I squeezed her hand in a promise before I started wandering and hugging and exclaiming over everyone's party couture.

As soon as Olivia departed, Claudette glommed on to me. "You look adorable, Kate."

"Thanks, you too," I gushed. "Fabulous shoes, Claudette. Really." She was sucking back a green apple martini that was not her first, by the looks of her. The festivities were being held in her father's limestone on Ninety-Fifth in Carnegie Hill. Completely unbidden, Claudette launched into a review of the party prep. Suffice to say that everything had been meticulously seen to, including the two bartenders, her sister's best dope connection, her dad's caterer, a hot DJ, and a security man stationed in her dad's bedroom and waiting to pounce if things went south.

"Smart. An off-duty cop?" I asked.

"No," she sighed. "It's Chris, my dad's personal guy."

Wow. Aside from surviving multiple marriages, I couldn't imagine what her old man had done to deserve *personal* security. Rich people were another species.

"Cool," I said.

Claudette warmed to me more with every sip of her drink. "Well, all sorts of crap happens at these things, and not just because of the mix." She eyed some of the public boys through her monster mink lashes. "My sister, Rachel, said that some weird stuff went down at a few parties last year. You take your chances with public-private."

"Yeah, places get trashed everywhere no matter what the mix, though. It's a timeless rite of passage for the brain-dead." I surveyed the town house. Claudette and I were with a few dozen kids on the open-concept first floor; the second bar and DJ were on the level below. Unlike Olivia's father, Claudette's dad came from the "more is more" school of decorating. Every single item called attention to itself. *Look at me—I am crazy expensive!*

"Some kids just run wild out of the blue." She waved her hand around for emphasis. "Like our dear Olivia. My sister said that she was on quite a tear for a while."

"Yeah, we've laughed about that," I lied.

"Wish I could have seen it." She sighed into her drink. "Then a few weeks later the party queen disappears and reappears this year as the ice queen. No rumors with any decent traction either, although Rachel did say that ice queen was more her MO as a junior and sophomore."

You could tell that Claudette would give her left arm to be considered an ice queen. Meanwhile, I was wondering if that was when Olivia had met the bad boy. Did he goad her on at parties? "Yeah, strange stuff happens. Hormones. Whaddya gonna do?" I was glad for the info but felt I had to put her back in her place. "I hear your sister is doing really well in rehab."

"Yeah, for sure." Claudette blinked at me happily. I swear, the girl's most distinguishing feature was her benign stupidity. "Hey, I really appreciate you girls making an appearance. I know it's the first party you've come to. I'm, like, so totally flattered."

I bathed Claudette in a few more compliments before extricating myself. Where was my ice queen?

Serena and Morgan were by the bar. It looked as if they were trying to explain some nuclear drink recipe to the bartender. Three Rigby boys were cheering them on. Olivia must have gone downstairs. When I turned to find the stairs or the elevator, or whatever they had in this place, I was accosted by a guy in a black T-shirt and black jeans.

Jesus. It was the bakery boy.

He was carrying a Michelob Ultra, which he promptly thrust into my hand.

"I've been scoping you out for almost an hour. You don't look like the green apple martini type."

How dare he? How dare he think that—especially since he was

right. I hated pretending that I loved Chablis and fancy cocktails. I was so furious, I could taste the fillings in my mouth. "What are *you* doing here?"

"Same as you, I'm guessing." Wicked smile. "Except I'm here as local color, and to make the private school boys nervous."

So he wasn't stupid.

At least three girls were tracking him. Bakery boy was a wow, and way worse, he so knew it. I tried to center myself. It was all so heart-thumpingly bizarre. How much did he know? How much could he blow? I didn't get any threatening vibes off him, but you could never be sure. "So I look like the light beer type?"

He ignored that. "I've missed you at the Chens'. Just as I was calling up the balls to ask you out for a coffee, you disappeared." He looked around the room. "You've moved up and on, I take it."

I ignored that. "Yes, I've been at Waverly since September. Olivia Sumner is my best friend, and I live with her." I was smiling but I said it through clenched teeth.

He shook his head. "Okay, if that's how you want it. Let me introduce myself—I'm Johnny."

He extended his hand and I put the beer bottle right back in it. "Johnny? No one names their kid Johnny anymore."

Johnny shrugged and leaned into me. He smelled like freshly ground coffee. "Is that so? What do I look like to you?"

"Like trouble," I said under my breath. I flounced off with a pounding heart and as much righteous indignation as I could muster. Even Rodarte knockoffs give good flounce.

There had to be fifty kids dancing, drinking and writhing on this level. Or maybe it was seventy, or a hundred. I sucked at judging that kind of thing. I finally spied Olivia cornered by a couple of publics. Johnny's friends? It took me at least twenty minutes and a dance with Taylor Ward from St. Joseph before I could get close to her. Claire was working it hard on the dance floor with what looked to be another St. Joseph boy. I remembered that Morgan had teased her about her crush being there. I gave her a little congrats hug and kept trying to make it over to the corner. A guy was all over Olivia, but it looked like she was more than holding her own.

"Back off, sweetie—that was another time and another me." She was laughing at him.

That's my girl.

"There you are! God, Olivia, we are so late. Gotta go."

"Thank you," she mouthed.

I grabbed her arm and pulled her with me all the way up the stairs and through the throng. "Boys are ignorant and pathetic," she yelled.

"I hear ya!" I yelled back.

We saluted the Wonders as we weaved our way to the front door. Johnny caught my eye just as we got to the vestibule. He raised his beer and nodded.

"Wait a minute! Seriously cute. Who is that?" shouted Olivia.

"Nobody," I said.

Who the hell names their kid Johnny?

OLIVIA

Olivia and Kate walked arm in arm to school. They were going to meet the other Wonders in the hall outside the Waverly boardroom. The Wonders had been instructed to wear their dress uniforms and wait for Mark Redkin to parade them around in front of the board members.

Olivia was still talking about the party on the way. "All I'm saying is he was gorgeous and he didn't take his eyes off you."

Kate hip-checked her. "Not interested. I won't go near that kind of distraction. Not part of *the master plan*. My eye is only on the prize."

"Yale?"

Kate nodded. "Yale, full ride. It's always about Yale, Olivia."

Olivia was in awe of Kate's single-minded determination, and a bit envious of it. She intended to go to Yale too, but given her legacy status, her mother's family history and her marks, she just assumed that barring a few hiccups, it was—like everything—pretty much a done deal.

What would it be like to *want* something so much?

Serena, Morgan and Claire were already stationed at their posts.

"Mr. Redkin popped out a second ago," said Serena, who, truth be told, looked a little buzzed. "Same drill as what we went through yesterday, except the intro spiels start with Claire, then Morgan, then me. We linger a bit longer with our Waverly royalty, Olivia, and then end with Kate's bit."

And that's how it went. Waverly's boardroom was almost medieval in its decor. The ornately carved school heraldry was meant to awe and intimidate. No one in the room seemed intimidated. Olivia had at least a passing familiarity with each of the board members—and more than that with Mrs. Pearson, who was a managing partner at her father's firm. These were her people. But her roommate probably had years of presenting to—and making her case in front of—rooms like this. Kate came off as compelling and sincerely enthusiastic. Again, Olivia's admiration rose. She had selected well.

When Kate finished, Mr. Redkin stood beside her to explain that the girls would appear at the Winterfest Gala and the various fundraising dinners, each hosting her own table, and that they would be the "face" of Waverly on all the school's online and paper promotional materials. He had that room.

But far more important, he had Olivia.

It caught her by surprise, but it was real. She knew this because as he delivered his spiel on the Wonders, Mark kept *almost* touching Kate. It was so natural, as if it were part of the presentation. Not remarkable in any way, really. What *was* remarkable was how much it bothered her. It was a straight-up feeling, and surprisingly intense.

Jealousy.

It forced Olivia to reevaluate, reappraise, *watch*. She paid close attention now. Mark Redkin was magnificent throughout the rest of his presentation. Confident and commanding, but not in love with the sound of his own voice like some of the others. Quick to smile but always on point. And so, so appealing. Mark bent the entire board to his will. Every one of his items was approved. By the time he was finished, Olivia was sure. Olivia *wanted*.

As soon as they were all excused, she caught his attention. "Mark, a word?"

"Of course." He drew her aside in the hallway. "That went beautifully, thank you. You were wonderful, Olivia."

You were wonderful. She wanted to melt into him against the wall. "Olivia?"

His lashes were dark, unusual for a blond man. He was inches away from her. No scent of cologne, no aftershave. Mark Redkin just smelled like himself—like a man was supposed to—and it was . . . intoxicating. Olivia searched for her breath.

"My father called just before we came. You can go back in and tell everyone that he's secured the new Whitney for the Winterfest Gala. I think Mrs. Sabre from the museum will call you about it tomorrow."

He smiled at her. Of course he did. But as he did so, Mark Redkin locked on to Olivia as if he had never seen her before, not really, and now that he did, no one else mattered. *Men* did things like that. Men like Mark Redkin.

"That's wonderful, Olivia. Let's talk about it soon."

As he thanked her, Mark grazed her arm. It was a nothing gesture, but one that electrified her, changed her.

"Yes, let's." Olivia didn't allow herself to smile until she turned to walk away.

WEDNESDAY, NOVEMBER 4

KATE

I've been itching since Monday, the kind of itch you can't get at because it's burrowed deep under your skin. Something was up.

Olivia was at her psychiatrist's. Maybe I should go too.

Yeah, right.

There's not a shrink on the planet I can't scam. I've been to psychoanalysts, psychotherapists, social workers and Dudley Do-Rights of all shapes and stripes. The system vomits them on you. I can feign shock, horror, despair and grief, all served up with a cup of crocodile tears. I cough up whatever's appropriate to the scenario, and I don't trust any of them. Stay sharp. Stay hard. Stay smart. I'd have been buried alive in foster care had I not managed them at every single turn. Scholarships, education, boarding schools, rich-kid environments—I knew even then that was the only way through. My mom hammered it into me: "You keep your eye on the prize, Katie O'Brien."

She didn't, but I will.

No distractions allowed. Especially not the bakery boy. Claudette let me know that he'd been trolling around for my contact info. I told her that if she or any of her crew gave it out, I'd dismember them. We laughed, of course, but Claudette is just a little afraid of me. As she should be.

God, he was cute, though. Exactly my type. I didn't even know I had a type until I saw him with that stupid beer in his hand. *Stop!* No one touches me. Not head, heart or body—not in *that* way. No one.

Which reminded me, Redkin had *almost* touched me a thousand times at the board meeting. But he drew back like he knew not to. Quick study? Too quick? Way too quick.

I was making too much of it. I get like that sometimes. It's what comes from being on hyper high alert. I had to get out of my head, so I fired up my laptop. I'd promised to help Olivia with AP History when she got back.

At some point, Anka walked into my room. She does that. Not to Olivia, just to me. I don't mind. I kind of like it. She spied me on the bed with the laptop and tsked as she flicked on the overhead light.

"Kate, no goot! You are blinding your eyes."

She placed an unasked-for mug of green tea on the night table. Did I thank her? I was still in the dark, sliding back to when my father found us. Back to when he grabbed me, reeking of rye and Coke and Camels. Back to when he was convincing me that I was like him. Had he already won?

I was worse than him.

"You're sure as hell not like your simpering mother. Uh-uh. Pulling a fast one on a nun. You're all me, sweet cheeks. Daddy's little con. Daddy's little liar. Admit it, Katie."

"No."

But it was true. WAS. But no longer, no sir. From here on in, I was going to be good.

I tried to remember the Act of Contrition, but the prayer got tangled up in my head right after the "O my God, I am heartily sorry" part.

Okay, okay, forget that one.

Our Father, who art in heaven . . .

I would march right in on Monday morning and tell Sister Rose the whole thing. Come clean.

Hallowed be thy name . . .

About all of it.

Thy kingdom come . . .

Daddy didn't move.

He was waiting.

I didn't move.

I knew better.

Thy will be done . . .

There'd be major big-time penance.

Something, daily bread something . . .

That's okay. I deserved penance. I could take it. But Sister would hate me. I couldn't take that.

And forgive us our trespasses . . .

No, no, she wouldn't.

As we forgive those who trespass against us . . .

Nuns take, like, a vow or something about that stuff.

And lead us not into temptation . . .

It's got to do with lost sheep or something.

But deliver us from evil. And I would never, ever lie again. Amen.

"Admit it, Katie." He clutched my hair tighter.

Suddenly I was indestructible. It was like I was all powered on and lit up from the inside.

"You're Daddy's little con. Girl, you are your father's daughter."

I am not! That would be a lie.

"Admit it. Admit you're me through and through." My father checked his watch. "I'll tell ya what, sweetie—say it and I'm outta here. Gone. No picnic. I won't screw up the little party you got going on. There's an oil rig with my name on it in Alberta, and my Greyhound could leave at nine thirty. But give me that before I go, give me that one little thing."

Gone? He'd really go? Just like that?

He let go of my hair, turned me toward him and crouched right down. "Katie, I gotta know I'm leaving a piece of me behind and I'm off."

My father's eyes were tearing up. He'd done that kind of thing before.

Mom started crying for real, though. Quietly. You wouldn't even know if you didn't know.

He put his hands on my shoulders, really gently. "Katie girl, you're just like me, aren't ya?"

I looked straight into his wet eyes.

Just . . . one . . . more . . . time.

"Yes, Daddy. I'm just like you."

Did I lie then or was it the truth? Did he break me or make me? I don't know. All I know is that night, my father got on the Greyhound.

I sold my soul for a bus ticket.

OLIVIA

Everything was better with Kate in her life. Maybe not a "let's flush the meds down the toilet" better—that had been a disaster—but better. Olivia was scrupulous about the meds, but the price to pay was insufferable flatness. That's how it was before too, and to be honest, *before* the before. It was like the world was out *there*, but she was covered in a filmy gauze that kept her from touching it. That, or she was too bored to reach out. So Olivia tracked Kate closely. She watched and tried to internalize Kate's hunger, her ambition, her *need*. She wanted some of that, to experience that. Sometimes when she was with Kate, an actual feeling pierced the gauze, and now since Mark—being near Mark—it was happening even more often. True, Olivia still didn't often know what she was feeling until after she felt it. But the time delay was improving. The impact-to-absorption ratio was better.

Instead of spending the weekend partying or grinding through material for midterms, Olivia found herself scrolling through sites for dog breeders and pet stores with Kate.

Olivia had never even thought about getting a dog until Kate began hinting for one. A dog would be perfect. Olivia *wanted* a dog. Last year, her father would have bought her a dog, a pony, a unicorn, anything. But she hadn't known then what she wanted, not really.

She did now.

And she also wanted a dog.

After some pro forma pushback, her father made a few calls from Brazil and came up with three "acceptable" pet stores.

Anka bought into the project heart and soul. It turned out that her family had always had a dog back in Poland. She loved dogs, especially the "too handsome for sure, very big dogs." The girls showed her how to refine her Google search, and Anka began bookmarking German shepherds, Dobermans, bullmastiffs and boxers. She campaigned hard for a guard dog. "Dey are a really *real* dogs and vould taking care of you ven I am not here. Nobody could kidnapple you vit a big dog."

"No one is going to kidnap me, Anka." She kissed the startled housekeeper. "I promise."

Kate meanwhile had glommed on to the rescue pages. "I know," she groaned, "too Freudian. But still . . . look at those faces!"

They were all in the kitchen, and Kate was winning over Anka with the rescue dogs.

"We can't handle a rescue." Olivia was adamant. "How am *I* the mature one here? Think, people! How could we possibly cope with a nutbar dog? I don't want it going to therapy with me. We have to start with a puppy. It has to have a clean slate. That way if it goes weird, it's on us and it would be *our* kind of weird."

"No." Kate shook her head. "We'd blame it on Anka."

Anka threw a dish towel at her, but reluctantly agreed that they weren't in a position to take on a rescue.

Olivia campaigned for an adorable dog. A dog that would be impossible not to fall in love with, so then maybe she would. She kept the bookmarks firmly on the "poo" dogs. "Come on! Just look. They're irresistible!" She kept scrolling through sites for Maltipoos, Shih-poos and Yorkipoos. Anka point-blank refused to look.

"Yeah, cute," agreed Kate. "But they're teeny. Hey, I'm all for little, Olivia—we're in a high-rise in Manhattan, I get that—but those guys all look like something the Kardashians would stuff in their evening bags, you know?"

"Ew."

"Yeah, ew."

Olivia sighed. They were getting ready to visit the three pet stores on her father's shortlist. "Okay, but it has to be super cute."

"I promise it will be super cute."

"Get a really real dog!" Anka called after them.

The girls walked over to Lexington Avenue arm in arm. When they got to Paws 'R Us, Olivia reminded Kate that they were going to be diligent about this. They would be thorough and dispassionate. They would ask a ton of questions, and most important, they would comparison-shop. "Ready?"

"Ready!"

They both inhaled as they stepped through the tinkling door and were greeted by the undeniable aroma of eau de warm puppy.

"Oh, look!" squealed Kate, racing to a pen full of little critters.

Olivia followed her and did indeed feel something stir as she gazed down at the furry, wriggling mass. Some were sleeping in a ball, wound up in and around each other, but others were playing with shredded newspaper, the wire pen or each other's tails. One bold little guy, clearly sensing the arrival of blonde destiny, waddled right up to them and got up on his hind legs, tail wagging furiously, before balance got the better of him and he toppled over.

"Look!"

"Oh, my God! Oh, my God!"

Their squealing caught the attention of a generously proportioned man who made his way over to them.

"Can we hold him?" asked Kate.

"That's what they're there for, to be cuddled."

Kate reached in and picked up the bold little puppy. He had big ears that stood at attention and a long tan body with four white socks. She placed him directly into Olivia's arms. The puppy promptly licked Olivia clean of blush and lip gloss.

"That there's a Pembroke Welsh Corgi," the waddling man offered. "Fine line. I got the papers."

"That's the kind the Queen has, right?" asked Olivia between licks. The royalty thing had an undeniable appeal.

"That's right." The man patted the pup's rump. "His littermates have all gone. This little guy's the runt. People can be funny about that, but he's great stock."

Kate looked pleadingly at Olivia. "So he's like a rescue!"

On cue, the rescue runt nuzzled into Olivia's neck, sighed and promptly fell asleep.

So much for careful consideration, investigation and comparison-shopping. Olivia bought him on the spot, as well as all the paraphernalia. They named him Bruce on the cab ride home. Bruce, exultant with relief, tripped over himself going from lap to lap and lick to lick the whole way home. Olivia couldn't stop giggling. She *was* giggling.

Proof positive. Everything in her life, about her life, was better because Kate was in it.

KATE

There was something different about my counselor, but I couldn't land on what. It was distracting. Over the past few months, I'd come to have a grudging respect for Kruger. Was she happy? Happier? Why would that be a bad thing? I had to focus, stay on top of this. I had to bring my A game to sessions, no matter how feeble the therapist or shrink, and Kruger was anything but feeble.

"So how's it going at the new address?" she asked.

She had the red file folder open, my folder. Sometimes she brought it out, sometimes not. Either way, Kruger would record session notes on paper and stick them back in the file. My secrets, and more important, Olivia's, were locked in that oak file cabinet. Old school but effective.

"Terrific, no hiccups," I said. "It's crazy how well it's working out."

Kruger smiled. "I'm glad. We all are, Kate. Nonetheless, we *should* have done an exit interview with your aunt."

"Well, sure, maybe. But remember, she isn't my guardian. My

aunt was just an address, and barely that." I was pricked by the memory of Mrs. Chen shoving the massive container of pork into my arms. "Actually, she was relieved to see the back of me." While this was true for the imaginary aunt, I was no longer sure that it was true for Mrs. Chen.

"I'm sorry to hear that."

"Water under the bridge." I shrugged. "Hey, I'm, like, a minute from the school, I adore Olivia, and you should just see where we live."

Kruger nodded at the file. "You'll be good for each other." She turned to her computer. "Your GPA is still stratospheric, and Olivia's marks, as I'm sure you know, are rising. Mark—Mr. Redkin— tells me that the Waverly Wonders are a real going concern. Your applications are strong." At this, she took off her glasses and smiled at me. "It looks solid. I'm very pleased."

"Well, I aim to please."

"Yes, yes, you do," she said. "And it's a quality that's been highly effective."

Huh?

I let that go and regrouped. "And to top it all off, we got a dog! Well, a puppy. A corgi, just like the Queen's got. Anka and I feed him and walk him, and we're trying to train him not to pee on the marble floors, though Olivia helps out with that part."

"That's a lot of responsibility."

"A day has to have bones, you know?"

"Bones?"

"I need a lot of bones." I crossed and recrossed my legs. Why did I start in on that? "Structure, responsibility. Stuff, you know, or I, uh . . ."

"Have too much time to think?"

Stay alert here, Katie girl. She's smart. "Bruce—that's our puppy—he

96

helps give the days more structure. I love him to pieces." And I did, even though I fretted that Bruce seemed to love Olivia at least as much as he did me. He was an equal opportunity lap-sitter and face-licker. It was a kick to see Olivia so happy with him, but still, he should love me more.

I'd taken to getting up in the night to feed him secret treats.

Kruger was busy noting it all down and smiling as she did so. She was definitely smiling a lot. "And Mr. Sumner?"

"He's cool, and apparently relieved big-time. He's gone, like, most of the time, and that's the way it's going to play for most of the school year, you know?"

She put down her pen. "I've scheduled a short meeting with Mr. Sumner when he's next in the city. I want to tell him how proud the school is of you—about your character—to reassure him about this decision." She looked up, anticipating my pleasure.

I stopped breathing.

"I understand that you're having a strategy meeting with Mar . . . er, Mr. Redkin to review student funding participation and the photo shoot for the Christmas mail-out." She waited for an appropriately Kate-like response.

It felt like my head was filling with sand.

"Kate?"

"Yeah. I mean, yeah, a Wonder meeting. Looking forward to it." *Get a grip, get a grip.* I couldn't. "Look, Dr. Kruger, the, uh . . . well, you know how critical that, uh . . ."

Concern displaced the good-natured smile.

"No one can know, all right? No one! I mean, yeah, we've talked about this, and you said . . . but still, like, I . . . it freaks me out that . . ." My mouth dried up. "No one can *ever* know. My parents . . . it would ruin me totally. Destroy everything, like all the other times. I mean, the point of the whole name thing and . . ."

"Kate"—the smile returned—"I'm aware of that more than anyone. I fully concurred with the process." She shut the file folder. "I've said it before and I'll say it again. I will say it as often as you need me to say it." Dr. Kruger got up, took the folder, placed it into the file cabinet and locked it. "It's privileged." She stood by the cabinet.

My heart was still pounding in my head.

"Only me and Ms. Goodlace—absolutely no teachers, no staff and certainly not anyone's father. I promise, Kate. Feel better?"

I got up as well. "Yes, ma'am. Thank you."

"Okay, then. Same time next month for assessment, but I expect to see you in here a lot for your exit thesis topic." Kruger walked around her desk. Before she opened the door, she leaned over. "You can bank on it, Kate, a hundred percent. Trust me."

I nodded and rewarded her with my most winning smile.

I trust no one.

SATURDAY, NOVEMBER 14

OLIVIA

The city had been bleached by an early winter. Bare branches scraped against an ash-gray sky. The muted browns and muddied grays of November comforted Olivia. The winter soot of New York mirrored her soul. She knew it shouldn't be so, wished it wasn't. Normal people—people who were not . . . *dulled* in some way— loved the other seasons. But spring, fall and summer with their garish, show-offy colors seemed to mock her.

Olivia knew where she stood with November.

She and Bruce padded away from the window. She had to get ready. Kate and Olivia had agreed to meet the rest of the Wonders for dinner at the Tent, one of the dozens of restaurants and clubs owned by Serena's father. Olivia would rather have stayed home with Kate and Bruce, but Kate insisted, and Kate was good for her. Besides, she'd find a way to tell Mark all about the dinner when she saw him at school. She'd work it and make it amusing. Mark. He had invaded her dreams, her thoughts. He did things in the dreams, ignited her. As Olivia got ready, she pretended she was preparing for him.

The Tent was entirely draped in saffron silks. The glow cast from the candles and the draping made the diners look way more attractive than they had any right to. Course after course of Indian fusion was specially prepared for Miss Serena's table. "It's scrumptious! Absolutely the best, Serena!" she assured her host. But it wasn't as good as the feast at that dive Kate had unearthed in Chinatown. The girls exchanged secret glances.

Since Serena had obvious pull in her father's restaurant, the Wonders were drinking a fair bit, with Serena leading the charge. Even Kate was on her second Kingfisher. Olivia nursed a Chablis while Serena, Morgan and Claire dove into pitchers of sangria laced with cardamom. They careened into truth-telling at record speed. It started when Kate complimented Serena on her father's vision.

"Yes, his oh-so-brilliant vision." Serena motioned for another pitcher. "My father's *vision* currently includes a twenty-three-year-old London assistant. And apparently this one is serious."

"Oh, that's hideous!" Morgan, the most effusive of the Wonders, threw her arm around Serena. "Divorce?"

Serena nodded. "Yeah, and since most of this"—she waved at the room—"is my mother's family, it's going to get real loud and real ugly, real quick." She took a gulp of sangria. "At least most of the tabloid stuff will be London-based."

"I wish my parents would get divorced," Morgan groaned. "They've split so many times it's a revolving door at my house."

"I don't know," said Claire. "My parents separated when I was two, and I see my dad *maybe* twice a year. The rest of them—my family—well, if you've read *Crazy Rich Asians*, those are my people. How about you, Kate?"

Olivia held her breath.

"Dead, remember?"

"Damn, sorry. I'm such a—"

"No, no, uh, it's . . . don't sweat it. It's kinda nice that you all keep forgetting."

Olivia felt obliged to leap into the lurch. "My mom died when I was eight. Old enough to remember, but not old enough to really remember, you know?"

They all nodded, even though they clearly did not.

"Then Dad married twice and divorced twice, both at the speed of light." Olivia waited until the server had refilled her glass. *Careful.* She had to watch the alcohol. "I almost liked them both, you know?"

Again they nodded, not knowing. All except for Kate.

"Dad says that's it. No more wives." She took a sip, shrugged. "Me? I wish he'd find someone who would make him happy." Truth was, it would take a load off her. She'd be less burdened if he had someone to—

Then she spotted them.

"OhmyGod!"

The Wonders inhaled as one. "What!"

"Don't anyone move. Serena, at your three o'clock—Claire, your four. Kate, right behind you. *Don't* anyone turn around. Draper has just walked in with . . . Mark Redkin!" Could they hear her heart pounding?

"Draper and Redkin? No way!" said Claire, gripping the edge of the table.

"Shh! They're at the bar," Serena reported. "Looks like they're just going to get a drink and some nibbles. He's asked for the bar menu."

Olivia's insides burned. It surprised her.

"Well, well, well." Claire picked up the pitcher. "Didn't you meet with him on Friday, Kate?"

Kate reddened. No one noticed except Olivia.

"Yeah, along with Ms. Goodlace. It was just for a minute." She drained her beer. "The logistics of the photo shoot, a bit about heading tables at the Winterfest Gala. I'm thinking that Goodlace isn't drinking the Redkin Kool-Aid, though. It's nothing obvious but . . ."

"No surprise there." Serena rolled her eyes. "She's the head, and she's immune because she's ninety."

"Yeah, that's probably . . . are you sure I can't turn around?"

"No!" Olivia and Serena said at once.

"Whoa!" Serena's eyes widened. Olivia was silent.

"What, what, what?" demanded Morgan and Claire.

Mark's hand was on Draper's knee and inching up her thigh. Then a squeeze.

No one peeked or peeped. They were as still as statues, even though most of the table didn't know what was going on. Olivia's own thigh warmed. He was touching someone else and she felt it. She *felt* Mark Redkin as his hand groped Angelica Draper. Serena looked like she wasn't breathing. Mark leaned over and whispered something to Draper. The couple downed their shots and popped a couple of their nibbles into their mouths. Then the director of advancement threw some bills on the counter and yanked up Draper with stunning force. Serena and Olivia both gasped.

"What, what?" demanded Morgan.

"They're leaving," said Serena, eyes still as wide as saucers. She turned to Olivia with a "did you just see what I saw?" look. "Methinks our director of advancement is a very, very bad boy."

As Serena duly recounted every gesture, elaborating on an

102

exchange she couldn't possibly have a clue about, Olivia partici-
pated, but from a distance. While she giggled with her friends,
Olivia clung to the burning sensation of the hand on *her* thigh.
She reveled in that sensation. But even in the reveling, she still had
enough possession of herself to note her surroundings, to note the
conversation and to note that Kate had not taken her eyes off her.

KATE

The air was thick with bullshit in Redkin's office. He was slinging it fast and furious, and I slung it right back. We were each the president and founding member of the other's mutual admiration society. This was my second one-on-one meeting with him in my role as chair of the Student Advancement Committee. So far it was even more "admirable" than the first. When we met last week, it was with Goodlace and in the morning. Redkin couldn't meet until five today. The place was a tomb at five; only Kruger usually stayed late. I prayed she was still in her office. Why? Why was I so squirrelly around him?

"Did I tell you, Kate, that the board was charmed by you all, but especially by you and your story? I hope you don't mind us milking it, per se."

He waited.

I delivered.

"Not at all, Mr. Redkin. I appreciate this opportunity. I realize that you put me front and center on this, and I can assure you that I take my responsibility seriously."

"It's where you should be always. And it's Mark."

"Sir?"

"And it's certainly not *sir*, remember?" He smiled. Redkin had full lips that curled when he smiled, but his cultivated facial stubble was enough to make the smile read heart-hurting, masculine. "It's Mark. I'm not your teacher or your dean. I'm just the money guy and my name is Mark. Say it."

"Mark."

"Good."

My Spidey-senses were firing blanks. *Not* good. Living the high life—being cared for—was making me stupid. I can usually read things, people, fast and clear, and I wasn't able to get a fix on this guy. What *did* he want? Agenda, agenda, agenda?

Mark got up, walked around his desk and leaned against the edge. His suit jacket and tie hung off the back of the chair he'd just vacated. His shirt was open at the collar. How could Draper resist this? I liked to think of myself as fully immunized against whatever he was putting out and even I "got" it.

"Apparently, I hit a home run with the board." He shook his head as if it were a surprise.

Nice move.

"Next item is that I want to feature you and Olivia in the big Christmas newsletter. The wild contrast in your stories and the fact that you became best friends is"—he paused—"enticing. We'll play up the whole 'only at a place like Waverly' angle. We'll also use it in the alumni package. It will make the old girls swoon."

"Well, sure, I see that." Made sense, sounded professional. "There's not an old girl in the city who doesn't recognize or revere Olivia's bona fides. I understand the Granfield clan helped build this place and kept it going over the generations. And their name is etched on half the buildings in the city."

He looked up at the ceiling. "You're such a smart girl, Kate. Smart in so, so many ways."

"Sir? I mean, Mark?"

He raised an eyebrow. "Oh, I think you understand me."

What?

He got up and walked around me and rested his hands against the back of my chair, but he did not touch. There was white noise in my head. Just as I stopped breathing the door flew open.

"Mark, I'm . . . Oh, Kate. Hello."

Mark straightened. "Dr. Kruger, come in. Kate and I were reviewing the Christmas mail-outs. We're going to highlight her story and contrast it with Olivia Sumner's. She's agreed. We'll arrange for a photo shoot next week with her and the Sumner girl. Come to think of it, we might as well shoot the entire Wonder team while we're at it and have those photos ready for the spring campaign."

"Well, that's splendid, and from my point of view, the timing works perfectly. We can supplement Kate's and Olivia's application packages with the mail-outs. That way, the schools get a look at them before selection and it's entirely credible, given their position within advancement."

She was genuinely happy for me. But it didn't matter. Not anymore. My heart seized. It was the way she'd walked in the door. The look on her face, her body language when she saw him. Before she saw me.

He had her.

"Well, I'll leave you two to the details." She stopped while turning. "I just came in to warn you that I'm leaving, and as last man out, you'll have to lock up."

"Duly noted, Dr. Kruger." Mark headed back to his side of the desk and made a show of shutting down his MacBook. No massive school clunker for this boy. "We'll be leaving in a minute."

"Well, good evening, all!" Kruger left the door wide open.

My throat closed.

"It will delight Olivia." He said it matter-of-factly.

"Yeah," I agreed. "You should probably lead with her. I'm better in a group. I juice up everyone else's game, you know? I'm a blender."

Redkin shook his head. "You're too modest. I'm good at this, at what I do. And what I see is a girl who has *never* blended. You're not *that* girl, Kate—the one who's lost in the middle of a crowd until you squint your eyes and say, 'Oh, yeah, there she is.'"

He got up and I got up.

Redkin reached for his tie and swung it around his neck. Then he slipped on his suit jacket. Dinner date? I made for the door.

"If that's all for—" I grasped the handle.

"I know what you are, and what you are not, Kate."

All the heat flew out of me. No. He couldn't know . . . *Calm, calm, calm.* I didn't turn around. *"Sir?"*

"Some of us are hunted," he whispered. "And some of us are hunters. It's better to be the latter, isn't it?"

What the . . . ? I pretended I didn't hear. "Thanks. Until next week, sir."

I shut the door and flew out of the school, and I didn't stop until I got to the penthouse. Bruce attacked me as soon as I cracked open the door. I sat on the floor so he could bathe me in puppy licks.

"That you?" Olivia came out of her room. "You are ruining that dog, you know. How'd it go with Mark?"

"Okay." I had to parcel out the words between Bruce's slobberings. "Photo shoot next week, all of us. But the Christmas mailing will feature just you and me."

"Oooooh, lovely!" Olivia clapped her hands. It was the most animated I had ever seen her.

It will delight Olivia.

"Isn't he incredible? The man has *it*. He's like that superhero in the Avengers movie, the blond one, right?"

Bruce was standing on my lap facing Olivia and wagging his tail furiously in my face.

"Yeah. Yeah, I know what you mean." But I didn't. I wasn't sure what Redkin's game was or what was going on. The only thing I was sure of was that being a superhero had nothing to do with it.

FRIDAY, NOVEMBER 20

OLIVIA

Kate posed herself on the stone coffee table. "Okay, ready?" she asked.

Olivia settled into the cushiest part of the built-in sofa. Both girls were swathed in the comfy fleece of their extra-large school sweatshirts and sweatpants. The Waverly sweats had become their "home" uniform.

"Ready, all ready!" She opened her book of *Immortal Poems* to the appropriate page.

Kate cleared her throat. "So his dad's dying. Keep that in mind for every single word. It's what all the raging is about. About not going gently, about not giving up with just a pitiful sigh, right?"

"Right, got it. Go."

"Okay, next line." Kate inhaled dramatically and threw her fists in the air.

Old age should burn and rave . . .

"Get it? Rave! That's the fight he's demanding, see?" Kate looked over to Olivia expectantly. Bruce rolled on his back, offering up his tummy.

"I'm totally with Bruce," Olivia said, nodding. "When you read it the way you read, it all becomes clear as glass from the first word on. Pray continue."

Just as Kate launched into the next line, Bruce leapt off Olivia. The front door flew open and the little dog attacked the incoming intruder with vigorous tail-thumping.

"Dad! You're early!" Olivia jumped from the sofa and ran to greet her father. "We weren't expecting you until midnight! We were going to order takeout."

Kate remained frozen on the coffee table, book in hand. "Hi, Mr. Sumner."

Olivia kissed her father's unshaven cheek. "Kate is reading Dylan Thomas, the one about his father dying. I really get it deep in my bones now. She should be onstage."

Mr. Sumner picked up the squirming puppy and smiled at Kate. "Looks to me like she already is."

"Sorry, Mr. Sumner, I shouldn't have . . ." She stepped off the coffee table.

"Relax." He raised his hand in a futile attempt to ward off an attack of face-licking. "If you've got Olivia digging deeper into poetry, you feel free to use any piece of furniture you see fit. This is the mutt I paid for?"

"Oh, Dad, come on. You love him already."

"Under advisement." He placed the squirming puppy on the floor and hugged his daughter. "I'm going to hit the shower, and then takeout sounds perfect. I'm beat."

"Sure, Dad. Just a lazy night at home with our men—you, Bruce and Bob Dylan."

"Dylan Thomas," corrected Kate.

"Whatever. We'll order from the best restaurant in the city. It's a dive deep in Chinatown that Kate's unearthed. We've got the take-out menu."

Mr. Sumner picked up his suitcase. "Kate, there's more to you than meets the eye. Speaking of which, you two look like sisters in those getups."

"Closer than sisters." Olivia stepped back and threw her arm around Kate.

Her father started for his suite, then stopped. "I'm assuming that Anka has already left for her weekend at her sister's?"

"Yup, apparently this round of chemo has been really rough on her sister. Remember to express concern when you see her."

"Right, thanks." Mr. Sumner headed off with Bruce hot on his heels, clearly eager to check out what the new interloper had in his bag.

They both heard a "Damn it!" from her father's room.

"He must've stepped on a chew toy." Kate bit her lip.

Olivia hugged herself. Puppy paraphernalia aside, she had made her father happy. She could tell. He was tired, sure, but there was no concern etched on his face. She could tell as soon as he'd opened the door. It felt good. *Felt* good.

"Come on, let's order a feast." Olivia marched over to the charging counter where they kept their plug-in devices and a stash of take-out menus. Anka never ventured near that area, convinced that all those devices emitted something marginally nuclear.

"Let's get a double of the spinach greens, that short rib thingy and . . . hey, Mark!"

"Redkin is not on the menu." Kate stopped checking off items.

"No, I mean, my father's going to be so pleased about the photo shoot and the latest Waverly Wonders news and how Kruger

111

is going to use it on our applications, etc., etc., etc." She smiled in anticipation of telling him all about Mark and how good he was for the school. *Mark . . .*

"You okay?"

"Never better." Olivia hadn't taken her Lexapro today, and no Ativan for two days. She felt herself awakening bit by bit. Sure, it was a little scary. But *this*—this *feeling*—was worth a bit of fear.

Mark Redkin was worth a bit of fear.

SATURDAY, NOVEMBER 21

KATE

They left at dawn. Last night, somewhere between the sweet-and-sour soup and the spring rolls, Mr. Sumner and Olivia got to talking about "the cabin" (which sounded more like a massive chalet) and how they hadn't set foot in it for over a year. Olivia's edges softened as her father reminisced about the place.

"Why don't you go tomorrow?" I suggested. "You said it's less than a couple of hours away."

"Dad? Why not? Let's go!"

Mr. Sumner shook his head but capitulated within seconds. They were adamant that I join them, and I was adamant that they go alone. Mr. Sumner's next trip was going to take him away until Christmas, and it seemed to me that they needed some time together. Besides, it gave me monster brownie points by making me look so considerate. When you're not paying rent, you have to think of a thousand different ways to "pay" your rent.

"Hey, I insist. You guys deserve some quality time. Bruce and I will guard the fort. Go!"

And go they did.

And I was home alone. *Home.* Whoa! I actually thought that. Dangerous. *Don't get comfy, Katie girl. Stay alert.*

I finished my physics lab work and the analysis of Dylan Thomas, and I even started making notes on my exit essay. It was going to focus on mental health issues, for sure. That way I had a bulletproof excuse to hover around Kruger's office. I reorganized the items in Anka's pantry according to size and expiration date. She wouldn't be back until late tomorrow afternoon. They were throwing everything but the kitchen sink at her sister in what seemed to be a hopeless situation. I called Anka with a cheery update and told her not to sweat it because the Sumners had gone up to the lake. She thanked me too much and cried. Slavs cry a lot. I walked Bruce four times, cleaned up my computer files . . . A day needs bones.

By three p.m. I found myself in Olivia's room. I had to smile at her wonky little altar setup. She'd told me that she hadn't prayed in months, but she couldn't get herself to trash the Holy Roller paraphernalia either. I made her bed on the second visit and had determined that there was nothing useful in there by the third. Except . . . I went back to her bathroom and opened her medicine chest. I knew Olivia always carried something with her, but the other bottles lived here. I took out the Lexapro, dumped out the pills and counted back to the issuing date. *Hmm.* A new bottle of Ativan, issued eight days ago, was almost as full as the Lexapro. There was no doubt about it. The girl was cutting down on the anxiety meds. It explained things. Olivia was *more* lately. I wasn't sure more what, just *more.*

Good to know.

It was probably a decent call. Her shrink, Tamblyn, was a meds slut. Most of them were. I never thought the combo she was on was doing her any favors, but then I didn't know quite what was up with her either. I'd have to get on that pronto. I should have gone through her files by now. *Chop, chop, Katie.*

114

Bruce and I started padding out of the bedroom, but I picked up a photo before I left. It looked out of place, since it was such a fussy pink and bejeweled thing. A frame picked out by a little girl. It wasn't the best shot, a little out of focus, but you sure got the sense of it. It was a picture of Mr. Sumner, a three- or four-year-old Olivia and a beautiful woman wearing a head scarf. They were outdoors somewhere, bathed in sunlight. At the cabin? The adults had their arms wrapped around the child, and the three of them were smiling into the sun.

A day needs bones.

Mother, father, daughter. I pressed the frame to me. I didn't have a single picture of us, not one.

I slid onto the floor leaning against the mattress. Bruce waddled up and settled into my lap. He wasn't interested in the photo.

Mother, father, daughter . . .

I knew it was a mistake. Even at eleven, I knew. But what could you do at eleven? Dick all, baby, that's what. Everyone else has the power. No one listens to a kid.

I'd thrown up three times already and there were almost two more days to go. It wasn't just the bus and the fumes—it was where we were going. I knew it would be bad. Why didn't my mother see? She was weak. He made her weak.

I hated that she was weak. But I still loved her. Didn't I?

"It'll be completely different this time," she said over and over again. "Daddy's got a good job, a great job with the oil rig. It's a big company. He's a supervisor, Katie! I'll only have to work part-time at the site's dental office. This is it. We'll finally be a real family—mother, father, daughter."

I had to leave Mary-Catherine, the only friend I'd ever had. And Sister Rose.

"He hasn't touched a drop since . . . since he surprised us in the spring."

I loved Sister Rose.

"He's a clever man, your dad—brilliant when he's off the drink. None smarter. He should have had his chance at university, that's all his problem is. Your father's just too smart for his own good, and the world is difficult for a man like that."

And Mary-Catherine's dad. He would miss me too. I was sure of it. They would all miss me. Yessiree, Katie's absence would be noted and mourned. I stared out the window while she talked. Dusk kissed the endless flat plains. I was trapped, pure and simple. Mile after mile of wheat and grasses and a sky that was way too big for its own good. There was way too much of whatever that was out there.

"And you've got no cause to fear on the schooling front. I have seen to all that. I know what you've got, Katie, and so did Sister Rose and the Mother Superior. Only the best private schools for you from now on. It's a gift, baby—a gift! It's your new life. My gift. You can always be the scholarship kid, no matter what. That's how good you are, and don't you ever forget that. You've got his brains. School, baby. It's your ticket. There's a prize at the end of it. We've talked about it. You keep your eye on the prize, because nothing else matters. Promise?"

The bus rolled on and night fell. Literally, just like that, it landed on the plains, sucking up the endless sight line, leaving nothing in its wake.

"Katie, do you promise?"

"Yeah, I promise, Mom. Really." What did it matter?

She smiled and sank back into her seat. "It'll be different, you'll see. Your father loves you so much. It'll be completely different."

No buildings, no lights, just all that darkness.

Bruce was licking the tears off my face. We both got up slowly. I replaced the photo: mother, father, daughter. *You're on your own, Katie.*

A day needs bones, is all.

TUESDAY, NOVEMBER 24

OLIVIA

Olivia had been looking forward to the photo shoot for days. She wasn't the only one. They all fluttered around Mark like butterflies to milkweed. That included Halston, the A-list photographer he'd drummed up. Ms. Draper was more restrained, but why was she even there? Supposedly she wanted to see how it was all put together so she "could speak to it" at the board.

Lame.

The Wonders were marched to the physics lab, the media room, the renovated drama center, the library and Mr. Cormier's classroom. Just when Olivia thought she'd drop, they were told to get into their gym gear and head for the Upper School gymnasium. The logistics were complex, especially with everyone keeping an eye on everyone else.

In each room, Mark took great care with the group and individual shots. Olivia could tell that each girl was on high alert. Each was tracking Mark tightly. Did his eyes linger for a beat longer on

Serena or Morgan than they did on her? No. Did he touch Olivia more than he did Claire? More than the others? Yes. Not appreciably, but Olivia certainly noticed and maybe Draper did too. She couldn't be sure. It was harder than usual to read that woman's expressions because she didn't have any. Olivia's money was on Botox, and probably a little filler too. How pathetic.

Olivia was relieved when they got to the big open space of the gym. She could finally breathe. The girls seemed to have doused themselves in their "signature" scents. Even Draper was dripping in Jo Malone. Olivia had been combatting a headache since the end of the first location.

The interesting takeaway was that Mark almost ignored Kate through the whole thing. So much so that Draper seemed compelled to make up for it. She kept fussing with Kate, putting her front and center. "Kate is the chair and our Waverly Scholar, after all. And just *look* at the child." Halston seemed to agree. Olivia didn't mind the focus on Kate, so long as Mark wasn't the one doing the focusing.

"Ladies, ladies, I need Mark in this shot too." Then Halston paused for an eternity, working out the scenario in his head. "Okay, off the top, Mark will be down and center under the basketball hoop. Wait." He frowned, looked unhappy, paced, looked at Mark, checked the gym, looked at the girls. "I've got it! Ms. Draper, darling, we need lots of identifiable pieces of sporting equipment."

Draper started heading for the storage room.

"I want a basketball, volleyball, soccer ball, the hockey thing the girls use. Do you girls play cricket? I want a baseball bat, rackets, uh . . ."

"We have an equestrian program affiliated with Central Park," offered Serena, who was in said equestrian program.

"Perfect!" gushed Halston. "Bring me a riding helmet and that stick you beat the horse with."

Serena took off for the crop and helmet like her life depended on it. She'd been like that all night. Desperate to please.

The rest of the Wonders raced to help Draper raid the equipment room. Couldn't have Serena looking like she was the only one who cared about Mark's photo shoot.

"Genius," Mark said, slapping Halston on the back when they returned with the gear. "You showcase the athletic riches of the school in one fun and campy shot."

Halston fairly cooed. "Exactly. Now, girls, pick up a sports item in each hand and put one foot on a ball. Mark, honey, you kneel with one knee down. Girls, arrange yourselves around him. And don't let me catch anyone posing hard."

"Come on, ladies," Mark groaned as he knelt. "Make the old guy look good."

Well . . . you can just imagine.

It took almost an hour of posing and rearranging before Halston felt he got the one picture that was more perfect than the dozens of others before. You could fire up a small country with the electricity generated during those shots. Even with Draper there, the girls got increasingly giggly, flirty, suggestive.

Not Kate, though, and certainly not Olivia. Olivia held herself way back. It was a gamble, but she was willing to bet that with a man like Mark, she had to make him come to her.

It was almost eleven p.m. before they were finally dismissed. The other girls scrambled to the dressing room. Olivia stayed back and surveyed the scene. It looked like a sports store had exploded in the gym. Draper was helping Halston with the photo equipment while they chatted about her vision for the slide loop at the Winterfest Gala. Mark was in the equipment room. Olivia paused, picked up a bat and a hockey stick, and headed over.

"Olivia. Hey, thanks, but you don't have to do this." He turned to her and, without the distraction of the others, *saw* her. "You

119

know, I was hoping that we might have a meeting before break on the gala proceedings. These are your people, so to speak. I've really appreciated your input so far. So how about a coffee next week?"

Bingo.

"Oh, I'd love that!" Was that too eager? She was startled by the emotions coursing through her.

"Perfect," he said. "I'll look forward to it."

And then Kate was by her side. "Time to go, amigo. Great shoot, Mr. Redkin." Olivia knew he hated being called *Mr.* Redkin.

Kate took Olivia's arm and dragged her through the door. When they were on the street, Kate lit into her out of the blue.

"What the hell, Olivia? What's going on? What is he looking forward to?"

"A coffee meeting," Olivia said, bristling. "What? Are you my mother? He's only taking an interest."

"I'll say! That man—" She stopped herself. "That *man* is a player of biblical proportions. We know about Draper and maybe other staff, and—"

"Kate, I don't want to marry him, I just want to . . ." No, Olivia would not venture there. Mark stirred things. She couldn't explain, couldn't trust Kate, not yet. "I just want a taste. It's like I told you— only men from now on, no boys need apply."

"Olivia, look, I have this real queasy feeling about him, about this, about whatever he's playing. Don't—"

"Don't? *Don't!* How dare you!" It was as if Olivia had been shot through with a hot spike. "Really, Ms. *Chair* of the Waverly Wonders?" They were in front of the condo building. "And do you know what they call that feeling, Kate O'Brien? Jealously! You're jealous! Mark barely looked at you the whole night. And you just can't handle not being in the spotlight for a single solitary second, can you?

Get something straight, Kate. Never, ever forget that I'm not part of *your* parade. *You're* part of mine!"

Olivia spotted Aftab craning his neck, looking at them through the glass door, puzzled. Whoa, whoa! *Exhale, girl.* Where did that come from? Even though she hadn't moved, Olivia sensed Kate shrinking from her. And that *felt* wrong. It was a misfire. She knew for sure that Kate was in her corner, and she was pretty sure the girl wasn't seething with jealousy either. It seemed that this brand-new feelings thing was still a bit wobbly.

"Uh, I'm . . . look, sorry, Kate." She took in a good deep breath. "That was way out of line." She reached for her friend. "I'm a little PMS-y lately, and I tend to erupt out of the blue. So far, only Anka has had to endure me." She was pleased with herself for pulling that one out of thin air.

Kate nodded but didn't say anything. She still looked a bit rattled.

"Don't worry," Olivia assured her. "I'm the one running this show with Mark, and I know exactly what I'm doing. I've been sort of out of it, and it's like I'm just beginning to feel human. Mark makes me feel human, and that's a kick. But I know what I'm doing and I'm so *not* going to lose my head, promise."

"Yeah, of course." Kate finally hugged back. "If you've got it locked down. As long as you're sure."

Sure? Of course she was sure. Olivia knew that she could handle this—all of it. *This* was thrilling. He wanted her. She had Kate, and she would have Mark too. Olivia Sumner had waited a long time for exactly this.

Bring it on.

MONDAY, NOVEMBER 30

KATE

I'd felt safe for a bit. Was that it? Was that the beginning? Safe makes you stupid. I never indulge in *safe*. Yet I blew off Olivia's little outburst, didn't turn it over and examine its entrails. I got distracted. I let Thanksgiving get to me.

Mr. Sumner was stuck halfway across the world in the Hong Kong office. Olivia played John Coltrane all day long in his honor. I got in a cab and picked up our preordered, ready-made feast from Dean & DeLuca, or the "Thanksgiving Special for Rich Losers," as Olivia called it.

We didn't allow Anka to lift a finger.

We set the table in the formal dining room. Mr. Sumner had sent a spectacular horn of plenty floral arrangement that took up almost a third of the table. I lined the rest with every single candlestick the Sumners owned and lit them all. We got out the Waterford Crystal, the Royal Crown Derby and the polished silver. We decanted seven containers of garlic-roasted fingerling potatoes, a wild mushroom salad, bacon-infused brussels sprouts, whipped sweet potatoes, lemon asparagus, a surprise dessert and a camera-ready, oyster-stuffed seventeen-pound turkey.

For the three of us.

It was ridiculous and pathetic and the best Thanksgiving I'd ever had.

But the glow wore off fast. On Monday I woke up knowing that I couldn't ignore the unease anymore. Ever since that stupid photo shoot, something had shifted. Olivia was sweet all weekend long, but more detached and preoccupied than usual. Dark stuff was gathering and I had to arm myself accordingly, but against what? Something. I felt like a bystander at an accident that hadn't happened yet.

Mrs. Colson's desk was covered with my research material, my laptop, my notebook and the library's rather pedestrian books on mental health, but I was waiting for something more substantial, the DSM-5. Kruger, Draper and Rolph, the head of the Upper School, were locked in Ms. Goodlace's office, probably discussing how to handle the inevitable blowback when winter-term reports were sent out next week. They finally emerged just before five p.m.

Dr. Kruger winked at me as she glided past my desk and into her office. She was wearing a dress, a nice fitted job, maybe Diane von Furstenberg. For the first month of school, Kruger had only worn pants. Now nothing but dresses. I smelled wardrobe overhaul. I smelled a lot.

"There you go, Kate." She plunked down the reference book, the nutbar bible, the *Diagnostic and Statistical Manual of Mental Disorders*. "Anytime you want it, just ask. But it can't leave the office."

"Sure, thanks! I'll always work at one of the secretaries' desks when I use it. Right now, I'll just skim, get the feel of it, use it for inspiration, you know?"

"Good plan." Kruger walked back to her office for her coat. Excellent, she was leaving. They all appeared to be leaving. "There's probably still staff around, but don't stay later than five thirty, okay? I don't want you here by yourself at all hours. Just leave the DSM-5 on the desk." And then—damn!—she locked her office. She was about fifty-fifty on doing that. We called out our "see you in the mornings." It had taken forever, but I was finally alone with the book in all its purple-covered glory. Just Googling various disorders hadn't been cutting it for me. I needed a starting point. With the book, I could begin to figure out what was up with Olivia. I thumbed through the index. Okay, let's start with major depressive disorders. I ran my finger down some diagnostic criteria. Hmm.

Depressed mood most of the day? No, not really. No. Well, maybe, kind of. But no, I was pretty sure, that was a no. Olivia wasn't deeply down or anything, as far as I could tell. *Significant weight loss?* Nope. The girl ate, and she was no more weight-obsessed than your average weight-obsessed high school senior. *Insomnia?* Everyone always has insomnia on the "are you crazy" lists. No on that one too. *Psychomotor agitation?* Whatever that means, no.

This didn't seem to be the right category at all. Sure, Olivia was detached or kind of flat at times. She hid it well, but I could tell when she was "working" her expressions and responses. She didn't do it with me so much, but out there in the world, Olivia Sumner had to make an effort. Wait a minute. There was something called "Specifiers for Depressive Disorders: With Melancholic Features," and that included something like a blunted reaction to things. I frowned at the rest of the list. Maybe, maybe not. Things fit, but not quite.

The book was a tough and confusing read. I changed tactics,

flipping to the glossary, which listed things like "Depersonalization," which talked about feeling all detached and being numb to stuff.

Maybe, kind of, but I needed more. There wasn't a handy "see *Acting weird*, page 140." So I flipped around glancing at stuff. Everything caught my eye. I lingered at borderline personality disorder. That was a scary one. It focused on feelings of abandonment, and there was the loss of her mom and her dad always being away. But none of the other criteria fit as far as I could tell.

I hadn't even noticed him coming in.

"Where have you gone, little girl?" It was Mark.

I had to admit it, the room warmed up when he smiled. Quite a trick.

"Nowhere." I shut the book and started to pack up. "Just trying to sort out my themes for the exit thesis."

"Stay, please." He tapped the desk. "I'll be in my office. I know you need staff around."

Was I relieved or scared? What was it about this guy? "Oh, thanks, but it's past five thirty and I'm . . ." *What, exactly?* "Late." First rule of Liars' Club—keep it simple. "But thanks, though." I grabbed my backpack and headed for the door.

"Next time, then. I'll always be here when you need me, Kate. Remember that."

Did I hesitate? Did he see?

"And, Kate?" he called after me. "Do tell Olivia that I'm very much looking forward to our coffee meeting on Thursday." I felt his smile on my back.

It was official. I was scared.

THURSDAY, DECEMBER 3

OLIVIA

Any doubts Olivia might have had on the way over disintegrated the moment she saw Mark at his table at the Last Drop Café. It was as if a spotlight was trained on him. Olivia made her way to him with her heart pounding in her throat.

The café was quite a few blocks out of school range, so it was new to her, and way more interesting than the Starbucks where the Wonders regularly met. The place was dolled up in deep Victoriana, with plush velvet mismatched chairs and ornamental antique side tables. Cozy, dark and comfy. Kate would love it.

"I hope you approve of my little find. I enjoy the vibe here."

Mark rose to greet her, and Olivia caught her breath. He was out of his "school clothes" and instead wore a pair of faded jeans and a fitted navy-blue T-shirt. He looked . . . he had beautiful . . . everything.

"May I get you a cappuccino? They do a good job here."

"Perfect." She watched his every move as he made his way to the barista.

"Skim milk, no sugar," he said, returning with a foaming cup. "Did I guess right?"

"Perfect." She was repeating herself.

"So I took your advice about only offering 'experiences' at the live auction this year." Mark raised his mug of black coffee to his lips, *his lips,* and held it for a heartbeat before he took a sip. She was mesmerized.

Olivia nodded, or she thought she nodded. Either way, he continued.

"The gala committee was wild about the idea. There was quite an infusion of excitement, and all because of you, Olivia."

She probably nodded again, or demurred or something. His arms were a work of art, defined, sun-dappled, strong. They looked strong.

How would they feel wrapped around her? God, this was . . .

"So far, we've got a dozen box seats to sporting events and four different sets of on-the-floor tickets for this boy band." He looked amused. "I forget their name, but I've been assured that the dads will go into a bidding frenzy just to surprise their little darlings. We've also got a bunch of vacation homes on offer for a week. One is in the Hamptons, and there are two chalets in Aspen and one in Whistler. Plus the Sanfords' villa in Aix-en-Provence. The Petersons arranged for a six-person spa weekend at the Grange, featuring some hot-yoga guru, and Serena's father kicked in a tasting tour of his restaurants in New York, Chicago and London, including airfare. Smacks more of a guilty conscience than a tax write-off, if you ask me." He raised an eyebrow.

"Probably," she managed to whisper. "Poor Serena, I think they're divorcing."

Mark nodded. "I suspected as much."

She was distracted by the sound of her own heart beating. Olivia had to strain to hear him. She leaned in closer.

"Then there's tickets to that Robert Downey Jr. play, including dinner and a night at the Four Seasons, as well as a helicopter tour of the city. I could go on and on, but . . . well, we'll break records because of you."

Were there other people in the café?

Mark asked about her and Kate's Yale aspirations. He listened intently and then insisted that they needn't concern themselves at all. He went on for a bit about his plans for the advancement committee in the coming year and how he had sold his platform to the board.

"Between the Winterfest Gala and the Wonders, the board thinks I walk on water—for the moment, at least." He moved imperceptibly closer.

Olivia willed him closer still. "Well, of course," she managed. "Creating the Wonders was a brilliant idea!"

"Yes," he agreed almost reluctantly. "Each one of you brings something extraordinary to the table. But especially you, Olivia. You have something even more—something that burns beneath that cool beauty and intelligence."

Her breath caught.

His hand grazed hers, carelessly. "I owe you, Olivia. You can count on me for anything and I will be there for you."

She was in danger of being flooded with emotion.

"Don't retreat."

"What?"

He took her hand into both of his. And she dissolved.

"I sensed it from the beginning. Maybe that's why I was so drawn to you."

"I, uh, I don't . . ."

The corner of his mouth played at a smile. She needed to reach over and touch that corner.

"Some of us have things happen to us, and then we guard

against it. We throw up walls that will never leave us exposed again." He squeezed her hand gently. "And it works. Sometimes all too well, right?"

He *knew* her.

Mark leaned back against his chair, taking warmth away with him. She wanted him to hold her hand again, to hold her. She so needed to be held.

"The pain's shut out or flattened, but so is everything else. All the beautiful light." He sighed then. "You are special, Olivia. So mature. The girls at the school must be like children to you. Am I wrong?"

"How . . . how did you know?"

"*Am* I wrong?"

"No."

"Let me help you find your way back." He leaned over again. "Let me help you find your way to feeling things you never thought possible. I can do that, Olivia. I *want* to do that."

She needed him to touch her, kiss her. She'd never wanted anything more.

Instead he rose. The café was no longer bustling. Somehow it was eight o'clock and the place was closing. People were preparing to leave. Mark offered his hand. He helped her into her coat wordlessly, tenderly.

They were nearing the door, and any words Olivia might have had were lodged in her throat.

"Do you trust me?" he asked as he opened the door for her.

The frigid December air bit into her.

"Olivia?" Mark took hold of both her arms before she could turn east and head for home. "Olivia, I need to know—*do* you trust me?"

"Yes," she said it clearly. There could be no doubt, because there was no doubt. She wasn't a child. It would be worth it. Whatever it was, whatever was coming. "Yes, I do."

"I'm glad." He smiled and let her go.

SUNDAY, DECEMBER 6

KATE

Olivia had changed her shoes at least fifty-seven times. She was just meeting a couple of her old high school friends for brunch. I didn't get it. She'd blown off every other attempt at get-togethers, and now, all of a sudden, the girl was deep into shoe frenzy.

"Too *too*?" she asked, trotting out in a pair of charcoal Jimmy Choo ankle boots.

"No, perfect. If you cuff your jeans, it'll be that expensive/casual thingy you rock so well." I could have shot myself. It led to her retrying her entire skinny jean wardrobe to see which one "cuffed" the best.

"You look spectacular!" I called into her room. Even though she hadn't seen Anita and Jessica, her so-called friends, since the summer, Olivia had never seemed to care that much about them or what they thought. She said they were as phony as rhinestones. So? Must be a rich-girl thing. Image above all else.

Anka and I got her out by 10:17 a.m.

"What a production!"

Anka looked grim. "I vas never to loving zose girls."

I, on the other hand, loved Anka more each day. It snuck up on me. The woman was such a force. "Hey, Anka, how about we go to Chinatown, you and me? We can get some great vegetables and maybe something nice you can bring to your sister this afternoon."

She made a face.

"What? What's the matter?"

"Zat place is full of immigrants-type peoples."

"Well, yeah, but aren't you, uh . . . ? Look, Chinatown is full of great stuff and great food. I know you're going to love it. I'll show you where I worked."

"Okay, zen." She bustled off to get our coats and her purse. "Ve go. I am to bringing za shopping list."

Even on a Sunday morning in the middle of winter, Chinatown was packed. The noise, colors and confusion were an assault on the senses after the perfect vacuum of the penthouse. I kept checking to see how Anka was faring. She was in her element. There wasn't a grapefruit, salted cod, carrot, Fruit of the Loom package (five for $2.99) or plastic change purse that she didn't pick up or run her hands over. If someone accidentally bumped into her, she smiled. Anka sucked it all in.

Maybe for us it was more home than the home we occupied.

I didn't know about her, but I could be *me* here.

I had to surgically remove her from Lee's kitchen store. Anka bought sixteen little blue-and-white bowls for a party Olivia was never going to have and last year's model of Vitamix blender for her sister. "She is too sickly to notice vat year model it is being." I steered her to the Chens' market, knowing full well that I'd never get her out once she spied their mind-numbing array of fresh fruit and vegetables. As usual, Mrs. Chen materialized out of nowhere.

Despite the weather, she was still sporting her trademark blindingly white apron and embroidered dragon slippers.

"Katie, ha! You come back!"

I stepped toward her.

She stepped back, clearly worried that I was going in for another hug. She examined Anka.

"Dis your mudda?"

"No, dhalink, I am to being za housekeeper."

I felt like I was trapped in an eighties sitcom. What was I thinking? There was no way that these women could traverse the highways of their respective accents and cultures. As if to prove my point, Mrs. Chen slapped Anka's hand, making her drop the Fuji apple she had reached for.

"Bah, no goot!" Mrs. Chen linked arms with Anka and dragged her to the back of the store and out into the alley. Wow, Anka was going to get to pick from the produce that hadn't been uncrated yet. This was an honor reserved for Chinatown royalty. Now what? Given Anka's proclivity for produce, we could be here for the night. I was stranded minding the haul from Lee's. The Vitamix bag alone was the size of a truck tire.

"Michelob? Michelob, is that you?"

I swung around and then around again.

"It is you!" And there, in all his irritating handsomeness, was Johnny. "What are you doing here? Couldn't stay away? I'm flattered."

"You know very well that I used to work here," I sniffed. Man, he got under my skin.

"Sure," he said, shrugging. "But now you live in nosebleed territory. So I have to assume you came back to get a glimpse of me." He tossed Anka's discarded apple in the air and then bit into it. Mrs. Chen would take him out with an iron pipe. "Glimpse away, Michelob."

What the hell? "I've glimpsed plenty, thank you. Anyway, never mind me—what are *you* doing here?"

Johnny extended his arm out to the street. "This, fair Michelob, is my domain, *my* turf. My people have a bakery on Mulberry."

"Hey, my name is Kate. I would appreciate it if you called me that, *Johnny*. And I say again, who the hell names their kid Johnny anymore?"

"It was my father's name."

Oh, damn. "Was?" I felt myself wince.

"Was." Johnny stopped chewing. "My dad, John senior, passed away a few months ago. I had to leave school for a bit to help out, but I'll be going to CUNY in January."

"OhI'msosorryreallyIam." The words tumbled and tripped out stupidly. I felt awful about his dad, about making fun of his name and about feeling whatever the hell I was feeling at that moment. "What's a CUNY?"

He shook his head and smiled. "The City University of New York. I'm taking paralegal courses, marking time and collecting credits before I apply for the NYPD. And you . . . ?" He eyed me. "I'm guessing nothing but Princeton for the *gweilo* princess?"

"Nothing but Yale."

He grinned. "You've got to admit I'm good."

"I'm not admitting any such thing, except . . . well, I really am sorry about your father. Really."

"Enough to call a truce?"

"Truce? There's no need. Look, Johnny, I'm not looking to—"

"Chill, girl. Just friends. Even though you have the Chens watching your back—and believe me you can't do better than Mrs. Chen—I've got a feeling that their little *gweilo* is even more out of her element uptown than downtown."

Out of my element? I was right back on fast burn. Who did

he think he was? If he only knew who he was talking to and how far I had . . .

"I'm cool with the Upper East Side party folk too, if you recall, and"—he surveyed the expanse of the market—"nobody knows the ins and outs of this place better than me. These people trust me. So I've got uptown *and* downtown cred."

Could he be more full of himself?

Just as I was about to take him down, I heard Mrs. Chen's slippered feet slapping behind me.

"Johnny, ha! Good boy!" She gave him another apple. "You like Kate? Very pretty, ha?"

Shoot me now.

Before he could answer and Anka could catch up, Mrs. Chen actually threw her arm around me. "You watch, she need. Always trouble, ha?"

What. The. Hell.

Did he bow? What was going on? How did this happen? I'd gone from eighties sitcom to "straight to DVD" thriller. Johnny turned to Anka and introduced himself as my *good* friend Johnny Donato. Wait, Donato? Of Donato's Bakery? I loved that bakery. Somehow, that just pissed me off more.

"It's a pleasure to meet you, ma'am."

Anka, in an uncharacteristic show of stupidity, was charmed.

"We've got to go, Anka." I began gathering up packages. "Your sister will wonder where you are."

Johnny handed me the huge bag containing the blender and the other one with all the bowls. "Nice to see you again, Kate. Now that you know where to find me, I'll be here waiting." Wink.

Yup, he winked.

Good, you just wait and wink away, because I for one was never coming back.

SUNDAY, DECEMBER 13

OLIVIA

Neither Kate nor Anka was home. Olivia let her purse drop, walked out of her coat and allowed herself to be adored by Bruce.

"It's happening, Bruce," she said to the puppy. "I knew it would." She giggled as he propped himself on his hind legs and placed his front paws on her chest to brace himself for exuberant face-licking. Was she drunk? No, she'd had just the one Bellini. She was always careful. "Okay, enough, you brute! I'm going to have a shower."

Olivia floated toward her room, and although she noted that she felt light and airy, she also noted how much she *felt*. God knows she had felt his kiss on the back of her neck as Mark helped her off with her coat at the restaurant. His lips barely touched her skin and yet her entire body ignited. He didn't touch her again—not once— but she was still radiating from that one sweet kiss. As she knew she would. Every move in the game was exactly right. And there would be so much more when . . .

She giggled again.

Olivia headed to the shower with Bruce hot on her heels. Again she stopped.

No, not a shower.

Olivia never took baths, only showers. Sometimes multiple showers. Sometimes scalding hot, sometimes freezing cold—sometimes both in successive order, just to remind herself that she could feel, that she was alive in her own body. Not today.

She padded to the linen cupboard and took out an array of candles, each one more prohibitively expensive than the last. Olivia arranged them around the bathtub and lit them all before turning the water to a warm, lovely temperature. She added a few drops of gardenia oil for good measure, and then she eased herself in, rejoicing in the sensation of being caressed by the scented water. Bruce couldn't quite reach the lip of the marble bath, so only his paws and ears were visible. He would stand guard there until she reemerged.

"Ahhhh," she sighed as she submerged into the water. It *was* everything she had hoped. And whatever the cost, it would be worth it. Olivia let the tap flow freely over her feet and legs, luxuriating in the sound of the running water.

Suddenly, Bruce yelped excitedly and tore out of the bathroom. They must have returned.

"Olivia? Hello? We're back!"

"I'm taking a bath," she called.

"A bath?" Silence. "You don't take baths. You okay?" Closer now. Kate's voice was in the bedroom doorway.

"Never better!" she called out again. She submerged herself once more and turned on the taps again.

Never, *ever* better.

KATF

The three of us were up to our ears in application remorse in the Waverly library. I don't know how we got started, but we were cranking each other up something fierce.

"I shouldn't have applied to Brown at all," moaned Serena. "I don't even want to go to Brown. My father wants me to go to Brown. He went full-court press and called in all his favors. I want to go to Pomona, damn it. I'll never get there on my own ticket." She was vibrating like a tuning fork. Come to think of it, the beautiful Serena seemed to have been running on raw nerves for the past couple of weeks.

Olivia and I had both applied Regular Decision to Yale. All the seniors had a team of college coaches and SAT tutors. I did the heavy lifting as Olivia's SAT tutor, but I also benefited from all her highly paid college adviser info. I was now second-guessing that paid advice. Olivia's college coach had insisted that Yale did not show enough love to its Early Action candidates, and that taking that route might choke other offers. She'd said that Regular Decision was fine. Thing is, Olivia was a legacy. Her parents had met at Yale. Her mother's people were Elis back through the mists of time. My parents would have been hard-pressed to tell you which state Yale was in. I should have gone with my gut and applied Early Action.

Did we blow it? Did *I* blow it? I thought Kruger looked nervous. Did she look nervous? The acceptance rates were terrifying. Brown took in a mere 10 percent of applicants. Pomona let in 13 percent, and Yale . . . Yale had a dismal acceptance rate of less than 7 percent. A new low. There wasn't a senior or junior in the school who couldn't recite college stats at the drop of a low-fat yogurt.

I'd also applied to Columbia, the University of Chicago and Stanford, plus a couple of Canadian universities, but Yale had been "the only" ever since my mom and I saw *Indiana Jones and the Kingdom of the Crystal Skull,* which was filmed there. "That's it, Katie. That's for you, that place. It's where you belong. That's the prize." We made a pact then and there as a result of that stupid movie. Well, that and watching reruns of the *Gilmore Girls* together. Serena and Olivia had each applied to more than twenty other schools. Each application cost money that I didn't have. They'd also toured their top choices.

I didn't have top *choices.* Just Yale. Nothing else mattered. My life would begin when I got to Yale, and everything would make sense. I'd kept my eye on the prize all these years above and beyond anything else, beyond all the horseshit. And then I blinked. I should have gone with my gut. I was done.

I buried myself in the stacks so they wouldn't see me shaking.

School would let out for winter break after tomorrow's assembly. We should have been out celebrating or shopping, but instead we were in the library and, speaking for myself, getting more nauseated by the minute.

"Ladies! What are my Wonders doing in the library? The sun is shining, and Christmas is coming!"

Mark blew in like a gust of fresh air.

I was deep in the stacks, but I could hear Serena and Olivia trying to draw him into the pity party.

"Uh-uh." Mark folded his arms. "No, you don't. I've been through a lot of schools like this and I've seen way too many sharp, talented and gifted young women drive themselves to despair over the admissions cycle. You girls will get into superb colleges that will be perfect for you. That's not a wild guess, it's years of experience."

"But—" they both stammered at once.

"No buts. I'm staff and I know exactly how all of you are doing. I also know that Pomona *and* Yale"—did he call out "Yale" loudly enough for my benefit?—"will be lucky to have you grace their campuses. Ladies, I have been at this dance before."

Deep as I was in the philosophy/psychology section, I could still hear them lighten up even as they protested.

"Enough! I'm not listening to another word," he said. "Field trip. Let's go see the tree."

"What? At Rockefeller Center?" Serena was aghast. "With all those crazy tourists?"

"Yup." I could hear the smile in his voice. "And if you behave, I may spring for hot chocolate. Let's go."

"I'm in," said Olivia. "Kate, come on. Mark is dragging us to Rock Center to ooh and aah over the Christmas lights."

I slid out from the stacks.

"Kate." He stepped toward me. "Please tell me that you of all people aren't buying into this nonsense. Nothing"—he looked directly at me—"absolutely nothing could ever get in the way of your goals. Don't tell me you're freaking out about admissions too."

He was, in that moment, so warm and open and . . .

139

"A little, I guess."

He shook his head. "It'll be okay, Kate," he whispered. "I promise."

"Let's go, girl!" Serena already had her coat on.

"I'll catch up," I said. "I've got to get a load of psycho books out so I can work on my thesis over the break."

"Sure?" Olivia asked.

"Sure." I nodded. "Go. Enjoy!"

I loved having the library to myself. I am inviolate in between bookshelves. Which is why I felt betrayed when I couldn't fight it off. It must have been the admissions anxiety. I grabbed one of the errant step stools to sit on. I tried to clear my mind and time my breaths, just as I had been taught.

It worked, until it didn't.

There was no Sister Rose at the new schools. Not at St. Ursula's in Alberta, or at any school I went to in the US. Sure, there were some nice teachers, a decent counselor or two, even one set of okay foster parents, but no one like her. Did I make her up? Eventually, I came to understand that Sister Rose had to have known each time I tried scamming her, but she loved me despite it. I would have been different had we stayed. Sister Rose was an anchor, as were Mary-Catherine and her father.

Oh, look at all that spilled milk.

I loaded up on new skills at St. Ursula's. Those girls were barracudas and I swam with the best of them. Had to. It was ugly when I didn't, I learned.

I also learned never to go to school when the bruises were obvious.

I could tell when he was "off" by the way my father opened the door or held his fork. I could read my old man at fifty paces, and I learned to read others the same way.

Survival of the fittest.

My mother did not learn. He made her not only weak but stupid too. Unbearably stupid. He did that.

Why did she serve us up on a platter? Why would my mom think that this time would be different from all the others? He could barely stand the sight of her. The more she tried to please and placate him, the more he despised her.

Not me, though. Even when he went at me, I knew I commanded his respect. Katie was his little "cockroach." Worse yet, he meant it as a compliment.

What time was it? Dazed, I grabbed my books, checked them out myself and then knocked on Mrs. Tanaka's window, mouthing "Merry Christmas" to the librarian. She smiled and waved back. I replayed the Yale application mistake over and over again. At least it was something I could get my teeth into. It wasn't until I was almost home that it came to me: Mark said that he had been through "a lot of schools like this." A lot? How was that even possible? It didn't scan. Surely he was too young to have already gone through a lot of schools. He must have said that to make the girls feel better. It was just Redkin trying to be soothing. Yeah, that was it.

Probably.

SUNDAY, DECEMBER 20

OLIVIA

Olivia's body hummed as she prepped. She was meeting Mark at their coffee shop to make plans to see each other over the holidays. *Really* see each other.

She had already formulated a list of excuses to whip out for upcoming absences. Kate would be cool, and she'd already promised the Chens that she'd put in some time over the holidays. So there was only her father, and surely he'd have a mad round of parties, business meetings and catch-up politics at the home office. So the coast would be clear. Well, clearish.

Except that it wasn't. Olivia had popped into Hermès on the way to the Last Drop to justify the excursion and buy Kate's Christmas gift. While she was there, her father called from Kennedy airport.

"Hey, Dad! Welcome home. I'm just out last-minute shopping. I'm thinking of getting a Hermès scarf for Kate. What say you?"

"Good call. I think Kate would love it."

"I thought so too."

"Look, honey, since you won't be home when I get there, I wanted to tell you that everything's arranged."

"Uh . . . ?"

"Our big plans for Christmas last year? Well, they're on for this year. We leave on the twenty-fourth."

"What?" Her stomach rolled over. "You mean Cabo?" God, they had talked about that way back in the summer! "For Christmas week?" Olivia almost tripped into the Salvation Army guy ringing his Christmas bell. She stuffed a twenty into his kettle on remote control.

"Dad, really? Uh, are you sure? I mean . . ."

"Absolutely! I promised you. I always keep my promises."

No, no, no.

"Dad, I know we always talked about it, and we almost got there last year, when . . ."

"We come back on the second. I know how you hate this season in the city."

"New Year's too?"

"You bet. And the Yardleys are making their way over from London, just like we planned last year. They're excited about seeing you."

Olivia picked out and paid for the scarf in a daze. She also picked up her pace. She couldn't be late. He didn't like late. "Yeah, me too them, but I . . ."

I what? she wondered. Her well-intentioned dear old dad was going to ruin everything. All her plans . . . Olivia had purposely begged off anything that came up. Even with Serena, who was no longer amusing. The girl had been throwing off a slightly desperate vibe for weeks now. Olivia had been making room, and lots of it. She'd carefully factored in the maximum allowable time with her father—it was the holidays, after all, and he wouldn't be back until the gala. But Kate was going to be schlepping vegetables, and Anka would be spending quite a few days with her sister.

And now it was all shot to hell.

"You've always wanted to go, and I needed to make it happen for my little girl." Checkmate. She could hear her father wending his way through the airport, out to the limo stands. "You and Kate have a suite and your own infinity pool."

"No, see, Dad, Kate really wants to earn a bit of cash over the holidays. She was quite insistent."

She heard car doors and trunks opening.

"Okay, I get that. But the Yardleys are arriving in full force, just like old times. We'll leave Christmas Eve afternoon."

The doors slammed again. He was on his way.

"Olivia?" His voice was softer now. Her father was tired. It was a fourteen-hour flight from São Paulo. "Honey, if it's not what you want, just say so. Maybe I shouldn't have sprung it on you like this. Look, I-I can get the office to—"

"No, Dad, it's great. I wanted to go more than anything, and then we had to cancel. You promised me even while I was in the hospital, and you made it happen. It's . . . it's a surprise, that's all—but a lovely surprise. I'll see you at home as soon as I get my shopping done, okay? Kate's home, and Anka's making beef Stroganoff."

At exactly half a block from the Last Drop, in front of a jewelry store, Olivia stopped, reapplied her lip gloss, threw back her shoulders and rearranged her face. Her expression should be one of anticipation tinged with dismay. She bit the corner of her lip and widened her eyes. There.

Of course Mark was disappointed when she told him. He even pouted. He looked so disarmingly boyish in that moment that she wanted to touch his mouth. And then she did, marveling at her boldness. "It will be worth the wait, I promise."

"Well, then." Mark intertwined his fingers with hers and then kissed them. "I will wait." He seemed to be searching her. "And when you do visit, well, discretion is everything, isn't it? This is important and I don't like repeating myself: you must remember to use the stairs, Olivia. Never the elevator. Got it?" And then he kissed her fingers again, and then again.

THURSDAY, DECEMBER 24

KATE

I was pretty much penniless. Even with my room and board totally gratis, Christmas wiped me out. It was why I had to go back to the market. Well, that and I sort of wanted to.

We did Christmas morning on Christmas Eve, and if I were a crier, I would have cried. All those years ... I always had to go home over the holidays, to whatever foster family I was nominally in the care of. None of them—not even the Petersons, who were halfway decent—included me the way that Anka, Olivia and Mr. Sumner did. It wasn't just the gifts. It was the way they made me feel like I was *supposed* to be there, opening my gifts with them. In return, I did my best to give them a show. You have to make people like that feel as if you're overwhelmed with gratitude.

Thing is, I was.

Anka gave me a gorgeous gray cashmere bathrobe, and that was from the housekeeper! Olivia surprised me with an Hermès scarf that was large enough to cover a family of four, and Mr. Sumner produced this amazing necklace crafted from Brazilian gemstones. I was going to be very, very careful with that one. If they tossed me out, I figured that whatever it would fetch on eBay would give me a livable sum until Yale. Damn, Yale. I started hyperventilating. Stop.

Stop.

Okay.

My gifts were a bit too. I gave Anka a grocery tote made of a patchwork of saris from Rajasthan. Mr. Sumner got a vintage fake Patek Philippe watch, which he put on immediately and kept on even as they left. I scored a "look what fell off the back of a truck" fuchsia Chloé bag for Olivia. Even with my world-class bargaining skills, it set me back big-time, since it was the real stolen deal from the Ugandans who peppered downtown and not a mere knockoff. Hence the need to get back to work, pronto.

Olivia and her father left for Cabo San Lucas at 2:07, Anka left for her sister's at 2:50 and I was working by 4:00.

Mrs. Chen, of course, gave me her usual exuberant greeting.

"You trouble?"

"No! No, Mrs. Chen, it's good. My friend went away for the holidays with her family."

She frowned.

"They asked me to go with them, but I said no. Look, I need to work, but everything is perfect."

"I smell trouble." She folded her arms, still frowning. "You lucky. I no rent room. Is yours when you come back. Blond girl not good."

My stomach lurched at the thought of those perpetually damp Spider-Man sheets.

"Honestly, Mrs. Chen, I've never been happier. Hey, Merry Christmas!" I handed her a very small bottle of perfume, Coco Noir by Chanel.

As soon as she opened it, she made a face and handed it back. "Too much. Get money back."

"No, it wasn't, Mrs. Chen. Really. I got it from the Ugandans."

She nodded, muttered a "ha" and snatched the bottle back. Yet another successful purchase on my part. All in all, it was a shockingly smooth transition back into my former life. The market does not close for the holidays. Christmas was one of the Chens' busiest times of the year, and I'd be pulling ten-hour shifts until the Sumners got back on the second. Work all day and do my readings and summaries at night. I needed the money and I needed the work.

Like I keep saying, a day needs bones.

The rest of the Wonders were a bit more problematic. They kept wanting to get together. Serena was relentless. Something was up with her. She wanted to "at least meet for drinks" before she left for London on the thirtieth, but there was no way I could afford the time or the price of the drinks, so I kept begging off. I had a moment of feeling bad about that. I almost liked Serena. I did promise Morgan that I'd go to the Sutcliffe New Year's Eve party with her and Claire, though. I'd find some excuse not to go at the last minute. I would *not* feel bad about that.

My cushy new life had made me soft. I was flat-out exhausted by the twenty-sixth.

Johnny turned up on the twenty-seventh.

"Heard you were back." He shared Mrs. Chen's sneaking-up-on-you skills.

"Yeah? Took you long enough to find me."

"Ooooh, do I detect a tone?" He grabbed a Bartlett pear in plain sight of Mrs. Chen and bit into it. Something I had not yet dared to do.

"I doubt you could *detect* anything, my once and future cop."

"*Your* future cop? Possessive case, so to speak?" A dark eyebrow rose.

"It's a figure of speech, so to speak. A riff on a book title."

"Well, I wouldn't know about that, being the product of a public school education and all."

Man, he was annoying, standing there all smirky and superior and gorqeous-like.

"How about a coffee break back at my bakery?"

"No."

"I'm not asking you to move in with me, just share a fifteen-minute coffee break."

"Can't."

"Hey, Mrs. Chen!" He was shouting and waving his arm to catch her attention way back in the Apothecary section.

To my horror, she waved back and smiled at him. That woman has not once—*ever*—smiled at me.

He pointed to my head. "Kate and me, coffee?"

"Sure, Johnny, sure!"

Adding insult to injury, she was still smiling as he hauled me out of the market.

It took us practically fifteen minutes just to get to the bakery. Johnny appeared to know every single human in Chinatown, and his place was at the outer edge. More perplexing was that everyone seemed to know me, or at least about me—even people at stores and stalls I'd never been near. "Ah, the Chens' girl!" seemed to be the standard greeting.

I was tired. Maybe my guard was down. I ended up blathering to Johnny about scholarships and how many times I'd had to move and the Yale debacle. Don't know why. Maybe I was in a mood. Maybe I was lonely. Maybe I was pathetic.

Johnny, in turn, told me about growing up in the market, and about the loss of his dad. And I listened. Don't know why.

He said he'd pick me up every day at 4:15 for our coffee break and I agreed.

Don't know why.

Just as we were heading back, I heard a laugh I recognized coming from up ahead and across the street.

"Hey, isn't that one of your uptown friends?"

I spotted her and my stomach seized.

"Yeah, you were with her at that party. You all came in together and blew everyone else out of the water."

My throat constricted.

"I'm sure she was with you." Johnny turned to me, puzzled. "Who's the guy?"

No.

The "guy" placed a protective arm around her waist. I stared at them, silent and stupid, until they disappeared into the crowd.

"Kate?"

Serena? Damn it, Serena! Where are you going? And why the hell are you going there with Mark Redkin's arm wrapped around your waist?

SATURDAY, JANUARY 2

OLIVIA

Olivia wanted to rush over to Mark's the moment they landed, but of course she couldn't, so she didn't. She texted him twice—once at the airport, once in the limo—and then promised herself that she wouldn't text again. The drive was agony. The whole trip was agony. The resort was spectacular, but the reunion with the Yardleys was hardly bearable. The Yardleys had somehow transformed into self-involved bores. Their last trip together was a lifetime ago. Olivia had transformed since then too. Several times.

All week long, she replayed Mark's every touch, kiss and glance, and fantasized about what was to come. What would Mark do? How would she react? How would she play it, manage it? It was the only way she got through the trip.

Olivia scrutinized her phone the whole ride home. Thank God her father was glued to his BlackBerry. The poor man had to do an almost immediate turnaround and be on a plane for São Paulo that night. She'd be free all evening. She would wait.

"Happy New Year and welcome home!" Kate showered them with streamers and confetti the moment they opened the door. Bruce barked and Anka tooted a ridiculous toy horn. All of them wore sparkling princess hats that proclaimed, "IT'S A NEW YEAR!" (although Bruce's fell off the instant he leapt into Olivia's arms).

"You know, I actually worry that he loves you more than he does me," said Kate, reaching for her friend. "I missed you so much! You too, Mr. Sumner. Welcome home, welcome home!"

"Not for long, I'm afraid, but thank you for, well, all of this." He appeared to be genuinely touched. "I've never had such a warm and . . . exuberant greeting."

Olivia had so missed Kate. Kate would have made the whole week in Cabo far more tolerable. Although they'd broken their standing rule and texted frequently, the phone was a poor substitute. The phone! She checked it as soon as she put Bruce back on terra firma.

Nothing.

When her father excused himself to prepare for Brazil, Olivia swept off to her room to "freshen up."

She didn't, though. She waited.

Mark wanted her. She was sure of it. She knew that look. Was she wrong? No. It was there. It was. She was always right about that kind of thing. But what if she was wrong? She felt nauseous.

Well, Olivia had wanted to *feel* things. Mark had done that. She'd known he would, and she was right about that. She'd been right about Kate too. And she was right about this. Sure, there would be blips, but Olivia knew what she was doing.

She checked again. She couldn't appear too needy, too clingy, too *too*. That would be the kiss of death for someone like Mark.

But she *was* all those things. So she texted again.

Home safe & sound. Can't wait to see you. What time?

Olivia stroked her arms. Waiting. There was a hopeful hopelessness about waiting. She smiled. Kate had got her through Samuel Beckett's *Waiting for Godot*. But she really got it now. Waiting was a tragicomedy. There was this whole absurdist, endless, excruciating quality to it. We distract ourselves in a million different ways to delude ourselves into thinking that we're not "waiting," because waiting is unendurable. Waiting has demands. It percolates with fear and potential rejection, and threatens you with despair. That's the "tragic" part that looms in the waiting, whether you're on hold with Bloomingdale's or waiting for your mother to die. There's always a wisp of hope in the hopelessness—the attendant will come back on the line and have your order, or your mother will recover, or he will text you back. She sat on her bed. Where was the "comedy" part? She checked the phone and then lay down.

Olivia slowly ran her hands up and down her body. It had been easier before. *Everything has a price.* Waiting cost her now. Why didn't he answer? In the cupboard of her new sensations, she felt like she was spinning in ever-tighter circles. She checked again.

"Olivia, I'm off, honey. The car's here."

She jumped off the bed, still clutching the phone, and went to her father. She, Bruce, Anka and, more shyly, Kate all bid him farewell.

"Hey, come on." Kate motioned toward the living room. "I've poured you a glass of wine. You can debrief me on the odiousness of the Yardley clan while you show me the pictures."

Kate was prepared with a hundred amusing Chinatown stories. Thank God for Kate.

"Hey, guess what? I saved the best for last. You are absolutely not going to believe it, but one of the times I was in Chinatown, I saw Serena *with* Mark Redkin *and* he had his arm around her! What did I tell you? He casts a wide, wide net, that boy."

The room spun. Serena? Olivia's head filled so quickly she felt as if it would explode. "Really?" she managed. "*Our* Serena?"

Olivia was certain she'd responded in the appropriate tone. Surely she'd gasped or giggled—after all, she had years of practice under her belt. Years of pretending. She swallowed an Ativan with her wine. She knew that Kate was watching her; she felt it. They looked at pictures and laughed about the Yardley girls, but she did so under an Ativan blanket. Later, when it was safe and Olivia didn't have to pretend anymore, she drifted off to the windows. It was dark and the lights of the city did their trick. And then, after she'd been home for hours, she finally felt her phone vibrate. She inhaled sharply, braced herself and then glanced at the screen.

Not tonight. Don't text ever. Not safe.

Olivia clutched the phone to her. She knew there would be blips.

WEDNESDAY, JANUARY 6

KATE

Kruger was glowing. It was the same stupid glow that had been radiating off Draper for months. Kruger, however, was married. I kind of got the thrill of flirting, but . . .

The possibility filled me with a tar-filled dread. Kruger knew *everything*—my whole sorry, sick mess.

Who else had he ensnared? Draper and Serena, for sure. Serena was getting weirder by the minute. The guy was all over the map on the age range. Redkin was going for power, information and amusement. What a trifecta. Maybe it would keep him too busy for Olivia. I had to keep her as clear as possible. Let's face it—she was my meal ticket and the roof over my head. I didn't much care who he had seduced before. Didn't pay close attention, wasn't alert enough. But now, as I examined Kruger, it became clear that his playground was dangerously close to mine.

He had my full attention.

I felt bad about Serena, but I swallowed it. Pity was a sign of weakness.

I faced my counselor. Kruger looked good. She wore a killer silk blouse. Oscar de la Renta, this season. She'd definitely upped her fashion game.

"What a beautiful scarf, Kate. Was it a gift?"

I stroked the scarf, which lay on top of my coat. "Olivia." I'd worn it to school today for a reason. Everybody noticed, and Olivia loved that everybody noticed. She carried her fuchsia Chloé bag today. Everybody noticed, and I too loved that everybody noticed.

Dr. Kruger and I rolled through the holidays, chatting about Christmas, the gifts, the schoolwork and how I was coping with all the "adjustments" thrown at me this year. That smelled like it was going to be the topic du jour.

"Hey, it's me. I thrive on *adjustments*. And let's face it, *adjusting* to living in a penthouse with your best friend is pretty sweet."

Kruger didn't look impressed. She should have. It was an impressive assurance. Instead, she was flipping through pages in the red file.

"And the memories, Kate? The flashbacks?"

Oh. We hadn't danced to this song in quite a while. I shrugged, which was stupid. It's what bored, defensive teens do in TV shows when they're being confronted with something uncomfortable. I knew better. *Get your gear on, Katie.*

"In control," I finally said. "I mean, *under* control. Totally."

Kruger clasped her hands and leaned forward. Her nails were freshly manicured. Not her regular OPI Samoan Sand, but a pale gray-blue shade. A youthful look? *Trying too hard, Dr. Kruger. Bad move. He'll smell it.*

"Kate, we both know that there are triggers: exhaustion, loneliness, stress . . ."

"Well, yeah, sure, and I think we'd both have to admit that I've managed those triggers well. Not least by landing in my current situation."

"Yes, Kate." She smiled and leaned forward even more. "But stressors come out of nowhere. As a clinical psychologist I can't prescribe, but should you ever find yourself in need of medication, well, I know the appropriate—"

"No drugs." I thought of Olivia. Every so often I'd catch her off guard and watch her float around, detached from the world in front of her. Maybe less so lately, but it was still there. "Not interested. Not necessary."

"Kate, your father's—"

"Yes, my father. Glad you brought that up. I think I'm going to change the focus of my exit thesis from students to dear old dad. I mean, not him, but his issue—whatever it was. Kind of a forensic exercise look-back. It might help me, you know. That cathartic thing." I knew she'd lap that up.

Dr. Kruger raised both eyebrows. "That's an excellent focus, Kate. And it's one that could indeed aid you in moving forward." She turned to her bookshelf.

The bookshelf. I'd been staring at Kruger's back wall for months— her books, the locked file cabinet, her pathetic knickknacks—and it never clicked until now. There it was, perched on three books lying horizontally on the very top shelf: the golden cup with the intricate Middle Eastern design. I'd even seen her drop her office keys into that little cup once before, and only now did it dawn on me that it must be where the key to the cabinet also lived. *Got ya!* I just needed the time alone.

Dr. Kruger reached for her copy of the DSM-5. "I feel positive about your interest in coming to terms with it." She handed the book over to me. "I'm afraid you'll have less than half an hour tonight, though, because I have to go soon and there's only Mr. Redkin in the office. And I believe he also has a meeting to attend to shortly."

I'll just bet he does.

"That's cool. I've already tried to look through it, and the DSM is kind of confusing on the topic of what I'm thinking his, um, issue was. So if you don't mind, I'll just use Miss Shwepper's computer and print off my gut hunch to start. I'll still keep borrowing both the printer and the DSM-5 in the next few weeks after school as I burrow in deeper."

She placed the book back on the shelves, right under the golden bowl.

"I promise not to abuse the privilege."

"Of course!" She logged off the computer. "I trust you completely."

What a fool, and in so many ways.

I gathered up my things. "Thank you, Dr. Kruger, that means a lot to me."

I had barely got to the website when I heard Mark open his office door. I did not turn around.

"Glad to have you back and researching, Kate. Let me know if there's anything I can help you with."

It was said with a lightness, just the right tone, and yet it was as if a steel claw had gripped the base of my spine. I knew that feeling. I knew to respect that feeling.

"Thank you, *sir*."

He sighed and returned to his office. I continued scrolling. There were some decent sites about Sociopaths, but it's a pretty controversial label and diagnosis. Shrinks seem to argue about it all over the place. Still, there were some okay sites including one that had an excellent "Profile of the Sociopath," which talked about superficial charm, manipulation, pathological lying and lack of remorse. But I wanted the official one, and the mother ship was the National Institute of Mental Health. There! I printed the relevant page and got bundled up to go, but I didn't turn off the computer. It would look as if I'd forgotten. Redkin would check before he turned it off. He would for sure search my history and then . . . bam! It would give him pause. Hey, I've seen this movie, had a starring role. It was why I reacted to him the way I did. My body remembered, but I didn't pay enough attention. Mark Redkin was a familiar species. Yeah, they were different in a hundred ways—education and polish, no substance abuse—but there was enough the same for me to pin him. Mark Redkin hid it better, but I'd bet my life on it. He was just like my old man.

ABOUT ANTISOCIAL PERSONALITY DISORDER

Antisocial personality disorder is defined by the American Psychiatric Association's Diagnostic and Statistical Manual of Mental Disorders, fourth edition (DSM-IV) as ". . . a pervasive pattern of disregard for, and violation of, the rights of others that begins in childhood or early adolescence and continues into adulthood." People with antisocial personality disorder may disregard social norms and laws, repeatedly lie, place others at risk for their own benefit, and demonstrate a profound lack of remorse. It is sometimes referred to as sociopathic personality disorder, or sociopathy. NIMH— National Institute of Mental Health

I collected the printout, tucked it into my backpack, and headed for the door. I did not exit the site. My heart was pounding way too fast. What was I doing? I should turn it off. I glanced back at the computer. No. Redkin needed to know that I knew. He needed to know to keep away.

SATURDAY, JANUARY 9

KATE

Something was coming, but I didn't know how to duck and cover. Cover from what? I couldn't decipher the most credible threat. There were so many potential yet vague launching pads.

I was pretty solid on the home front, even though Olivia had weirded out when I told her I was going to continue to work at the market. She seemed to take it personally. It is absolutely impossible to talk to the rich about some stuff—like not being rich, for example. I might as well have been addressing Bruce.

"Why? What for? What do you need? Just tell me. You're not paying room or board, you've got that stipend thingy *and* you're still working in the stupid office every morning. I mean, whoa already! We can't even walk to school together as it is."

I tried explaining that the stipend only took care of books, school supplies, field trips, uniforms and application costs. Grooming supplies, clothes, drinks and even our coffees had to come from elsewhere.

"Oh." Her face fell. You could tell that Olivia had never once in her life thought about any of those items as something that you *pay* for. "Well, okay. I get it, I guess. So I'll give you mad money, like, on a regular basis. We can set up an account, and that way you won't be all creeped out about it." She and Bruce had started pacing. "My dad doesn't even have to know, if that's what you're worried about. It'll be a total secret!"

She'd offered with an open hand, no strings attached. It threw me.

"Olivia, I love you to pieces." I had to get up and pace with her. She was making me dizzy. "You're crazy generous and a life-saver, but this is something I need to do for me, for my own self-respect."

She made a face.

I couldn't very well tell her that there was no way I was handing *that* much power over to another person, even her. I couldn't be that beholden to anyone, no matter how prettily the offer was wrapped. Besides, I kind of missed the market.

"Hey, it's just four hours on Sundays, and if we have plans, Mrs. Chen will let me off. See, it's really important to—"

"You mean tomorrow?" She stopped pacing so suddenly that Bruce and I almost bumped into her.

"Yeah, starting tomorrow."

"Okay, yeah. Well, I get it, I guess. If it's, like, such a big deal for your self-esteem or whatever, fine."

Quelle turnaround.

Olivia wasn't home when I got back. The afternoon hung on me like a smelly sock. Despite putting in my hours at the market and finishing a physics lab, I felt it pressing. The walls closed in on me, and given the size of the penthouse, that's saying something. Bruce and I made an executive decision to go to the park.

We had the same argument every single time: I wanted us to

have a nice leisurely stroll through the park and Bruce wanted to chase after every big dog he saw. Bruce barked and lunged at German shepherds, boxers and Dobermans. The little dogs, the bichons and terriers, were invisible to him. It was a pain, but I had to admire him. Bruce knew where the real threat would be coming from.

We liked to end our walk sitting on one of the benches near Fifth and close to the Met. We always chose the one that was right in front of the stone bridge with the beautiful ironwork.

We both noticed the man sitting diagonally across from us. He was definitely Upper East Side material, so it wasn't that. What caught my attention was that he held his cigarette the exact same way my father did. Smoked it the same way too. That's all it took to transport me back to dear old dad. I understood my father—"got" him—by the time I was twelve. But I was the only one. And it wasn't all that helpful.

Everyone—my mom, his cronies, his many and varied employers—labored under the misguided assumption that in the end, it was my father's drinking that led him to unconscionable actions. I knew better. My father used alcohol as an excuse for actions he would have happily committed without a single drop. I'd see him ruminating over a cup of coffee, stone-cold sober at 6:15 a.m., giving us both the gimlet eye, and sure enough, the cops would be called that night. Or not. But there would be pain.

Even at his most inebriated, my father did not leave marks on my mother on the days she had shifts at the dental office. He saved that kind of thing for when she had four days off in a row.

He rarely left marks on me.

Was any of that in Kruger's locked file cabinet?

We were very, very secretive, Mom and me. We thought the shame would kill us. What idiots. Did anyone guess? Was anyone paying attention? Sister Rose would have, and she would have done . . . *something.*

But that last move, I swear to God, we didn't even know where we were. Who could we have told?

"Stephen, please, please . . ."

He unfastened his belt with one hand, holding a cigarette between his thumb and index finger with the other. "Cockroach, you go fix your daddy a drink. You know how I like it. Go on, baby. Don't make your daddy mad now."

And I did. Every time. I'd go to the kitchenette. I'd shut the kitchen door and open the fridge door, wide. The old Amana made an unearthly electronic wheeze every time you opened it, and it just got louder the longer you kept it open.

But not loud enough to drown out the sounds.

Not nearly enough.

I would get the Coke but leave the fridge door open because the wheeze was better than nothing, right? I'd retrieve his glass. It had to be his glass. Then, ever so slowly, I would reach for the ice. Four perfect cubes—not three, not five. Plop, plop, plop, plop. Three fingers of Canadian Club splashed onto the cubes. The Coke can always gasped when I pulled the tab. Five fingers of Coke. And then I would wait with his glass in my hand. Had to wait until the noises, the pleading, softened. I always waited by the open fridge door. Praying to the interior lightbulb, of all things, because God had not followed us to this address. Praying that my mother wouldn't be hurt badly. "Please, please, please . . ." Praying that I wouldn't throw up. And worst of all, praying for forgiveness, because I was so relieved that it wasn't me.

When the noises stopped altogether, I would close the fridge and open the kitchen door.

"Here's your drink, Daddy."

OLIVIA

Olivia suppressed a gasp when he opened the door. Mark Redkin lived in an "artisan" loft at the edge of Tribeca. Artisan meant "authentic restoration," which in Mark's case apparently meant that everything was bleached and painted white. The brick walls, the exposed pipes in the ceiling, the ceiling itself, the kitchen area, the sofas—it all gleamed with a bright coldness . . . *no,* she corrected herself, not cold, just clean and crisp. Yes, it was clean. Olivia liked clean. "It's beautiful, Mark!"

"I'm glad you like it." He leaned over and kissed her temple. "Sit, make yourself comfortable. Can I get you a drink? You like Chablis, right?"

"Yes, please." How did he know? She stepped into the living area. Every surface was clear. There were no books or accessories other than clear glass bowls. A couple of outsized art posters of Mondrian exhibitions in Europe dominated the space. Her father hated Mondrian. *Well, good thing he's not here, then.* Olivia giggled. She was nervous, very nervous.

"What?" asked Mark as he returned with two huge goblets of wine.

"Nothing, I-I was noting the Mondrians."

He kissed her temple again and sat in a white Le Corbusier chair directly opposite her. "This apartment suits you. It's as if I had you in mind as I completed it." He shook his head, looking a bit sheepish. "*And* I kind of did. To tell you the truth, I just bought those stupid Mondrian posters in hopes they would impress you."

"Really?" Olivia hugged herself. This was better than the thousands of scenarios she had imagined.

"Yeah, and I think I hit a home run. This place, *my* place, is a perfect blank canvas for your beauty. You do know how exquisite you are, don't you?"

She so had the upper hand in this. She would obliterate the others.

"You see, I find that truly beautiful women know they're beautiful, but they have a great need to be told so. They flourish in the telling, and so I'm telling you, Olivia. You are absolutely exquisite."

Her heart hiccupped. No *boy* could pull off that line. No *boy* would know how true it was. A shiver of fear competed with the thrill of being there. Mark was not a boy. She took a sip from her glass. Then another.

"Mark, I—"

"How's your wine?" He leaned back into his chair, but not once—not even for a second—did he take his eyes off her.

"Perfect." She took another sip and dared to look directly at him. His eyes were full of *her*. It was as if he had never beheld such a creature and would never want for another.

"I'm glad you came, Olivia. I've imagined you here, like this. There is so much I want to show you, teach you."

His voice was a caress. She felt light-headed in his words and leaned back.

"Don't." Mark took a sip of his wine and smiled playfully. "Please stand up again." He ran his fingers through his hair. "Please? For me?"

He smiled just enough to unearth a dimple on his left cheek. How had she not noticed that before? Was there ever a more attractive man? More powerful? He thrilled her, scared her. Conflicting feelings coursed through her, but they didn't cancel one another out. They existed side by side.

"Put down your drink, please."

Olivia looked vainly for a coaster, gave up and set the goblet on the glass coffee table.

"Good girl."

What was he thinking? What was he going to do? What did he want? She held her breath, was going to explode. More than anything, she wanted . . .

"You are so beautiful in that dress. You must only wear dresses. Turn around slowly."

She did so, desperate to please him, and in the turning realized that she had lost the upper hand.

"Yes." Mark nodded, as if to himself. "Yes."

Olivia dared to take a breath and then resumed her perfect pose. She knew how to pose. She had been doing it all her life.

"Now . . ." His voice was low, hoarse. "Take off your dress."

THURSDAY, JANUARY 14

KATE

It was almost five thirty. I was sitting at Shwepper's desk, flipping through the alphabetical listings at the back of Kruger's DSM, basically just waiting for the meeting to start. The meeting would be in the little boardroom just off the admin office. We, the Wonders and Redkin, were going to review our gala instructions. The Winterfest Gala wasn't until the end of the month, but the prep was monster and involved a phalanx of mommy committees. Today, Redkin would present the final seating lists. We were to memorize the biographies of the guests at our individual tables.

Redkin was in his office, which made me hyperalert, but at least I knew that Goodlace was also still in hers. And as was increasingly the case these days, her door was wide open.

"You forgot to turn off the computer the other day."

He was behind me.

He waited for me to react.

I did not.

"I'd say I've got my eye on you now, but then, I have since the moment we met."

"Time to go?" I stood up.

I felt his smile. "You still don't see it, do you? I tried to tell you before—"

"Mark?" Draper stepped out of the meeting room. So she was here too. Why? Keeping tabs? "We're ready to start."

He stepped over beside me and leaned in ever so slightly. "Surely you see it?" He said it softly, gently. "If not now, you will soon. It's why I'll wait. It can be lonely for people like us. I know what you are. You and me, Kate, we're *exactly* the same."

My heart stopped beating.

Fruit don't fall far from the tree, Katie. You're just like me, through and through.

"Mark? Mark?" called Draper. "We're ready."

"Coming," we said.

SATURDAY, JANUARY 30

OLIVIA

Olivia was buoyant. Her father was able to make the gala after all! He had to head to the Far East on Monday, but he would be here when it counted. Olivia knew that having her father by her side added to her currency at her events, and that she did the same for him at his. Of course her father had sponsored and headed a table, as had Joanna Shipley, his first ex-wife. Joanna and her new husband, a hard-driving thoracic surgeon, had a little girl who had just entered kindergarten at Waverly. Olivia was fairly neutral on Joanna, as was her dad, but the seating arrangements at these functions were usually a nightmare waiting to happen. Try as you might, you could never prepare for all contingencies.

Olivia glided among the guests, practiced gliders all. Cocktails were held in the spectacular lobby of the new Whitney Museum. The lighting accentuated every shimmering jewel, every glint of gold. She caught Kate's eye and gave her a discreet thumbs-up. Kate was busy enchanting the Newbiggings and Mrs. Kimbault, major donors to the Waverly Foundation and, more important, to the Waverly Scholar Fund. Olivia was proud of her; Kate was holding her own in this rarefied air. She just hoped that Kate wouldn't trip up when they pressed her about which colleges she had applied to. The Yale thing was her Achilles' heel. To Olivia, it was a shrug—they'd get in, end of story. She had complete faith in her college coach's advice and in her father. But Kate totally shut down on the topic. The word *Yale* was verboten. The way the word *Mark* seemed to be.

Kate also looked sensational. Again, this pleased Olivia; she took it as a reflection on her. She had insisted that Kate go "shopping" in her closet, and she was delighted that her friend had decided on a knee-length, red-lace, full-skirted Dolce & Gabbana. "I've only worn it to a partners' event with my dad, so you're safe with this crowd."

"But won't everyone be in gowns, including the rest of the Wonders?" Kate had asked while she was admiring herself.

"Exactly!" said Olivia. "We'll look young and fresh and *très* adorable. Trust me, *we'll* be the standouts, Kate. This is where I'm the tutor and you're the pupil."

It was true. Olivia "got it" even as a child. She just knew how to look and how to *be* at these things. Her own dress was a gold metallic mini by Stella McCartney that she had scored at Bergdorf's. Olivia knew she looked beautiful, but Mark was right—she had an unquenchable need to be told. She unfurled in the compliments that flowed her way.

"You look especially enchanting tonight, Olivia." It was Mr. Cartwright. The Cartwrights would be at her table later. "All grown up. And it's Yale, I hear."

"From your lips . . ." She shuddered just a bit in a show of expected trepidation.

"I have no doubt whatsoever. I'm on the board. You know to have your father call me if there's a hiccup."

"I will. Thank you so much, Mr. Cartwright."

Her father joined them. He handed Olivia a tall, clear glass that looked like it was full of Perrier. She made a face.

"It's Stoli, soda and sweet lime juice," he whispered as he led her away. "Just the one."

"Of course. Thanks, Dad."

"Well, your advancement guy is all the rage," said her father as he caught sight of Mark mobbed by Waverly matrons.

He was heart-hurtingly handsome in black-tie.

"I told you so. He's so amazing."

Her father raised an eyebrow. "I'll take your word for it."

Olivia knew that she would likely not exchange two words with Mark that night. They each had their roles. His was to charm, cajole and dance with every anorexic old biddy that cast a sideways glance at him. Hers was to captivate her table and extol his virtues. And the virtues of the school, of course.

They retrieved Kate, and then Mr. Sumner escorted both to the lower level, where the entertainment and tables were set up. The room was breathtaking. The walls were bathed in indigo, and laser art was projected onto them, making the entire space both surreal and intimate. Crystal sparkled off the tables, adding to the light show, and each centerpiece featured elegant branches of forced white magnolia blooms.

The Wonders were strategically positioned throughout the room. But wait, Serena was at the same table as her own father. How did that happen? He must have bought his way into that table while he was still in London. Mrs. Shaw was at a table anchored by the Van Kemps and headed by Morgan. The Wonders were supposed to be separated from any parent/relative/guardian, as part of a divide-and-conquer strategy. No doubt Mr. Shaw wanted to impress his only daughter with his generosity as step one in a bid for a rapprochement.

Serena wasn't looking at her father or anyone else at her table. She was staring—no, make that glaring—at the table anchored by Mrs. Pearson, the chair of the board. That particular table was stacked with heavy-hitter old girls and . . . Mark. Before she had to turn her attention to Mrs. Kreighoff on her right, Olivia caught Serena downing something in a martini glass. *Stupid girl.* Olivia did her best to amuse both Kreighoffs while she fumed inwardly. *Not done, Serena. Not in this venue.* She sipped her glass of adulterated soda. When she glanced back at Serena, she noted with alarm that the girl had a fresh drink in front of her.

Everything else proceeded flawlessly. As champagne flowed, so did the conversation and laughter. Her tablemates happily devoured their dinners of either Chilean sea bass or rack of lamb, and all the women made a show of "splurging just this once" on a hot chocolate brownie cake with marshmallow frosting. Olivia sang the praises of their new director of advancement and giggled enthusiastically about the stupendous auction list. "There's never been a list quite like this one, and we have Douglas Rainey from Sotheby's doing the honors." She directed this comment at Mr. Cha, but made sure that the entire table was being primed.

By Olivia's count, Serena was on her third drink, and she was still eyeing the Pearson table hard. Enough was enough. Olivia excused herself, got up and headed toward Kate's table, stopping here and there to receive or bestow a compliment. Her friend was a hit. At least there was that.

Olivia leaned down to Kate's ear and, still smiling, whispered through gritted teeth, "Don't turn around, but that idiot Serena is getting shit-faced on martinis and looking grimmer by the minute. She'll listen to you. Can you take care of it before the bidding starts? Laugh now."

Kate laughed.

Olivia returned to her table and let the group in on the secret that she hoped her father would bid hard on the long weekend in Paris at the George V. Five minutes later, she saw Kate head to Serena's table and then lead her to the ladies' room.

Ten minutes later, Kate returned alone.

The "experiential auction" was a huge success. Mark Redkin was a success.

When the Peter Duchin Orchestra took to the stage, Kate approached Olivia's table and introduced herself to everyone. "Shall we show them how it's done?" She extended her hand to Olivia and led her onto the dance floor.

"Nice work," said Olivia once they were safely away. "What happened?"

All eyes were on the two gorgeous girls dancing with controlled abandon.

"I sent her home using your car service. Hope you don't mind. Jackson promised he'd deliver her to the doorman."

"Perfect." Olivia swayed. "What was up?"

Kate turned her palms up and shrugged in time to the music. "You know, her dad being here, her mom at another table, everyone knowing . . ."

"Sure." Olivia nodded, pretending to believe her.

She didn't look, but she knew that Mark had not taken his eyes off them since they took to the dance floor. She playfully threw her arms around Kate, knowing they were the personification of all that was best about Waverly. Too bad, really, that Serena wasn't here to see how it could be done, *should* be done. She was such a child, really.

Serena, Serena. Little girls should not play with matches.

THURSDAY, FEBRUARY 4

KATE

5:50 P.M.

Serena was a no-show at our gala postmortem at Starbucks. After we stopped congratulating ourselves, which took us into second cups all around, we got to her.

"Like, what was up with that?" asked Morgan. "One minute the girl was there, and then she wasn't."

Olivia shot me a look.

"I think the whole family situation got to be too much for her, poor thing," I said. "She was at her dad's table. Did you know that he actually wanted to bring his new . . . uh, what do you call a twenty-three-year-old assistant who breaks up a family?"

"Conniving bitch?" said Claire helpfully.

"Whatever." I shrugged. "I think Serena felt sucker-punched."

"Well, I wouldn't know about that," sniffed Morgan. "But even Mark found it odd."

"Mark?" Olivia turned her attention to Morgan. "When did Mark say anything to you?"

Was Olivia's voice clenched in the asking?

"When I danced with him." Morgan looked spectacularly satisfied with herself. "While you lot were helping distribute the winning auction bids, I asked him to dance. And yes, ladies, it was positively dreamy." She sighed dramatically. "He said he was very pleased with me."

We eyeballed her.

"Okay, he said 'us,' but he was holding *me* very, very close at the time, so . . ."

We groaned.

"You're just jealous. Any one of you would jump him if he so much as looked at you twice."

"Got that right," said Claire.

"Not my type," I said.

"No, but poor wannabe cops are, right?" That was Olivia. Was that a jab? If it was, it pricked. "The guy from the party? She sees him every week."

"For coffee only."

"Oooh, the dark cutie from Claudette's do? By the way, we have to go to more parties this semester." And Morgan was off. Thankfully she couldn't hold a thought in her head for more than a breath. "The Westover girls are having a thing in NoHo this Saturday."

"I'm booked up this weekend," Olivia said, shaking her head.

News to me.

"Well, Claire and I are going to go. And Nikita is planning this massive bash near the High Line at the end of the month. I insist we all go to that, including crazy Serena. I'll let her know."

We spent a good amount of time reviewing the best and worst dressed at the gala, and which of the parents had indulged in too many glasses of wine or too many longing glances at the wrong spouse. We had, after all, been allowed into the perfumed sanctum of grown-ups at play. I liked that part a lot. But then they ended up gushing about Mark. The man was a virus.

"Serena is such a fool," said Olivia as soon as we were back on Fifth Avenue.

I didn't know where to go or what to do with that. Olivia and I had been speaking in a bizarrely intricate code over the past few weeks. I excel on the "taking cues" front, but it was making me dizzy. It was as if she knew that I knew about her thing for Mark, whatever that was, but it would sever something if I dared to acknowledge it.

"She's absolutely no match for . . . Look, she's in three of my classes, and I think Serena's unraveling."

God, I wished I'd never mentioned seeing them together in Chinatown.

"She's crazy naive about Mark." Olivia slipped her arm through mine.

"Yeah, maybe, but she's not the only one. There's Draper, for sure, and I'm worried about Kruger. And I bet Serena is not the sole senior."

She paused, collected herself. "Old ladies and children."

My stomach cramped. How deep in was she? I couldn't shake the feeling that he was coming at me through her. Hey, even paranoids have enemies.

I kept my mouth shut as we strolled past the Plaza and on through the fifties and sixties. It wasn't until after Aftab cheerfully retrieved the elevator that I risked it.

"So you're booked up this weekend?"

At least she had the grace to look away. Olivia examined the floor indicator as if it held the keys to the rest of her life, but she didn't say anything. She didn't say anything when Bruce attacked us with his atomic greetings, or when she took off her coat and started for her room.

I don't know what came over me. It was like I had misplaced myself. I should've left it alone. Instead, I followed her into her room. "So this weekend?"

Olivia sat in front of her makeup table. "I'll be away." Her reflection smiled, a satisfied, secretive smile.

"Don't, Olivia. Just don't, please. He's ... Mark's a viper or something. I can't explain it, but—"

"Then don't." She crossed her arms. "Because you can't. Mark is an amazing man who understands me like no one else in the world."

"Sure, he's slick and—"

"Look, Kate, I'm sick of your superiority complex. Being an orphan doesn't render you a genius on the hearts of men." She sighed. "Besides, how would you know? You're so buttoned-down in your virgin, queer or frigid self. What is the matter with you anyway?"

"With *me*?" I wanted to slap her. What's the matter with me? I know a sicko when I see one, that's what. Keep your mouth shut and leave the room, Katie girl. Turn around. "He's using you, Olivia."

She stood up so fast that she knocked over the chair. "You jealous bitch!"

"What? No!"

"You just can't leave it alone, can you? You think you're the hottest, most mysterious thing in the whole school! Ooooh, what does Kate think? Will Kate be coming? Where's Kate? Everybody wants Kate." She took a step toward me. "You just can't take it! He wants *me*. Me above all others. He *adores* me."

"I'm anything but jealous! He makes my skin crawl."

Bruce came between us, wagging and whimpering like his life depended on it.

"Well, if you're not jealous of *me*, you must be jealous of *him*. Is that it, Kate?" She was yelling now. "Is he getting in the way of us?

Are you worried that he'll mess up your gravy train? Ruin it for you somehow?"

And there it was.

And it was probably true. So I had nothing. No comeback.

"You're not getting in the way of us. He wants me and I want him. Deal with it." She was calmer now, colder. "If you value our relationship, don't risk it. You've got a lot to lose. Don't you *ever* mention his name again, or you'll be out on your ass."

I turned away before my head exploded. I wanted to scream, *Don't worry yourself, Olivia. I won't make the mistake of giving a crap again.*

I settled for slamming the door.

THURSDAY, FEBRUARY 4

OLIVIA

6:35 P.M.

The remorse was instant and uncomfortable. Olivia's skin felt like it was on too tight. Remorse? She flipped open her laptop and Googled.

re·morse \ri'môrs\ *noun*

1. deep regret or guilt for a wrong committed: *they were filled with remorse and shame.*

synonyms: contrition, deep regret, repentance, penitence, guilt, compunction, remorsefulness, ruefulness, contriteness; pangs of conscience, self-condemnation, self-reproach; guilt complex

e.g., Have you no remorse for what you did to your friends?

Yup. That'd be it in black and white. Olivia spent the next few minutes righteously cataloguing how and why she was the aggrieved one. But nothing had traction. She had never cared for or about a friend more than she did Kate, and she was sure that none of her friends had ever cared more genuinely for her.

Yeah, Kate needed her.

But she needed Kate more. Much more.

Olivia slumped deeper into the chair. Bruce had deserted her. Now what? Kate was mental on the topic of Mark and she couldn't allow her to trash him at every turn, but . . .

"Oh, hell!"

She got up and walked into the living room. Not there. She went over and knocked on Kate's door before entering. Not there. *Oh, God, what if she . . . ?*

"Kate? Kate!"

"We're in the kitchen."

The relief was almost as instant as the remorse. Olivia hustled to the kitchen. Kate was on the floor with Bruce, laptop open.

Olivia joined them. "Look, that . . ." She stopped. Why hadn't she prepared what to say? "That was, well, unfortunate. We—*I*—said things that aren't . . . Kate, you're my best friend. So except for the part about never talking about Mark again, can we pretend it never happened? Please?"

Bruce crawled into Kate's lap and bathed her face in licks.

"See? Bruce and I would both be grateful."

Silence.

"Fine," Kate eventually groaned. "I can't fight both of you."

"Thank you." Olivia rose and extended a hand to Kate. "I, uh, also need a favor."

"About this weekend."

"Yes." Olivia began to pace around the island. "I'll be away Saturday, returning sometime on Sunday. I'm going to tell Anka that I'm off to visit Jessica in Boston and get a taste of college life."

Kate inhaled and nodded, but she didn't say anything.

"So if my father calls on the house phone . . . ?"

"I'll tell him you're with Jessica."

"Yes, thanks. And I'm going to need your notes on the readings for AP English when I get back."

Kate nodded again, but it was like she was on autopilot.

Olivia exhaled. "That's great! Really, Kate, it means a lot. I'm going to go pick out my wardrobe before we have dinner." She spun around and started for her room with Bruce at her heels. "Honestly, thanks a mil!"

"S'okay," Kate called. "What are friends for?"

THURSDAY, FEBRUARY 4

KATE

6:55 P.M.

There was collateral damage in the aftermath of that little confrontation—me. What just happened? I'd ignored the early warning signals and now it felt like there were missiles raining down on my head.

How dare I risk everything, this whole setup? Who cared if he chewed her up and spit her out? Caring was dangerous and sloppy. It got in the way. Sure, I had to keep an eye out, but caring was for losers.

Yet aside from Sister Rose, no one had ever been kinder or more openly generous to me than Olivia had.

So I cared. Big mistake.

I had to get back on survival footing, which meant war footing. I needed to find out everything there was on Olivia, because I was pretty sure that Mark already knew. That had to be his game. I had a gut feeling that he *knew* stuff and then played accordingly. Yup, information had to be his trump card. He must have got to Kruger by now. Between her and Draper, all the files were there for his pickings. Mark probably knew everything there was to know about me, about my dad, about it all. He was just biding his time. But how was he going to use it? Jesus. My stomach seized. I felt my way to the bathroom.

I turned on the bath taps but threw up before I stepped into the tub. Sinking into the water, I realized that I'd have to start with him. Mark. Who was he? Where was he before this? He'd said he was at a lot of schools. What did that mean, exactly?

I couldn't sit on the sidelines and just watch this play out anymore. I needed to arm myself. I'd had this sense of pure dread before, but I didn't know what to do about it. How to act. I was a kid. Not this time. No, sir.

Then I got out of the bath and threw up again.

OLIVIA

It was as if someone drew him. He was that beautiful naked. Olivia watched Mark slip smoothly out of bed and into a pair of khakis and a black T-shirt.

He turned to her and put a finger to his lips. "Don't say anything."

Olivia propped herself up on one elbow, her legs winding around the immaculately white silk sheets.

Mark groaned. "Just nod. I'm going out for coffees and bagels to feed my queen."

She nodded.

Mark smiled, but he didn't start for the door. He stood still in the simmering silence, taking her in. He reached over with the back of his fingers and stroked her from collarbone to ankle with a touch so light she wasn't entirely sure that he had made contact. But he must have, because her body began to respond. Again.

"Don't move, not a muscle. You're glorious. I want you just like that when I return."

Olivia nodded.

She didn't even exhale until she heard the front door close.

She wanted to prance around the room, giggle, squeal and scream. She wanted to admire herself in the mirror and hug herself. What a night! What a morning! She was drunk with pleasure. Mark seemed to know everything about her. About who she was and how she was. He "got" her like no one else possibly could, and despite all that, he loved her. He more or less said so.

"There is so much about you that I love, Olivia."

But she shouldn't move. Mark was so serious about his commands. No, not commands, per se, but wishes. That's it, he *wished* her to do certain things.

But she had to pee.

And she had to take a pill. She hadn't taken one yesterday, and she would be two behind if she didn't take one right now. Where was her backpack?

But he said not to move a muscle.

She smiled at herself in the closet mirror. Yes. This was more than anything she could have imagined. She was wildly alive, every nerve ending sparked. Mark had awakened everything.

He loved her.

But she really did have to go to the bathroom. Olivia got up carefully. She went to the bathroom and then tiptoed into his immaculate living room, where she found her backpack and retrieved the pill bottle. Eyeing the door, she dry-swallowed the tablet. Olivia then tiptoed back to the bedroom giggling, because for the life of her, she didn't know why she was tiptoeing.

Mark Redkin's bedroom was opulent, but discreetly so. Anything you touched or laid your hand on was sensual and perfect—the silk sheets, the suede headboard, the honed ebony side tables and the stainless steel dresser.

How she wanted to open just one drawer.

Better not.

She cautiously rearranged herself back into position, taking great care to place the sheet around her in the exact replica of her original pose.

"You are the most beautiful creature I have ever seen. I'll never tire of looking at you, touching you. Knowing that you're mine."

He *loved* her.

And of course, she loved him. Did from almost their very first meeting. She'd understood even then that he could bring her fully to life. That's why Olivia would do and be anything for Mark Redkin. Anything at all.

She heard the front door open. "Honey, I'm home!" Mark chuckled to himself and it made her smile.

Yes, she would gladly, willingly do anything to make him happy. She already had.

SUNDAY, FEBRUARY 14

KATE

There had been a shift, a big one. Most of the time, Olivia was with me in body but not in spirit. Oh, she was as charmingly distant at school as ever, but now she was charmingly distant with me too. We still did our homework together. We still bitched about the other girls and the teachers. She still teased me about Johnny—even insisting that I invite him to the High Line party (no chance). And most of the time, we still walked Bruce together. It was so *us*, but ever since our blowup over Mark, it was not us.

The unspoken was deafening.

I tried to spoon-feed her possible exit thesis topics all week. We were supposed to choose something that affected us personally but had global applications, like the calming benefits of having a pet during senior year; an emotional cost–benefit analysis of uniforms versus street clothes; or the comparative private high school experiences in New York, São Paulo and Singapore. I figured her dad could shovel her some great info on that last one. But Olivia went and picked "The Hidden Value of Fund-Raising in the Private School System."

Atta go, Mark Redkin.

Shoot me now.

Worse yet, I was probably going to have to write it.

We toasted each other with a Valentine's Day coffee first thing in the morning. "At least we have each other," she said.

Liar.

About half an hour before I had to leave for the market, Olivia decided to take a bath. She'd gone from being a multi-shower-a-day girl to a big bath girl, at least on the days she saw *him*. Always when she saw him.

I'd tense up as soon as I heard the water running. She was slipping down some weird rabbit hole, and if I couldn't figure out something soon, she'd take me down with her, I just knew it. But what? I couldn't risk another blowup about Mark. I'd be on the street.

Bruce and I were in the living room chasing anxiety bubbles while Olivia bathed. I was the one who needed the Ativan now. Wait. I knew about the meds bottles in the bathroom, but surely she kept a stash on her as well. The backpack! I'd been looking for a chance to go through it anyway.

I tiptoed into her room. The backpack was on the floor by her bed. I reached into one of the side pockets: lip glosses, tampons, keys. Damn. Other side pocket: ID and credit cards. The girl had a million of them. Why didn't she keep them in her wallet like normal people? Next, the center pocket. The water stopped. I heard her sigh and I stopped breathing. Bruce came in to give me a helpful lick in the ear. I couldn't risk shooing him away—she'd hear. There, two bottles. I opened the Ativan, popped a pill and returned the bottle before carefully picking up the other one. This one I hadn't seen before. Olivia didn't have its twin in her medicine chest.

Bingo.

This was the serious stuff—something called risperidone, 2 mg. What was that? What was it for? I replaced the bottle and zipped up the bag, and then Bruce and I crawled back to her bedroom door.

I was going to be late for my shift.

"Olivia," I called, "I have to go now."

"Okay." I heard splashing. "Don't work too hard. See you tonight."

Sure.

I smiled at everyone in the store. I smiled at the vegetables, at the pineapples and at Mrs. Chen nonstop. My face hurt from smiling. It didn't hit me until halfway through my shift that I was stoned out of my gourd. Mellow doesn't begin to touch how I was feeling. Wow, how high a dose was she on? I'd taken the odd scrip before from other girls at other schools—bennies, Adderall, ecstasy—just to be social. But this was a trip all on its own. *Groovy.*

Mrs. Chen eyed me nervously. Or I might have imagined it.

When Johnny came to get me for coffee, I giggled the whole way over to his family's bakery.

"Nice to see you so chill, Michelob."

"I like that name." Was I grinning at him?

"I thought you hated it. I just call you that to get a rise out of you."

He was a handsome guy, that Johnny. He would look yummy in a cop uniform. I was supposed to ask him something. I had planned to ask him something, something important. Instead, I giggled again.

"Naw, I've never had a nickname before."

Cockroach.

"Least not one that wasn't ugly." And then I giggled again. I am so *not* a giggler.

189

We made our way to our table at the bakery, and Johnny nodded to his uncle as he always did. Dominic brought us both espressos, but instead of our usual pastry, he brought me a massive almond cookie in the shape of a heart with "Will You Be Mine?" scrawled in red icing. All I registered was that it was pretty and that I was starved. What *was* I going to ask him?

I realized that both Dominic and Johnny were looking at me intently.

"Oh! The cookie." I started breaking it up into bite-sized chunks and shoving them in my mouth, so hungry. "Great cookie."

Johnny winked at Dominic before he left. "I just thought it'd be a kick if . . . but hey, you know, dig in and everything."

Digging, that's it!

"Johnny, you'd have to dig into a person's background before they'd be allowed into a school system, right? Have you come to that part in any of your classes?"

"How's the cookie, Kate?" The boy was looking aggrieved.

I took a huge bite. "Dlishus," I offered with my mouth still full. "They'd need some kind of a check to have, like, a senior position, right?"

"Can we remember that I'm not an actual cop? But yeah, I do know that schools would require a standard police background check."

"Excellent!" I took another bite. "This really is good, best cookie ever. And the results would be in the school admin file or something, huh?"

He frowned as if he was having trouble following me.

"You'd better get some before I eat it all." I kept breaking off cookie bits and shoving them into my mouth. "So records . . . they'd be in a file someplace, right?"

"Not necessarily. If they're in the school, it pretty much

guarantees that they've got a clean record in New York. Maybe a DUI might turn up, but they'd be clear, you know. What's this about? You worried about someone at Waverly? That'd be rich."

"Just New York?" Okay, that was disappointing. I finished off the cookie and was pressing my finger against the crumbs. Mark, I seemed to remember, had bopped around all over the place. "Not the whole world?"

He laughed then.

"No, Kate. There is no global criminal record database, unless we're talking Homeland Security. Don't they feed you uptown?"

"Homeland Security, huh? And you couldn't get into that?" I was still pretty spacey but also still starving. "Can we get another big cookie?"

"Well, surprisingly, Homeland Security doesn't let first-year criminology students muck around their top-secret database, and yes, you can have another big cookie." He motioned to Dominic.

"So how would a person find out about someone's, uh, potential naughtiness in other places, then?"

The cookie arrived and I dived in, even though it didn't have the pretty red icing on it.

"What the hell, Kate? What have you got yourself into?"

"Nofing!" I might have sprayed him with a couple of crumbs.

"You do it the old-fashioned way," he sighed. "You track the name and the last-known address, and you Google the local papers over the correct time period. Laborious but effective." Johnny leaned back into his chair. Wow, his bakery T-shirt fit ever so nicely across his torso. He crossed his arms. Such nice arms. All guys should know that all girls like arms. *Keep your eye on the prize. You have no room for this, Katie O'Brien.*

"You're so cute." What the hell? Was that *me*? It must have been because he was shaking his head and grinning.

"You're a trip, you know?"

More like I was *on* a trip.

He glanced at his watch. "Time to go back. Let's go. I'll get you one more for the road." Johnny got up and went over to the counter.

Okay, okay, okay. Our advancement director's past "accomplishments" were strewn all over school, and his resume had to be in Draper's clunker of a computer. I'd start there and work my way back—when I had a chunk of alone time and my head was on straight.

Johnny proffered another outsized almond cookie wrapped in a sheet of waxed paper. I bit into it as soon as we got outside. He was still looking a bit put off.

"Brilliant cookies, Johnny. I mean it. I've never had better. Really!"

He groaned as he steered me back to the Chens'.

There's just no pleasing some people.

OLIVIA

It was Presidents' Day, no school. But no Mark either. Kate was doing a holiday shift at the market, so it would have been perfect. But Mark was otherwise engaged. All day.

He was a busy man. Of course he was. Olivia understood this. She also knew not to whine or pout. That was for the others. And she was pretty sure that there still were *others*.

For now.

It's just that today was special—actually, not special but hard. It was a hard anniversary. A year ago today, Olivia left for Houston. It had been bad for weeks, months beforehand, but today was the day they'd left. A bullet of shame pierced through the meds.

She looked at her watch. When would Kate get home from that stupid job? She needed Kate. Her place was here beside her, especially today. Olivia popped another Ativan.

She could call her father.

She worked out the time in her head. Her father was in Singapore for three days. No, he'd be asleep now. She knew he'd call as soon as he was awake. He would call for sure. Because today was today, and he knew it.

What if Kate didn't come right home? What if she decided to go somewhere with that Johnny or one of the Wonders? What if she'd driven Kate away? It was possible. Olivia winced, remembering what she'd accused Kate of when they argued. That, and she had been a bit of a bitch of late. Was Kate distancing herself? The possibility alarmed her.

She had to get Kate back on board, make her understand. Not about Mark—and certainly not about everything, of course. Kate wasn't ready for that. But about today and why it was so important. Yeah. And then Kate would completely forgive her for everything and go back to being all understanding and caring and . . . devoted.

Anka was tracking her. Anka knew about today. Even though she had the day off, she had not gone to her sister's place. Anka wasn't going anywhere.

The housekeeper stole into the living room brandishing a feather duster.

"Anka, you're hovering."

"Vat hoovering? I don't know vat dis is meaning."

"Yeah, you do, and you're doing it." She walked over to her. "Kate will be home in a few minutes. Go then."

"But—"

"I'm going to tell her about today."

Instead of looking relieved, Anka looked skeptical.

"She's my best friend and I trust her completely." And it was true. That she'd only realized it at that moment didn't make it any less true. Kate would understand and be sympathetic, the way Mark was. Best friends shared secrets. Besides, secrets were what tied people to each other, forever. Secrets were good that way. She looked at her watch again.

Bruce began barking and running in circles. He had become an early warning system, since he heard the ping of the elevator long before anyone ever reached the doorway.

"Hey, Brucie! Hi, Olivia. Should we take him out?"

"Sure, in a minute. But sit down for a bit. I want to talk to you."

Alarm streaked across Kate's face. "Uh, okay."

Anka bustled by them. "I vill coming to home eight o'clock." She turned to Kate. "Zer is a chickens pie in za oven."

As soon as the door shut, Olivia patted a spot beside her on the sunken sofa.

"What's up?"

"I want to tell you about today."

"Today?" Kate plopped onto the couch.

"Yeah, today is sort of an anniversary for me." Olivia tucked her legs under herself and faced her friend. "You see, a year ago today, we left for Houston."

"For the hospital?"

"Well, eventually, yes."

"I'm so sorry, Olivia. I shouldn't have gone to work. You shouldn't have been alone. What a downer. I shouldn't have . . ."

That was better. "S'okay. You didn't know." Yes, she loved Kate. She had never loved a friend before. Oh, she had faked it, professed it, pretended it, like she did with everything. But she had never truly *needed* a friend the way she needed Kate. Need, love—it was much the same thing. Olivia turned and glanced back out the windows. Dusk was settling on her city and she was safe here in her home, with her friend. Even though she couldn't see Mark today— even though he knew what today was—well, it didn't matter.

Olivia had Kate.

"Daddy rented a charming little house right near the hospital, and that's where we lived until . . . the hospital. Daddy didn't do a single international deal the whole time. He'd just fly into New York for the day or at most two days." Olivia seemed to lose herself in that quaint house with its normal furniture. It was how regular people lived. She nodded at no one. "Just the two of us. And Anka, of course."

"And . . . ?" Kate whispered.

"And what you don't know is that we had to leave a year ago today because, well, I felt I was starting to show."

"To show?"

"Yes." She spoke so softly that Kate had to lean over to hear. "You see, it wasn't so much that I had issues—that's more or less acceptable in our circle, *n'est-ce pas*? I swear you're the only person I know who isn't medicated."

Kate nodded, but she was clearly confused.

"Remember I told you about the public school boy?"

Kate nodded again.

"Well, we had to leave because I was pregnant." Olivia swallowed and turned back to the windows. "And I wouldn't consider an abortion. Don't ask me why—I can't tell you to this day. I don't know, I just don't, but I couldn't. I refused. So . . ."

"Houston."

Kate had not moved, did not blink. No interjections or audible gasps of shock or surprise.

"So now you know. I feel better, even though it's excruciating for me to talk about it, to revisit the details, the . . . shame."

"But what happened to the . . . ?"

Olivia's hands trembled. "Please, let's not . . . I just can't. Not yet. But I needed you to know. I need you to, uh, try to understand me or, I don't know, forgive me . . . Kate, say that you do. Please, please."

Kate threw her arms around Olivia. "Shh, it's okay. It's all okay. It will be okay. I promise." She hugged her tighter. "Remember what I told you all those months ago? Only look forward, right? Just today and tomorrow. The rest is horseshit."

Olivia stopped trembling in the embrace. She had been calmed. Yes, Kate was worthy of her.

WEDNESDAY, FEBRUARY 17

KATE

Dr. Kruger leaned forward on her desk and clasped her hands tightly. "You're in the running, Kate. Yale is not out by any means. Your marks, your preparation, your story alone . . ."

She was trying to hose me down. I was radioactive on this issue. But this was about Yale. Everything was about Yale. Kruger knew that I'd sworn it to my mom as she was dying. A promise is a promise.

"You're in the general pool, and I know you have more than a fighting chance, as does Olivia. Of course, she's a legacy, but you are definitely in the top tier. I also think the other schools will go after you. Do not despair."

Easy for her to say—and so she did, often. This was our dance. Kruger would pretend to assure me and I would pretend to be assured. She said more or less the same canned thing every session, and she would keep saying it until the bitter end. I noted that today the shrink was shrink-wrapped in a Diane von Furstenberg. How long had she been doing him? Was it from her change of wardrobe on, or before?

Kruger spent the rest of our session examining me while trying to look like she wasn't. Something other than her concern about my concern was evident in those hands gripping each other like a vise.

"Everything else under control?" she asked.

"Sure. Midterms are a ways away, and let's face it, we're all just trying not to drive into a ditch with senior slump." I glanced over at the photo of her and her husband and their small son. Was it recent? Was the small son still small, or was he old enough to ask questions, notice changes in Mommy? What about the husband? He taught clinical psychology at NYU. Was he oblivious to the obvious?

Kruger unclasped herself and leaned back in her chair. "And how are the Wonders?"

"We're cool." I shrugged. "I mean, we're not on call as actual Wonders until the spring board meeting and working dinner. But we still hang at school and over coffee. We're going to a party en masse at the end of the month. So if you're worried about me not socializing enough, I've got that covered."

Kruger nodded, but she was frowning. Shrinks should get a better hold on their facial expressions. They all look at us, but they forget that we're looking at them. I lost her for a minute. It was as if she had left the room. I took in the locked file cabinet in the pause. The urgency to break into it had ebbed since Olivia coughed up that seismic fur ball about being pregnant. I was spending too much time processing that one. Mistake. I had to smarten up, had to get in the files to see if my girl had any other surprises. There had to be more.

"And Serena?" The cords on Kruger's neck tightened into visible ropes. "Have you seen much of her?"

Hmm. "Well, not so much after the gala, I guess. Just around, you know? We were together yesterday. Why?"

"How did she seem to you, if you don't mind my asking?"

But I did. I minded a lot, all things considered. Dr. Kruger was no longer the trusty shrink with my best interests at heart.

"She was a bit distracted." Truth was, Serena was a seeping, leaking mess. Mark was done with her. Finished. She was impossible. Truth was, I had to skip physics yesterday and get her out of the school, she was that strung out. Serena had always dabbled in prescriptions, as did half the school, but she'd slid fast and furious from dabbling to drowning. She was into him way too deep. How had Mark allowed it to get so rabid so quickly? Hell of a misstep, if you ask me. He'd picked the wrong screwup to play with. This would get ugly. And then, just when I didn't think it could get any sicker . . .

It did.

"I admire your loyalty, but I suspect you won't be surprised to learn that Serena is leaving the school."

"What? When?"

"Yes." She cleared her throat. "I think I can confide in you, since you know that Serena has been under increasing family pressures and, as you say, distractions."

Confide in me? Come on! Since when does the school shrink confide in a student?

"Couple that with the potential substance issues I suspect you are aware of and, well, it has made her situation at the school untenable. Her father is taking her back to London with him. She'll be under his care and will likely finish out the semester there."

"Her father? Not a chance! London?" Then it hit me. How convenient. "When?"

"Tonight. She's leaving for London this evening." Dr. Kruger sighed, but the cords in her neck looked like they were going to break free. "I . . . we at the school hope that we can count on your discretion, but we'd also ask you to convey to those who care about her that London is the very best option for Serena, for her physical

200

and emotional health. Tell the other girls that Ms. Draper and I both feel, *blah, blah, blah, blah, blah . . .*"

It was as if I were listening to her underwater.

He *was* a genius. I had trouble locating my breath.

Kruger *had* to do his dirty work because he had her in so many ways. She had a job to protect, a family to protect and, probably, him to protect. I had a moment to consider the fact that Draper and Kruger were working in concert for him. Did they know about each other? He was a snake. My father was a snake. I bet Johnny was a . . .

"Poor Serena."

In response, Kruger reverted to her classic hand-clasp pose. Her face had all the color of uncooked dough. She spouted pap like "healing venue with her father," "support from that branch of the family," "healthy psychic distance," "excellent care" and "Serena's remarkable resilience."

Weasel words. Rinse and repeat. Serena was about as resilient as a wet paper towel. Her father must have been jubilant to be able to swoop in like a white knight and "save" his only daughter. Better a damaged daughter than no daughter at all.

I felt the bile rise within me along with the enormity of what had just happened, of what they had managed to do. There were more words.

"We can count on you, can't we, Kate?"

I must have nodded. Of course I nodded, and I kept nodding as I left her office. Mark was standing by Miss Shwepper's desk, glancing idly at back issues of the school newspaper. He did not approach me or say anything. He just looked up and winked.

I started running as soon as I hit the hallway. What in God's name was I thinking? That *I* could outmaneuver Mark Redkin? I was punching way above my weight.

And he knew it.

SUNDAY, FEBRUARY 21

OLIVIA

He lay down beside her and brushed a wisp of hair off her face. It was a gesture so tender that it almost crushed her. "You're an angel," Mark whispered. "I feel like I'm at peace with you. You do that."

How could she not be enthralled? Olivia shifted slightly to be able to see him better. "Nobody knows me or has ever known me the way you do, Mark."

"I know the inside of you, *all* the secret parts, the best parts." He kissed her eyelids. "Don't ever be ashamed of anything. Everything about you is beautiful."

Olivia flinched. *Shame.* Yes, there was that.

"And what I know for sure is that you're a wonder." He chuckled at the word.

She braced herself. "Are you going to replace her?"

"Who?"

"Serena," she said. Her eyes locked on to his. "As a Wonder, I mean."

"No." He nuzzled her neck, then rolled off the bed and walked over to her side. He moved like a Ferrari. "There's no need. Spring break will be here in a minute, and then it's wind-down. My four Wonders will be plenty wonderful enough." He kissed her temple. He began dressing, preparing to go out and forage for their sustenance. She loved that about him. Loved so much about him. She would love to cook for him. Except, of course, Olivia didn't know how to cook. But she would learn for him. She'd make Anka teach her so she could make intimate dinners, the envy of Le Cirque, and then they would . . .

"You know the rules." Mark zipped up his jeans. "I need to think of you exactly like that on my bed as I brave the big bad city and the lineups at Zucker's. I don't want you to move a toe."

Olivia giggled.

"Imagining you here like that will give me the required strength."

"Not a toe," she promised.

She faded as soon as she heard the door shut. That was happening more and more, this thing. Olivia was never more alive and present than when she was near Mark, but as soon as they were apart, it was as if she was put on a dimmer switch and half-formed questions almost floated to the surface. Almost.

She studied her position, memorized it and then got up. So Serena was gone. Too bad, so sad. Who else was there? Draper didn't concern her, nor did Dr. Kruger. It was obvious that he was only using them. It was understandable, really—Mark had his career to think about. Neither was a threat to her. They were old, and Olivia was sure they couldn't do what she did. What about the other Wonders? Morgan would jump at the chance, if she hadn't already, but she was hardly a threat, and nor was Claire. They wouldn't be enough for him. That left Kate.

Kate would have been a problem, but her best friend seemed to despise Mark more with each passing day. Oh, she tried to muffle it around Olivia, but Kate stiffened if she even caught sight of him in the hall. No, Kate would never be a threat. More important, Kate would never do anything to hurt her.

This she knew for sure.

And this made her smile.

But what if there were others? Someone more important to him than her? The thought stuck in her throat and made her gag. When he was with her, Mark made her feel like no one else existed. He filled her lungs with pure oxygen. But when they were apart, all that was left was an anxiety-filled smog.

Olivia stepped gingerly to his dresser and started opening drawers. She didn't dare touch anything. She left his sweaters, T-shirts and accessories undisturbed, caressing the items only with her eyes. She performed the same ritual with the night tables. What was she even looking for?

She opened his closet, which looked like the men's suit rack at Saks. Everything was immaculate. Anka would swoon. Shoes were lined up and perfectly cared for. Ties placed on a rack in order of hue. Summer wear neatly folded in clear plastic boxes in the back. Wait. Way in the back left-hand corner, underneath a wicker basket. Was it a book? No, but it could be a photo album. Who had albums anymore? Then she remembered that Mark was older. It could be from his childhood or—she could hear her blood pumping in her ears—it could be more recent. It *could* include photos of his romances, of the girl who had shattered his heart. For Olivia was sure that there was such a girl. It would explain so much, and she would dedicate herself completely to making him forget that other one.

Thankfully, even lost in her reverie she managed to hear his key in the door.

The bed was too far away.

There was no way she would make it in time.

She wasted precious seconds in frozen panic. It was only when she heard him enter the living room that she shut the closet door and willed herself to leap for the bathroom.

Why was she so afraid? It was silly. Olivia gulped down air and flushed the toilet. She ran the faucet and arranged her expression.

He was already in the bedroom when she opened the door.

"Hi, you're back so soon. I'm glad."

Mark didn't respond. He stood at the foot of the bed, watching as she climbed back in.

Olivia beckoned to him with open arms.

Again, Mark did not respond.

"I just had to . . . I know you said not to move, but I had to go, and I didn't think—"

"You didn't think?" His voice was measured.

"I'm sorry, Mark. I didn't think you'd—"

"You didn't think," he repeated.

She *was* afraid. It was his voice, that stare, his blue eyes dark with something unknowable.

"You're right. I didn't think."

He smiled then and her heart leapt. She smiled back at him.

Mark began to unbuckle his belt.

"Well, then, little girl, Daddy will have to punish you now."

TUESDAY, FEBRUARY 23

KATE

I'd taken to texting Serena on the way to my admin duties at the school. Her texts were largely incoherent, especially before she went "in treatment." Still, I had to keep that line of communication open. The girl had firsthand intel on Redkin, and who knows, maybe one day she'd cough up something useful. Besides, I kind of missed her. I think we all did, except for Olivia.

Every single conversation with Serena ended with the same desperate warning:

Mark way weird sick stay away!!!

Yeah, well, tell me something I don't know.

I promise just get better grl.

I got to the school by 6:30 a.m. Mr. Jefferson had to let me in again. I told him it was a big push to get to as many files as possible by spring break.

He told me I work too hard. Mr. Jefferson had a mottled

butterscotch complexion and the best smile in the school. I felt guilty about lying to him.

I got over it.

I was in Draper's office by 6:35 a.m. And even on that ancient computer, I was into her files by 6:38. Like I keep saying, I'm that good.

I gambled that Draper would be the keeper of the staff resumes along with all the student records, and bingo, there he was—Mark Lawrence Redkin. There was a long version that weighed in at four pages, including an impressive list of references, and a summary that was barely a page. Both were right up to date. Good practice? Or ready to leap at a moment's notice? I shut off Draper's computer as soon as I'd sent the one-pager to the office printer.

MARK LAWRENCE REDKIN

A highly creative and results-driven nonprofit management professional specializing in independent schools. Almost ten years' experience and expertise generating revenue and increasing support for expanding school programs. Enhanced international and national exposure with a proven track record.

AREAS OF EXPERTISE
- Donor Development
- Board Development
- Strategic Planning
- High-End Event Planning
- Program Development
- Major Gift Solicitation
- Direct-Mail Marketing
- Communications/Branding

HIGHLIGHTED EXPERIENCE
2015   Executive Director of Advancement and
         Community Relations, The Waverly School,
         New York, New York. Reinvigorated and
         redefined the advancement team and program.

2014–2015	Advancement Director,
	The American School, Lucerne, Switzerland
2013–2014	Advancement Coordinator,
	The American School, Lucerne, Switzerland
2012–2013	Assistant Director Development Office,
	St. Mary's School for Girls, Melbourne, Australia
2010–2012	Director of Communications,
	The York School, Sydney, Australia
2009–2010	Senior Development Officer,
	The Pilot School, San Francisco, California
2008–2009	Donor Services Associate,
	The Pilot School, San Francisco, California
2006–2008	Advancement Associate,
	University of California, San Diego,
	San Diego, California

PROFESSIONAL AFFILIATIONS

Association of Fund-Raising Professionals
Young Nonprofit Professionals Network
National School Foundation Association
Chase Brookings & Associates

EDUCATION

Proposal and Grant Writing Certificate—New College,
New York, New York
Master of Arts, Psychology—University of California, San Diego,
San Diego, California (Phipps Scholarship, Anderson Fellow)
Bachelor of Arts, Psychology—Tufts University, Boston,
Massachusetts (Truman Scholar)

I read it as it came out of the printer. Who are you, Mark Redkin?
His resume was a testament to the power of moving around in your

career. Every single move was a significant upward push. It was aggressive and opportunistic. I got that, understood it. But why? Was he the black sheep with something to prove? Poor bright boy made good? Yeah. That smelled right. He was a scholarship kid at both universities. Dear God, would my resume look like that one day? Was he right after all? Were we alike?

No. It couldn't be. Could it?

I tucked the sheet inside my binder before heading off to the file room like I was supposed to. It was 6:51 a.m. I allowed myself to slump against the wall of cabinets, waiting for my heart to slow. *Think!* Okay, every move was a big step up. There was nothing suspicious in an ambitious young man pursuing advancement all over the globe. At least now I had specific markers to search: schools, cities, dates. But how, and for what? The Serenas of Mark's world were hardly going to turn up on the front pages of *The Sydney Morning Herald*. What was I doing?

I was talking myself out of digging in, that's what. My gut screamed that I couldn't afford to do that. I flipped open my binder to my research notes on sociopaths. There was a copy of an old *Psychology Today* article written by a self-admitted sociopath, as well as other first-person quotes that I'd pulled from the Net. I skimmed them all but rested on these:

I have never killed anyone, but I have certainly wanted to . . . Remorse is alien to me. I have a penchant for deceit.

like to imagine that I have "ruined people."

Handsome, confident, charming . . . Congrats, you have just had the pleasure of meeting my mask.

There are only two major motivations in my life: desire and rage.

I shut the binder. The quotes left me slick with sweat. They could have been written by my father. When he was sober and moving out and about in the world, people admired him, trusted him. The alcohol threw him off his game, messed with his control. As far as I could tell Mark Redkin didn't drink, and he never lost control, ever. I'd barely survived my father.

I didn't stand a chance against Redkin.

SATURDAY, FEBRUARY 27

OLIVIA

Olivia had planned the evening with her usual precision. She'd organized the car service to take them all to the party. They'd picked up Morgan and then Claire on the way to the Spice Room and headed off to the Meatpacking District at precisely 9:25 p.m. It was clear from the moment they giggled themselves into the car that the other half of the Wonders had indulged in some pre-party drinking along with their pre-party primping.

Olivia had arranged for champagne in the car and got a kick out of the four of them clinking their glasses and being seriously silly throughout the murderous traffic across town. She didn't even mind when Claire insisted that they toast Serena. "To absent friends!" By the time they got past Chelsea, Olivia had to admit that she'd enjoyed every single minute of the ride over.

"Sweet!" said Kate as they entered the Spice Room.

With the restaurant's warm glow of lanterns, Eastern exotica and hand-painted screens, it was like they had just stepped into Burma.

The party was a combination Waverly–Brinksome event, with the Sanchez family footing the bill for their daughter, Nikita, and their son, Estevez. Selected seniors from both schools were invited, with the necessary publics thrown in for color. Morgan's family was tight with the Sanchez clan, even though Morgan herself wouldn't be caught dead near the fatally airheaded Nikita.

The Wonders were met with squeals and hugs as they were herded over to the bar area. The drink crafted specially for the evening was a Singapore Slingback, apparently a more potent and spicy reinvention of a seventies-era cocktail. Kate looked at it dubiously while Claire and Morgan inhaled theirs.

"Hey, Kate! Kate, over here!"

Olivia had to nudge her to pay attention. The noise level in the place was formidable. But there, at the far end of the bar, was Kate's bakery boy, Johnny, waving a Michelob Ultra in the air.

"I got ya covered!"

Kate groaned loud enough for the Wonders to hear. "How did *he* get in?"

"That boy is smokin' hot," said Morgan, whistling. "If you ask me, he got in on looks alone."

Olivia turned to Kate with a raised eyebrow.

"Okay, so, yeah, I maybe invited him a few Sundays back." Kate winced. "Now what?"

"What do you mean you *maybe* invited him? You either did or you didn't, goof."

"No, see, I was stoned out of my mind on Ativan."

"Ativan? You, Kate? I don't believe it." Olivia would have paid to see that. "Where did you get it?"

"Uh, Serena gave me a couple before she left. That girl must be on some hell of a dose. I was fondling pineapples and grinning my whole shift."

"Well, from now on, come to me! God only knows what garbage that girl gave you. Go! At least have a drink with him. He probably had to smuggle that bottle into the place." She pushed Kate over to Johnny, with Kate protesting the whole way.

Morgan appeared with another round of Slingbacks. The girls downed those and headed to the dance floor. They were into their fourth dance when a familiar voice called out to Olivia.

"Well, if it isn't the ever-glorious Ms. Sumner!"

Matt Holbech strode toward them.

"Matt!" Olivia threw her arms around him, which was a challenge since Matt must have clocked in at six foot four. "It's been forever! I thought you were at Oxford. Did they turf you out?"

"I'm just here for a few days, my gorgeous girl. But I was hoping you might put in an appearance, so I put in an appearance." Olivia screamed out introductions to Morgan and Claire, and then to Kate and Johnny when they joined the group. Their dancing circle widened, intertwined and enlarged, with more boy add-ons. The last in were dispatched to retrieve more drinks. Olivia and Kate went for a reprise of their gala dance number as soon as the electropop blasted on. This was met with sincere and loud appreciation from every boy in the circle. Whenever the girls came in close, Kate entertained Olivia with screamed fashion commentary.

"Check out Tamara's puce leather pants. They're making my eyes bleed."

"I think Shawna's implants have left her unbalanced. She can't dance with her new breasts."

"Oh, look! Surprise, surprise, our hostess is beyond plastered already. So's her brother. Sharp as bowling balls, the whole family."

Matt didn't take his eyes off Olivia, and that felt good. Better than good.

They danced, drank, laughed and danced some more. And then it was 11:45. Olivia's heart lurched. She'd be late.

But she didn't want to leave. Olivia did not want to leave.

Yet she headed to the door like someone had yelled, "Fire!"

"Whoa, hot stuff! Wait!" yelled Matt, but he was held back by the crowd.

Kate was not. Using her elbows as weapons, she caught up to Olivia at the front lounge. "Hey, roomie! What's up?"

She couldn't explain, because it didn't make sense. Olivia wanted to *stay*. She had never wanted to stay before. But she had to . . .

"I gotta go. Don't ask. I'm taking a cab. I've arranged for Jackson to be here for you guys at two. He'll wait if you want, but . . . don't you wait up."

"Olivia, don't. Please. Please stay. You belong here with us, with *me*. That guy back there has got it for you bad. I know you want to stay."

The look on Kate's face almost stopped her. She seemed to know Olivia better than she knew herself.

But she couldn't be late. There would be consequences.

"I need to. I mean, I *want* to. I have to go." She couldn't be late. She gave Kate a quick squeeze. "Love you lots. Have fun."

"Olivia! Come on, talk to me!"

She could *not* be late.

Olivia jumped in the first waiting cab. When she got to Mark's building, she ran up the three flights with her heart in her mouth. By the time she reached his loft, she was dead sober. She knocked on his door.

Olivia was late.

214

TUESDAY, MARCH 1

KATF

The DSM-5 weighs over four pounds. That's a lot of mental disorders. I was relieved that Kruger wouldn't let me use it outside her office. It would have thrown out my back lugging that baby around. I finally found where the whack-jobs on the DSM committee had stuck the details on sociopaths and psychopaths. They lumped them into a category called antisocial personality disorder (pages 659–63). Well, lock me up, but that just sounded wrong given how "social" sociopaths tend to be. Not only that, but the info wasn't all that helpful. The Internet was better.

I was perched at my research station—in other words, Miss Shwepper's desk—trolling through the mental health sites that Kruger had recommended. I got to one on "appealing sociopaths." It said that people with this illness may seem charming since they're often highly intelligent and can read people like a book.

Ha! Dear old dad ditched the charm, at least with us, within a couple of months of our arrival. He was less and less charming with each passing week. I knew something was building—the air was thick with it—but aside from being scared, I didn't know what to do. I was supposed to be so smart, but I never knew what to do. It made me feel like I was full of holes.

We were in the kitchen, my father and I. You could cut the air with a scythe. Mom was at a training upgrade for dental hygiene. He hated it when she wasn't home and he was. And God forgive me, so did I. On the one hand, I was freaked that he'd go after her when she was there. On the other, I was freaked that he'd go after me when she wasn't. Lose-lose, in other words.

My father was chain-smoking and on his third Coca-Cola, no rye. But he was ruminating. Ruminating was trouble, drunk or sober. He'd suck everything out of the apartment except for my fear. He barely touched the dinner. Couldn't really blame him—I was a lousy cook. He leaned back and studied me while I washed up.

"You got your smarts from me, you know."

"Yes, sir." No beats, no pauses allowed. I rinsed off the CorningWare and started loading the dishwasher, quietly. My father did not care for loud loading.

"We didn't have fancy scholarships in my day. So I didn't get a chance to run off to some whoop-de-do boarding school, like they're giving you in Calgary next year. If I'd had half your chance, I wouldn't be in this shithole. But you, you're destined for better, cockroach. You are going places."

I had to gather myself but not pause. "Yes, sir." Rinse and repeat.

"I'm glad for you. Yes, I am. You're going to make something of yourself. What does the old lady always say?"

"Keep your eye on the prize."

"And what's the prize again?"

"Yale, sir."

There was a long pause, then he chuckled. "Every so often even that dishrag gets something right. You'll do it, kid. No doubt, no sir. You've got all the best parts of me. You're gonna make me proud."

See? Every so often he'd throw you a curveball. Make you think that he gave a damn.

And I was deeply, deeply ashamed to admit just how much that meant to me. How much I craved it.

I heard the bottle cap being unscrewed and the glug, glug of the rye, followed by a splash of Coke. Here we go. We were in very dangerous territory. My father went from sweet to mean in a heartbeat. I heard him snort. Without turning, I knew that he was shaking his head.

"Shit for brains, that's all you got from her."

It was because of her that I was planning to turn down the scholarship. Neither of them would know until it was too late. My mom wouldn't last a week without me. That I wouldn't be going filled me with a rage that made me incoherent. Whenever I thought of it, as I did in that moment, my mouth filled with ashes.

I heard him get up, leave the room, open drawers in the living room and return to his throne in the kitchen. I was rinsing the knives and forks so hard I could have passed them to a surgeon.

"I wonder if your mother is doing that dentist she works for? I bet she is. I bet that's where she is right now. Why else would he hire her? Isn't that right?"

Say it, say it! The words crawled up my throat but got caught in the ashes. Too many beats.

"I said, isn't that right, cockroach?"

My hand found the paring knife, gripped it.

"She's not worth spit!"

The scholarship, the fear, the beatings—all surged into the hand gripping that knife. "You're the one who's not worth spit!"

I spun around.

And I would have killed him. I swear to God.

217

Except that he held his drink in his left hand and a gun in his right. A gun.

He laughed and laughed when I dropped the knife. "You got my fire too, I'll give you that, cockroach." He took a sip and let out a satisfied burp. "Now, either you set up for a proper beating or . . . you can lick my feet."

We stared at each other. I did not move.

My father took his finger off the trigger guard.

He must have been a handsome man once.

I knelt down and took off his shoes.

There were tears on Kruger's DSM-5. A handkerchief appeared out of nowhere. Mark Redkin pulled up a chair near but not against Shwepper's desk.

"Momentary truce, okay?"

My stomach seized. Was there anyone else in the office?

"Wipe your face before you start blotting the pages. Don't worry about it. Lots of people have cried trying to understand that stupid book." His handsome face was etched with concern. His voice was gentle, warm.

"I-I needed . . . I just have to, uh . . ."

He sighed, then got up, shut the book and turned off the computer. "I'm thinking that's enough for one day. Things bubble up, memories burn, you can't see straight. It's an order, Kate. Go home, get some air, have dinner, watch a reality show, regroup."

"But . . ."

"Go on." He shook his head. Did he look sad? "I promise, we'll live to fight another day. *You'll* live to fight another day. Go. That's enough for you for now."

See? It was almost as if he gave a damn.

That's how you get twisted by them.

It wasn't until I was slobber-greeted by Bruce that it dawned on me. Of course he knew. Mark Redkin knew about all of it.

But still, in the knowing, he was so completely there. He got it. *He's in your head, Katie. Get him out. Stay cold, stay sharp.*

I ran a bath before dinner, talking to myself the whole time. I learned a lot from my old man—what to do, what not to do, how to duck, how to lie. My old man was a walking, talking master class. But in the end, the main thing I learned the best thing—was never to bring a knife to a gunfight.

SUNDAY, MARCH 6

OLIVIA

The water ran freely over her calves. Hot. When the bathtub threatened to overflow, Olivia pulled the plug to release some. She did not turn off the taps while doing so. After a while, she stopped replugging the tub and just let the water flow and drain at the same time. It was a metaphor, she thought, but didn't know exactly for what.

"Olivia?"

She dunked her head. The voice was very far away.

"Did you hand in your physics lab? I can do the poem synopsis for you when I get back, but you're on your own with the physics thing."

Olivia had already had one extension on the lab and one in AP Calculus that Kate didn't know about. Then there was that stupid exit thesis. He said he would help.

Help.

She dunked once again and then proceeded to get out of the tub. Slowly, because Olivia got dizzy if she moved too fast. Sometimes.

She wound a towel around her head and began to pat herself dry. As she did so, she could feel his whispers against her skin and she smiled.

She massaged in the cinnamon-scented body oil with great care. He liked the cinnamon the best. That done, she wrapped herself in a snowy white towel, dry-swallowed a pill and headed back into her bedroom.

A knock. "Are you decent? Sorry, I just want to check that you want . . ." Kate walked in.

"S'okay." Olivia shrugged and padded over to her closet. He liked her in dresses and only in dresses. She hadn't bought anything new in quite some time. The spring lines had been out in the stores for weeks. Olivia remembered thinking how much fun she'd have taking Kate to all her favorite haunts. She also remembered how flat-out happy Matt was to see her at the Spice Room. She once had a bit of a crush on Matt. A long, long time ago.

"I'm going to bring back some fusion Indo-Vietnamese from this new place that Johnny raves about. Do you think you'll be back for dinner? Bruce and I will wait."

"Where is he, our fearless protector?"

"Anka took him for a walk and then she'll head out." Kate hadn't moved from the doorway and Olivia hadn't stopped staring into her closet.

"So Indo-Vietnamese?"

Maybe the purple cashmere dress. He hadn't seen that one yet. "Sure, sounds good, especially if *Johnny* says so."

Kate stepped over to the bed and tossed a throw pillow at her.

"Ooooh, a little touchy on the topic of Johnny, are we?" Olivia picked up the pillow, tossed it and then another one back at her friend. For a heartbeat, they were *them* again. But in the toss, Olivia's towel had loosened.

The pillows landed at Kate's feet. Kate didn't retrieve them for another throw. She looked stricken. "Olivia, my God."

Olivia turned to the mirror. There were the bruises, the tiny scars—dozens of them. Some were pink, some red; some looked silver in this light. Her body was his canvas, he said. She hadn't looked in weeks. She had skillfully avoided *seeing*. Now, Olivia couldn't stop. Kate sucked in air but didn't speak. The bruises were dramatic. They bloomed and faded in different hues. A couple were fresh and reddish, while most looked like faded rainbows. But it wasn't the bruises—they would disappear. It was the scars that shredded her, all those scars . . . ugly, ugly scars.

Tears pooled in her eyes.

"Olivia . . . Jesus."

She readjusted the towel and turned to her friend.

"I love him, Kate."

Kate took a step toward her and then stopped. "No, Olivia. No, you don't." She took another step, paused. "Mark drew you in, understood things no one could understand about you, and now . . ." Kate seemed to be weighing each word, parsing it against another blowup. "Now, he's using that to hold you, to play you. He's twisting you. Some part of you knows it. You're stronger than this, I promise."

Olivia wanted to slap her. It would feel good to hurt Kate, to hurt someone.

"I told you never to talk about him." Her voice was flat. It was as if she was trying to remember something. "My house, my rules. If you have a problem with that, leave." She turned her back on Kate. "You could never understand a man like Mark."

"You're wrong, Olivia. I understand Mark plenty," Kate called out as she was leaving. "And I'll be right here when you do too."

Olivia shook as she returned to her closet. She examined dress choices mechanically. The purple cashmere, the fitted Céline, the flowered silk jersey, the blue-and-white Prada—he would approve of them all. Mark would love them all. Yet she didn't reach for any of them. He had *scarred* her. Minutes slid by. She would be late. And still she didn't move, didn't breathe.

Finally, Olivia exhaled into her decision. She reached deep into the back of her closet and retrieved her favorite Rag & Bone jeans and then shrugged into her comfiest cashmere sweater.

"Perfect!" she whispered to the mirror. But she had to hurry or else she'd be late.

MONDAY, MARCH 7

KATE

Olivia, Bruce and I were snuggled deep into dueling couches, laptops open, books and photocopied papers spread across the stone-and-copper coffee table. Anka came in at half-hour intervals to replenish espressos and admonish us over something or other. Every so often Bruce would rouse himself from my stomach to waddle over and settle himself onto Olivia's, and then back to me again.

It was like the best of before, but not. We both pretended that I hadn't seen what I'd seen. We were doing a lot of pretending. And even though that was more or less my normal state of play, I felt myself fraying at the edges. I knew too much, and then not nearly enough. I had to break into Kruger's file cabinet this week, no matter what. I'd been putting it off, but why? Not like me, really. Maybe I didn't want to know. God, I was getting squishy. *Stop!* I needed to know what Mark knew. I needed to know it all. Speaking of which . . .

I Googled risperidone.

What?!

Risperidone is usually used to help treat the symptoms of conditions such as psychosis, schizophrenia, schizophreniform disorder and hypomania. It can also be used to help manage confusion, dementia, behavior problems (e.g., in ADHD) and personality disorders. It may also be used in smaller doses to help treat anxiety, tension and agitation.

Whoa. What a smorgasbord of crazy. I was going to have to look up each one of those things. Is that what Mark had on her? Did he know exactly what it was, the whole story? I switched to a gossip site to collect myself and then glanced at Olivia. She looked content in her sweats, both lapdog and laptop balancing on her outstretched body. She was deep into a long-overdue math assignment. I reached into my pocket and slid out my phone. We still kept up after a fashion.

hey Serena u there?

of course ☺ whats up?

i miss u, u ok?

ya better, outpatient now.

congrats! u rock ☺

not so much
I miss you Kate but better here, even with dear old dad. was drowning there. you know the score.

i hear u. Mark?

yup bad bad scene

can't u report him?

no way!!!!! Imagine the scandal on top of my family scandal ☹
besides he knew stuff
collects secrets and cuts u with them?
Pure reptile.

for sure so sad for u, sucks big time

shudve known better.

NO! u didn't stand a chance!

Thanks babe. is he after you?

not bad so far

really? surprised. was all ocd about you

steering clear, but olivia . . .

i know, how bad?

I looked over. She was happily cursing at her screen. Bruce was snoring.

way bad. cant stop her.

he's like a drug, gotta find a way
a girl in Melbourne killed herself while he was there.
my cousin was there then
don't think suicide was a coincidence, seriously.

My mind emptied.

kate you there?

yeah just scared.

you should be, probably not the only one. you sure about you?

yeah, biding his time . . . i guess.

I swear he likes you best. dangerous Kate, very.

i know.

"Kate O'Brien, are you actually texting? You hate texting. I'm jealous! Who're you talking to?"

I gtg sweets. later.

np, miss you. stay safe!!!!

Sharing the panic xoxo

Here if you need me xoxo

"Believe me, no one," I groaned. "Just this mouth-breather from my last school. Never hear from her, and then, presto, she's coming to New York during spring break with her folks and wants me to show them the sights, be a private tour guide." It was good to remind myself of just how *good* I was on the fly.

"The nerve! I hope you said absolutely not!"

"I graciously declined, yes."

"Good! You've got to watch that, Kate. You're the type that dweebs feel they can take advantage of." She didn't lift her eyes from her laptop. "You're always there for people, even when it doesn't serve you at all. You were all soft on Serena, for instance."

Then again, it was good to be reminded of just how *good* Olivia was.

"Well, not anymore," I said, getting up. "I just care about you, me and our son here. I believe it's my turn to take him for a walk."

At the word *walk,* Bruce stopped snoring, sprung from Olivia's stomach, leapt over the coffee table (kicking my laptop closed in the process) and headed straight for the door. When we stopped laughing, Olivia got up too.

"Come on," she said, swinging her legs to the floor. "I'll come too. Let's walk over to the Nespresso on Madison. You hold him and I'll get us some cappuccinos and those little chocolates."

Like I said, so like before and yet so not.

OLIVIA

Olivia wanted to go home. It was late. She was exhausted. He was not. Kate had written the response to the Hamlet soliloquy for her, but she should at least read it over before she submitted it tomorrow. Shouldn't she?

So tired.

Mark had just left the room to retrieve more Chablis. Olivia didn't want any more Chablis. She risked getting up out of bed. He hadn't ordered her not to move, after all. She caught herself in the mirror and looked away immediately. She ran her hands over her stomach, down her ribs and over her protruding hip bones. He liked to touch her bones and his marks.

He had pronounced her "flawless" not ten minutes ago. Olivia wanted to be flawless for him.

Didn't she?

She padded naked into the living room. Once she disrobed, Olivia was not allowed to put on any clothes or cover up until it was time to leave. Though shirtless, Mark wore a pair of chinos. He was bent over, absorbed in his phone. Seeing him unaware and un-guarded, Olivia was transported back to when she first caught sight of him, and her breath slipped. His tanned upper body was toned and muscular but lean. Blond curls fell over his eyes as he texted. He was an oil painting.

He looked up. A flash of annoyance almost broke free. She saw him catch it and produce a smile instead.

"Hey, babe, I'm just freeing up my Sunday for us. I'll be right back."

"I was just getting a glass of water."

"I poured you another glass of wine. It's on the credenza."

"But I—"

He sighed. "Take the wine and wait for me in bed, my darling."

"Yes, Mark."

She couldn't quite get a deep breath in. Olivia tried. She in-haled as deeply as she could, but her breath caught on the ever-expanding block of granite that seemed to be wedged between her lungs and the top of her stomach. Worse yet, she was out of Ativan.

She crawled under the immaculate white sheet and drew her knees to her chest. Olivia had been so hell-bent on feeling "real" feelings that she'd wanted to master this game, master Mark. *Stu-pid, stupid girl.* What she wouldn't give to rewind and go back to roaming Chinatown with Kate, having coffee with the Wonders, going to a party or two, just hanging out together and bitching about everybody else. Long, rambling conversations with her dad were over. She had to keep it short because her father had picked up something in the tone of her voice. Her father . . .

Mark came into the room and yanked off the sheet.

"My father," she said.

He got out of his pants, carefully folding them and placing them on the bureau. "What about your father?"

Mark was not in a good mood. Olivia gulped and then was afraid that he'd seen her do so.

"My father wants me and Kate to join him for spring break in Rio." A *life raft.* "He's got a place overlooking Copacabana. Kate will just—"

"No." Mark walked over to the bed.

"No?"

"Make it *not* happen. Don't arouse his suspicion, but make it go away. And don't have Daddy jetting home because he's all worried about you. I want you here."

How could she possibly do that? How could she make her father understand? Kate would have loved Rio.

"Understand?"

Olivia nodded.

"Good." He straddled her. "It's time to make me happy."

"Yes." She adjusted herself. "I would love to."

"No, not just in that way." He stroked her hair with a caress so gentle and loving that she would have melted and promised him anything . . . before. "I'm growing a little frustrated."

If she could only get one good breath in.

Mark leaned over and kissed her forehead, and then her eyelids, and then her cheek, and then he whispered, "It's time, my love."

"Why her? I'll do *anything.* You know I'd do anything to make you happy. Besides, she won't come anywhere near you."

"I have faith in you." Mark smiled, exposing one adorable dimple. "And if she doesn't . . ." He kissed her. "I." Kiss. "Will." Kiss. "Tell her." Kiss.

No. She commanded a breath, and then another. Then, with a courage she didn't know she was capable of, Olivia went for the bluff. "I told her. She knows already."

Mark laughed as he settled himself on top of her. "Come now.

You may have told her a *version* of the truth, but I'm sure she doesn't know the whole truth. Nor do the rest of the staff. Nor does the admissions board at Yale."

The shame was blinding.

"There, there." He kissed tears that Olivia didn't even know she'd shed.

"It's time." He pinned her arms against the mattress. "Deliver Kate to me." He tightened his grip. "Do you understand, Olivia? Do you really understand how much I want this?"

"Yes." Olivia closed her eyes. She had to please him or she wanted to? Which was it? "Yes," she said. "I understand."

WEDNESDAY, MARCH 9

KATE

Poor old Mr. Jefferson had to let me in again. It was 6:47 a.m., and he was not pleased. "They gonna work you to death, girl!"

"Almost finished, sir. And it's my choice, really. I like to get in while it's quiet. I can get ten times more done."

"Young lady, you're going to be wrung out before you even get to college. You gotta lighten up. Don't let 'em get you."

"No, sir, I won't."

I got it then. Mr. Jefferson knew I was the scholarship kid. He wasn't pissed. He felt sorry for me. Just like Johnny. Johnny could tell something was going on. But nobody gets in for the real story, ever. *Nobody* gets to feel sorry for me. We'd argued about it all the way back from coffee on Sunday.

"Okay, fine! Don't tell me. Who cares? I don't!" He yelled at me right in front of the mangoes before stomping away. So mature. Mrs. Chen caught it.

Tough.

I was still working out why it bothered me so much.

I dumped my stuff onto Miss Shwepper's desk, turned on my laptop for effect and headed for Kruger's office. I had to will my feet to move with every step. *Let's go, let's go.* I couldn't risk turning on the light. The castoff from the administration office would have to do. For the first time in years, I made a sign of the cross and headed for her bookshelf. The little gold bowl was still perched on top of the books on the very top shelf. What if I was wrong? *Please, please let the key be there.* I felt beads, coins, a ring and . . . a key!

Straight to the oak file cabinet. My hands were ice cold, my fingers stiff and awkward. Precious seconds were wasted trying to get the key in the lock. Done! The first drawer was packed tight with file folders. They were all alphabetical and all marked "Confidential." I ran my fingers across the tabs. They were current students. I snagged on that for a bit. How many secrets do we have in this school? Fingering my way through the alphabet, I froze on O: O'Brien, Katherine. Man, it was thick. I didn't have time to stop and examine it. I mean, I knew what was in there, but the knowing made my hands shake. I reached in and pulled out one of what had to be dozens of press clippings, reports and hard copies of Internet dreck. I shoved the clipping in my pocket. Why? A souvenir? I put the file back. I was breathing hard now.

Okay—P, Q, R, S. Sala, Salinsky, Stephens. Sumner, Olivia. Not as thick as mine, but thicker than most. I glanced at my phone; it was 7:12. There wasn't enough time for a good look. Draper could be here at any moment. I teased her file up but not out and flipped through pages and reports. I didn't know what I was looking for until I saw a name I recognized: Dr. Russell Tamblyn, MD, PhD. Olivia's shrink. It was a letter dated August 12. I tried to expand the file enough to give me a sideways sight line; I couldn't risk slipping it right out to read it.

Further to the attached report from Houston Medical, I concur with the diagnosis, the instigating events and the prognosis . . .

Something, something, something . . . schizophreniform disorder . . . first psychotic break . . . something, something.

My heart beat in my head. Psychotic?

An episode of acute primary psychosis led the patient to believe that she was pregnant. A full medical workup revealed that the patient was still a virgin.

Jesus.

Mitigating and inducing factors . . . the temporary psychosis could have been instigated by several factors: although the client continues to deny it, it is likely that she had discontinued the risperidone as prescribed eighteen months prior (first onset of possible symptoms) in reaction to the anhedonia. (Attached please find a summary report relaying Miss Sumner's account of how the medication left her feeling flat and "without any decent feelings.")

. . . the client's recent bout of depression and feelings of dislocation might have been exacerbated by a virulent case of mononucleosis. The attendant stress of loss of school time, coupled with self-reporting of experimentation with "party drugs," is a possible causal factor . . . in light of possible noncompliance with medication . . .

I fully concur with my Houston colleague's assessment that the presenting psychosis has been well treated and is likely not to be a chronic factor in the client's school term.

She will remain under my care and is fully compliant with the maintenance regime.

Oh, my God, Olivia. I was running out of air. I shoved the file drawer closed, then had to hang on to it to steady myself. Was it better to be pregnant than crazy? Maybe. As sympathetic as the Ivies were to modern emotional issues, the word *psychotic* still had that hard thunk to it. Just keeping this kind of secret would cost her plenty. I knew what it did to me.

So this was the thing Mark was playing her with. This knowledge, these secrets. Bastard!

Get a grip. Who cares?

I did. I was in too deep. Apparently, there was still enough of Sister Rose in me that had not been beaten to a pulp. Olivia had given me a home, a dog, a life with open arms.

A rage welled up and took over, leaving no room for the fear. To hell with him. To hell with Waverly and Yale and scholarships and keeping an eye on the goddamn prize. She was the only family I had. I would see him burn before I'd let him destroy her.

The outer office door rattled.

Raw fear ricocheted right back, shoving out the anger and leaving it in a puddle on the floor. I locked the cabinet drawer as quietly as I could, grabbed the DSM-5 and left. Who could it be at this hour?

"Ah, my favorite Wonder!" Mark Redkin looked amused. "Good morning! Is there anything in particular you were looking for in our good doctor's office?"

I raised the book in my left hand. My right was gripping the key so hard it threatened to break skin. I'd have to return it before Kruger got in. "Dr. Kruger said I was welcome to use it whenever, so long as I stayed in the office."

"Right." He smiled at me. "Still working on your sociopaths?"

"I have an intense personal interest."

"You're looking stressed, Kate. I'm concerned." And I had to admit, he actually did look concerned. "Life is a game." He crossed his arms. "I believe you have an innate talent for it. In fact, you're the best I've seen. I wish you'd let me show you how to play with the rest."

My stomach roiled. I would have hurled, but thankfully there was nothing in there. I hadn't even had time for a coffee.

"Good morning, all!" Ms. Draper breezed into the office. She was wearing a brand-new floaty dress. They were still at it, then. Still timing their entrances. That meant Draper was still useful to him. "How pleasant to find the office not deserted. Mark, Kate!"

"Good morning, Ms. Draper." I took this as an opportunity to sit at Shwepper's desk before my knees gave out. "Thank you, Mr. Redkin."

I spent the next half hour staring at the DSM-5. All I needed was to hold it together and not give in to the cramping that was clawing at my gut. At precisely 7:45, I made a show of sighing, shutting the book and returning it to Kruger's office. I placed the book on her desk, but the spasms were so bad by then that I had trouble reaching up to the bowl to drop in the key.

The cramps didn't disappear when the immediate threat did. I minced into the file room and played at reorganizing the next batch for logging. The inhabitants of our little nucleus in the administration office came in, called out greetings and chided each other good-naturedly. I didn't leave the file room until it was time for class.

"Oh, Kate"—Mark came to the threshold of his door—"I have something that may aid you in your paper. I know our library doesn't carry this." He held out a book.

"Thank you very much, Mr. Redkin." I walked over and took it from him, eating the strain with every step. "I really appreciate it, *sir*."

I didn't even look until I got to the third floor. *Snakes in Suits: When Psychopaths Go to Work* by Paul Babiak, PhD, and Robert D. Hare, PhD.

I was late for AP French.

Turns out, you can puke long and hard even on an empty stomach.

THURSDAY, MARCH 10

OLIVIA

1:50 A.M.

What was that Plath poem? The one way back at the beginning of the year? The one that Kate got her through? The one about dying being like an art or something. She strained to retrieve it. It was important, maybe. Dying, living, the scars, it was all art.

Olivia got it now. Ha! She *got* Plath. Kate would be so proud. Kate. She had threatened Kate about even mentioning Mark. Olivia got up on shaky legs, avoiding the mirror at all costs. She would see them. They were worse than those of her Houston roommate, the cutter. With some pride, the girl—what was her name?—had outlined the ritual, the necessity, the release afterward. Olivia couldn't listen. She was so completely freaked out by the scars. Whatshername had made them with a special paper cutter, or a kitchen knife, or in worst-case scenarios any old pair of scissors or sharp object. The thing that terrorized Olivia was that you could still see cuts that had been made months and even years earlier.

"Marked" forever. That's what *he* said. Olivia chugged back the dregs of her wine before she slipped into her clothes. Mark lay on the bed, his head propped up by his beautiful sculpted arm.

She shuddered.

"Remember"—his voice was low, gravelly—"I'm growing impatient."

Olivia nodded, finished dressing and stumbled out of the apartment and into a cab.

Somehow she got into the penthouse and into her room and into her bathroom. She stripped and turned the taps to scalding. She forgot to look away. On her way in, she saw.

THURSDAY, MARCH 10

KATE

2:46 A.M.

I shot out of bed like a bullet. The keening, piercing howl was animal-like. I scrambled in the dark, desperate to locate Bruce, but he was there right beside me. Ever since Olivia had started coming home at all hours, he'd taken to sleeping in my bed. Bruce did not like his bedtime routine disturbed. I switched on the light. He wagged his tail at me, but you could tell he was annoyed. Did I dream it?

There again. A cry from hell.

Olivia! I sprinted to her room, stumbling over dog bones and squeaky toys. Then complete silence, just the chugging of blood in my ears. I knocked.

No answer. Nothing. I opened the bedroom door and walked in, hovering at the foot of her bed. It was empty.

Bruce headed straight for the closed bathroom door and started pawing at it. I could hear the taps gushing at full blast. I knocked gently. There it was—a keening, though much softer now.

"Olivia?" I knocked louder. "Olivia, it's me and Bruce. Are you okay?"

The crying stopped. The water did not.

"Olivia?"

"Sorry, guys. I'm okay. Too much wine and hit myself on the counter. I'm okay. Go to bed. Really, I'm good. Promise."

Bruce and I looked at each other. "Okay. If you're sure."

"Promise."

I stopped panting and turned around. Her new Zac Posen dress was crumpled on the floor like she'd just stepped out of it. He liked dresses. I bent over to retrieve it and lay it on the bed. It was ruined. The white silk lining was covered in strange little splotches. What? Was that blood?

Oh, God.

"I'm here, Olivia. Do you hear me? I'm here and always will be, got it? Whenever you're ready. Olivia?"

"Please go away."

FRIDAY, MARCH 11

OLIVIA

5:03 P.M.

Olivia was panicking and in heavy pacing mode. Anka had come in "for to dusting" the artwork and lingered.

"It's okay, Anka. I took it this morning."

"I did not for sure be saying noting!" Anka did her best impersonation of someone being falsely accused. Bruce sidled up to her, recognizing her for the soft touch that she was. "Okay. Za dinner is in oven. Ven Kate is coming, please eat. I am taking za doggie for a big valking now."

Olivia watched her housekeeper and house pet depart, and then she resumed marching. *How could she do it? She couldn't do it. Wouldn't do it. Kate was her best friend, her lifeline. Couldn't, shouldn't, wouldn't.*

She didn't have a choice.

At 5:35, Kate finally rolled in from doing her research on the crazies. She caught Olivia in mid-stride. "Hey, what's up? Where's . . . ?"

"Anka took Bruce to Central Park, or at least that's what I think she meant when she said 'a big valking.'"

Kate smiled.

"Let's eat, Kate, I'm hungry. Want to eat?"

Kate slid out of her backpack and school jacket, eyeing her friend warily. "Sure, especially if you're actually going to ingest food. I'll pour you some wine."

The girls settled themselves at the kitchen island, doling out cutlery, grilled salmon, salad and wine. Olivia downed her glass in two gulps.

"Whoa, friend of mine, what's up?" Kate's smile faded. "Do you have to see him tonight?"

Have to.

"At eleven," she said, pouring more wine. "And 'have to' isn't fair, Kate. You . . . you so haven't been fair to Mark from the beginning. Right from the start, you threw up roadblocks, even though he was so great about you chairing the Wonders and so concerned about you and . . . well, he cares deeply about us—about you, in particular—you know?"

She watched Kate swallow whatever she was going to say.

Olivia got up, holding on to the counter with one hand and her glass with another. "Not only should you cut him some slack, but you should, uh . . ."

Kate stood. "What's going on, Olivia?"

Couldn't shouldn't wouldn't . . .

"I'm just saying, well, he's so smart and he can be incredibly sweet, and if you'd just give him a chance . . ."

Kate walked over and put an arm around her. "Olivia, stop. Why are you crying?"

She was crying?

Kate wrapped her arms around her friend. "Shh, it's okay. It will be okay."

"No, Kate." She pushed her away. "No, it won't. He wants *you!*

He wants me to deliver you to him, like gift-wrapped or something." Now she was shaking as well as crying. "And no, I'm not jealous! Not anymore—well, not much—but if I don't, you have no idea . . . if I don't, he'll . . . oh, Kate, he'll . . ."

Kate took the wineglass from Olivia and placed it on the island. "He'll what?" Her voice was soft. "Tell me that you had a little gone-nuts episode? Tell me that you weren't pregnant at all? That Houston was a psych ward stay? Is that what he's threatening you with? Is that it?"

Olivia fell into the chair.

Kate took her hands. "It's okay. I know it all, and I love you even more, I broke into Kruger's secret files two days ago, and believe you me, this school is sitting on a crapload of 'For Your Eyes Only' stuff. You and me, girl, are the least of it. Listen, Redkin has access to our stuff because he's been playing Kruger like a violin."

"What?" Olivia could not stop shaking. "What?"

"It's official—Redkin is a horror show. And he's probably left a trail of crap at every single school he's been at. Are you listening? It's not just you. It's not your fault. He is a MONSTER!"

Olivia reached for a paper towel and blew her nose.

"The man is a predator, pure and simple—and oh so proud of it. He knows I'm on to him. I let him know. In his warped world he thinks we're alike, sick soul mates or something. Wait 'til you see the book he gave me." Kate dashed out of the room and then dashed back, brandishing the copy of *Snakes in Suits*. Olivia took the book because it was expected of her, but in truth, she was several steps behind. She was still way back at the "I know it all, and I love you even more" part. She looked at Kate, trying to discern deception. All she saw was searing anger.

"Focus, Olivia. It's time to focus! I know of at least one suicide at a school where's he's been, and I'd bet my soul that there are more. He gets off on it, on us, on girls and women like *us*."

Us? That confused Olivia. The important takeaway was that Kate still cared about her.

"Turf me out or whatever, but pay attention. Redkin is dangerous—really, really dangerous."

It was like being enveloped in a warm bath. "You really forgive me? Mark, the lies, my illness?" She felt her heartbeat accelerating. "If Yale finds out, I . . . they said it's not likely to happen again. I'm really good about the pills—I really am—but . . ." She scrubbed her face with her hands. "Sure, the others have stuff, but I, like, really checked out from reality for a bit there."

"I don't care! *This* is our reality." Kate squeezed her hand. "I'm not just patting you on the head. Everybody has something. *Everybody*."

Kate reached into her purse and retrieved a newspaper clipping.

Olivia looked up at her, confused. "Who is Stephen Medvev?"

"Read it."

THE CALGARY TRIBUNE, SATURDAY, AUGUST 13
"You Can't Kill a Cockroach!" Says Murdering Father

Stephen Medvev was led away in handcuffs from 322 Bolger Avenue in Fort McMurray. His wife, Janet Medvev, 41, was pronounced dead at the scene, after what sources say was a brutal beating and multiple stab wounds. His daughter, thirteen-year-old Katie Medvev, was medevaced to Centennial Hospital in Calgary with life-threatening injuries. Neighbors called the police just after midnight when they heard screams coming from the Medvev house. Mr. Medvev was heard to say to a police officer that "they had it coming."

Mr. Medvev is a supervisor with Energo Extraction. Colleagues and neighbors have expressed shock and dismay.

"Steve was the total package—smart, on top of things and totally in control," said John Tilsdale, an executive vice president with Energo. "We offer our heartfelt prayers to the Medvev family in the face of this tragedy."

Neighbors describe Mr. Medvev as charming and helpful. "Everybody loved him."

Sources say that Mr. Medvev laughed as his daughter was being loaded into the ambulance. "Kid'll be fine," he reportedly said. "She's like me, man. The kid's a cockroach. You can't kill a cockroach!"

Mr. Medvev was taken into custody without bail. Katie Medvev is listed in critical condition.

Olivia looked up at Kate. "What's this? This isn't . . ."

"Yes, it is. It's me. It's us—my father, my mother. I'm the cock-roach." Kate's eyes looked hot. "As you can see, he was right. I made it. And I *didn't* come through that circle of hell just to let Mark Red-kin take me down. I promise you, Olivia. He won't get either of us."

"Medvev?"

"That's his name, and it was mine." Kate got up and then sat back down. "He'll get out eventually and search for Katie Med-vev. So she doesn't exist anymore. He killed her in so many ways." Kate hugged herself. "PTSD doesn't begin to cover it. On the heels of that nightmare was the trial nightmare and the child services

247

nightmare and the foster parents nightmare, and I know how this will sound, but"—she put her head in her hands—"after all that, the thing that almost broke me was the nonstop hounding by the press. I guess Cockroach Katie, indestructible kid, was too sweet a story to let go. They hunted me down wherever I went, wanting a 'where is she now' update, taking pictures, sticking mics in my face. And then it would start all over again—I'd become instantly untouchable."

Kate stood up again and stayed standing. "I changed schools three times. Each time because a staff person let it slip or some kid Googled my name. And each time was uglier than the one before. I couldn't go through it one more time." She turned to Olivia. "It all got worked out at Trinity Prep. We legally changed my name. My mom was Irish, so O'Brien."

Olivia was having trouble digesting this. It was as if the words came close to her but fell to the floor before they penetrated. Kate?

"Olivia, pay attention!" Kate snapped her fingers. "So Trinity Prep and Waverly both swore to secrecy, and other than Kruger and Goodlace, no staff would ever know the whole story. To tell you the truth, I don't think Draper knows the story to this day. Look, I can take just about anything, but not my story coming out. Ever. People knowing, looking, the press, having to relive it all . . . and Redkin knows that."

It was too much to take in. Olivia inhaled and caught herself. The rock in her chest was gone. She could breathe. At least she could breathe. She crumpled the newspaper clipping and tossed it in the garbage.

FRIDAY, MARCH 11

KATE

9:47 P.M.

We talked for hours. When Anka and Bruce returned from their walk, much of the talking was actually whispering. We talked and whispered while we pretended to eat. Then we moved to my bedroom and pretended to be absorbed in something on my laptop. There, we talked and argued and cried. But I finally got to her, I think. Olivia's eyes were clear of worship and filled with abject fear.

As they should have been.

"What do we do? We have to do something. We have to nail him," she said as soon as the coast was completely clear. "That bastard has marked me for life. *Scarred* me. You don't know the half of it. Neither of us is safe, Kate. I know where his tastes run. I know what he's capable of. And to think what a bitch I was to Serena. I was actually happy that . . ."

"Sit down, Olivia." I patted the bed beside me. She sat. "You've got to cancel tonight."

Confusion and relief chased each other across Olivia's face. "But we . . . it's too late."

"Look, we're waist-deep in quicksand. Nothing short of a black ops playbook is going to get us out of this." As I said it, I knew it was true. What were our chances? "No way for tonight. You've got to get yourself together. You walk in like this, you'll either sink us both or get us killed."

"Killed! Come on, Kate, don't be—"

"Remember the *suicide*? It was actually a friend of Serena's cousin's. How creepy is that?"

The color drained from Olivia's face.

"There's got to be others. I'm sure of it. Everything I know about his type and how he was pressing Serena . . ." I looked at her hard. "You've got to message him and cancel."

Olivia grabbed her phone and started pacing around my bedroom. I didn't move. Trying to think. Coming up empty.

"I can't message him." She was vibrating. "I did it once and was told in no uncertain terms never to do it again. No messages, emails, texts, nothing. No leaving a voice mail. We . . . we make arrangements in the halls at school. If it's really important, I can call Mark on this other number. I think it's a burner. But even then, either he picks up after two rings or I hang up. Those are the rules. He's, like, super paranoid."

"No, he's super smart," I groaned. "He won't have left any kind of cyber trace. So much for hacking into his office computer. I'm sure his laptop is as pure as a boatload of virgins." I grabbed a pillow and shoved it into my stomach. "Hey, I wonder if maybe he'd have keepsakes, like of his conquests. Some of them do—jewelry, photos, something. Maybe we could somehow trace them back to his schools and then . . . and then . . . God, I don't know, maybe blackmail him into leaving us alone or something."

Olivia stopped pacing and fell onto the bed beside me. "Photos?"

"Yeah, photos. Like trophies of his worshippers. I know you binge-watch *CSI* and *48 Hours*."

"He has a photo album. Maybe, I think." Her breathing grew more and more rapid. "A while back, I saw something that looked like one in the very back of his closet, under stuff." She gulped. "I remember thinking how weird it was for anyone to have a photo album, and then I thought that it probably had pictures of *the One*, you know? The girl who had broken his heart and turned him into such a player." Tears pooled in her eyes. "And stupid, stupid me would be the one to make him forget her. I would heal his broken heart, and oh, God, instead he destroyed me."

"No. No, he didn't, Olivia. Nowhere close."

Her tears didn't break free. She straightened up and looked fierce. A little drunk, sure—the girl cannot hold her liquor—but still fierce.

"I'm sure it was a photo album, Kate."

We didn't say anything for a long while, just nodded at each other.

Finally, I took her hands in mine. "You'll have to go back one more time." Her hands went cold. "The performance of a lifetime. Does he ever leave you alone?"

She looked choked on the shame. "On Sundays, if I'm, uh, 'good,' he'll go out for bagels and coffee for us. I, uh, haven't been good enough the past two weeks."

I had to look away.

"I know," she said.

"It's our only chance. There might be names or locations or something written on the back of the photos, and then we can work back. I'll get Johnny to help."

She looked alarmed.

"We don't have to tell him why. But he's bound to have access to some good search engines at his college—he's taking criminology, for God's sake—and I think he'd do it . . ."

"For you?"

"Yeah." I took her glass from her. "But first you have to call and cancel tonight."

We both looked at her phone. She was clutching it so hard her fingernails were white.

"What does he really, really want, more than anything?"

She looked away. "You."

Neither of us made eye contact. "Then promise him that you're getting somewhere on that front. And say you have to stay with me tonight, to keep selling me on him."

"He'll know."

"No, he won't. Not if he wants it—me—bad enough. They all have a *thing*, a blind spot, and they think they're invincible. Look, we'll prep you for the call and then we'll prep you for Sunday. I'll cancel Mrs. Chen." I took the phone from her. "We can do this, Olivia. We *have* to do this. I've already had one of him in my life, remember?"

What I didn't say, could barely think, was that booze made my old man sloppy, vulnerable. That was his thing. But Redkin? That man had total control of himself. Redkin had no discernible weak spots, no access points—except for, possibly, me. Would it be enough? Would *I* be enough?

We role-played conversations until Olivia just stopped and threw her arms around me.

"Kate, your mom, you—damn, your whole . . . I'm just so . . ."

"Let's table that for another time. We have to call him now."

It was almost eleven. I knew from the terror in her eyes that he'd picked up on the second ring.

"Hi, lover." She was whispering, as instructed.

"Yeah, me too."

"Sorry, my love. Sorry for the late notice. But it's a bad news/ good news thing. I can't make it tonight."

"Of course not!" She giggled.

Good girl.

"It's her—Kate. We're, uh, talking, if you know what I mean. Uh-huh, about that." She nodded. "I think I'm really getting somewhere. I'm . . ." She shot me a look of naked desperation.

I smiled hard and mouthed, "Keep whispering."

"No. Real headway, I mean it. I said all the things you told me to. It's at a delicate place, and I feel that if you want her—"

Olivia stood up. "Well, you know I'd do anything for you. *Any thing.*"

She was good. The hairs on my arms raised at that *anything.*

"Yes, yes, of course. I'll count the minutes. Sunday morning. It's so far away, my love." She closed her eyes. "You'll see, I promise. I'll be such a good, *good* girl."

The pooling tears freed themselves and slid down her face.

"Yes, that too. I promise."

I turned away, ashamed for us both.

SUNDAY, MARCH 13

OLIVIA

9:05 A.M.

Brunch with the Wonders was agony. Kate had insisted they go. She said they had to do their regular things, appear normal. She also said that Mark would be eager to hear of any news from that front. Reporting to him would be part and parcel of being a *good girl*.

Even though they were at Balthazar before nine, they had to line up, since none of them had thought to make a reservation. When they were finally seated, they instantly reverted to type. Claire was chronically giggly, Morgan was manic, Kate was hyperalert and charming, and Olivia, well, Olivia was highly medicated. It was hard to pay attention. Snatches of conversation and orphaned phrases dropped down and around her eggs Benedict.

Morgan: "Don't worry, I wailed on him big-time. Nobody does that to me . . ."

Claire: ". . . it was an entirely dumpable offense."

Morgan was breaking up with what's-his-name? What was his name? The dumping conversation took her through one of her two eggs and half an English muffin.

Kate: "I don't know, guys."

Claire: "Come on, Kate. It's all arranged. Serena was insistent."

Wait! Serena?

Morgan: "Mr. Shaw is taking care of your flight. And the rest of us have got your incidentals. It's like an early birthday present from us."

Huh?

Claire: "Serena's dying to see you. Mr. Shaw has arranged everything. Her dad will do anything to make her happy. So spring break in London, ladies—the stores, the clubs. And the drinking age is eighteen, so no fake IDs required!"

What? London? With the Wonders? Oh, she would love that! Olivia knew exactly where to go. She'd take Kate to the boutiques on Beauchamp, show her Notting Hill and Selfridges. Then she winced, remembering Mark's reaction when she'd brought up her father's Rio offer. But this would be even more fun. They could—

Stop!

They had a plan, she and Kate. Had to stay put.

They had a plan.

"Sorry, guys," she said. "We can't." This was met with protracted groaning. "Really, you girls go. Have a great time and cheer up Serena. Kate and I are going to meet my father in Rio." She caught Kate's eyes. The eyes urged her on. "I haven't seen him in weeks and weeks, so he's arranged this whole Copacabana thing."

Eventually they stopped pouting and protesting. It was an airtight excuse, solid and impenetrable. Everyone would be away during spring break but them. Olivia was pretty sure that she had handled that well.

Brunch took almost two hours in all. Once free, Kate and Olivia grabbed a cab to the Meatpacking District. Olivia started hyperventilating in the car.

Kate reached for her hand. "Take a pill."

"I've already taken two."

"Take another one. You're freaking out. You've got to hold it together."

Olivia dry-swallowed half an Ativan. How could she go through with it? She felt herself failing. He would cut her again, she was sure of it. Of all the *things* they did, the marks scarred her in body and mind. Could she take one more cut? And after all that Olivia did for him, all those nasty things, it turned out that she was just the warm-up act for Kate. Everyone wanted Kate.

But she had her.

Kate was hers. They would be forever bound by their secrets. Fortified by this, Olivia nodded.

The panic reappeared and clenched hard as soon as they stepped out of the cab. They scurried to Starbucks, where Kate would wait for her. Olivia had been practicing her breathing with such intensity that she was now hiccupping.

Kate rolled her eyes. "Come in and get some water before you go up."

She downed most of the water in one long, slow gulp.

"Remember, you've got to pretend you're in a movie or one of your *CSI* episodes. It's important, Olivia. You're watching it—you, him. It's on film, *not real*. You are *watching*. You're not in it. You have to climb right back into that dissociative groove you were in when I first met you."

Olivia's breath snagged. "You saw?"

"Yeah, I saw. Let's not get hung up on it now. We'll table that for later too. I need to know that you get it. It's serious protection, this movie thing. We'll bring you back, but up there, with that monster, you are the director, not the star."

Olivia nodded. "Is that what you did? With how bad . . . I mean, did it help with your father?"

"Where do you think I got it from?" Kate took the plastic cup from Olivia and finished off the water. "Look, I've had years to embellish on that night that didn't need any embellishing. The movie thing blurs stuff. My father tried to kill us both. I saw him gut my mother, Olivia. It's *still* a movie. It has to be. I couldn't put one foot in front of the other if it wasn't." She grabbed both of Olivia's arms. "*Can* you do this?"

A *movie?* Of course she could do a movie. Olivia had been starring in a movie for years now. She broke free of Kate's grasp.

"Just watch me."

SUNDAY, MARCH 13

OLIVIA

11:23 A.M.

Olivia hit the stairs at 11:26 a.m. with reluctant legs. *One last time, one last time . . .* She knocked on his door at precisely 11:30 a.m.

"There's my girl." Mark's smile matched his shirt, a beckoning white. "I love you in that dress." He drew her into him. She did not allow a single part of her to recoil; instead, she *watched* herself. Olivia wore the capped-sleeve purple cashmere dress. Kate had picked it out.

His hands glided down her body and then up again.

"Hmm," he growled. "Now take it off."

She giggled and pushed him away. "Of course, my love." She bit a corner of her lip. "But don't you want to know about my brunch with the Wonders first? I have news. Appetizer news."

Mark raised an eyebrow. He led her into the living room, seated her in the Le Corbusier chair and poured her a glass of wine before he sat down. He was pleased. "Appetizer?"

For the first time, she saw the elegant white-on-white room for what it was—a mask. Olivia leaned back and crossed her legs.

"Spring break is the entrée." She sipped her wine in an effort to collect herself. "And dessert is my roommate."

"Ah!" He leaned forward, arms on his knees. "Do tell, little angel."

Olivia obliged, playfully recounting the Shaws' invite to London. "The Wonders were even going to pay Kate's fare. Just think of it," she giggled.

Mark stood up. "Were they now?"

Did he pause? *Ah, when worlds collide.* Surely he'd be concerned about what "crazy" Serena might say, but he was so guarded. She waited for him to speak. He didn't.

"Of course, I told them there was no way we could go, because Kate and I were headed to Rio!"

"Olivia . . ."

"It's okay." Could he hear her heart pounding? "I worked out the perfect compromise."

He leaned in closer. Olivia caught an unmistakable whiff of Jo Malone Orange Blossom. Kate had been complaining for weeks that both Kruger and Draper were dousing themselves in the stuff.

One or the other had been here with him—in this apartment, this very morning. Olivia raised her eyes to meet his. Her body clenched. She could do this.

"Well, as you suspected, my father was all set to fly back home for break when I told him we were swamped with critical catch-up, so . . . I told him that we would wrap up all our schoolwork and join him for four days, missing the first Monday back at school, because who cares about the first Monday back in senior year? That gives me five whole days to delight you."

He leaned back and away from her, considering. "Not bad."

"I knew you'd be pleased." *Smile. Remember to smile.*

"And the most important news?" He looked at her with an open curiosity.

"Yes, Kate." And then she did smile. They had rehearsed and rehearsed this part. "Well, she's skittish, to say the least, and as you know, stubbornly resistant to your charms."

He frowned.

"But that, no doubt, is a part of the attraction for you."

"A very small part."

Was that annoyance? She couldn't risk annoyance.

"Well, as I said, we had a yummy chat about how wonderful you really are, how you want to help her—us—and how you have so much to offer." *Smile more.* "And we're very, very close, my love." She risked standing up without being asked to. "Very. I'm thinking that you should just casually drop by that first weekend of break. The weekend is better because my housekeeper won't be there; in fact, she'll probably take a few days off to be with her sister. Brilliant?"

"Why the change of heart? I *know* her, Olivia. She fears me at best and loathes me at worst." Mark looked amused, but then he seemed to be searching her, suspicious. She tried to rein in the panic. They hadn't prepared for this.

"Yale," she gulped.

His expression softened instantly. "Ah!"

"Yeah, I, uh, strung her a story about you having strong, um, ties to an old flame on the acceptance committee, and I said that you might be willing, uh, to . . ."

"Pull them on her behalf?"

"Yes. You know how demented she is about Yale and, well, it's in your court now. I have no doubt that you can convince her of your powers. So like I said, come by on the weekend."

"Olivia, you know that I can't be seen—"

"No, no, of course not. I'll let you know how to get in through the parking garage, and you can use the dedicated move-in elevator. No doorman, no cameras. See, I've thought it all through. And then you'll just chat and be yourself, all sweet and generous and full of promises, and she won't stand a chance. Maybe even that afternoon, in my penthouse . . . she's that close. She wants Yale that much, and you know it."

Olivia circled him, her hand trailing behind her, touching him the way he liked. She was very, very afraid. Kate insisted that she stay afraid, stay alert. No worries on that front.

"Oh, and you were right, of course." Mark turned to face her. "She's a virgin. I'm not even sure she's ever been kissed. She's mega-weird about guys touching her. I don't know why."

Finally a smile, the left dimple flashed. "You've done well, angel. Now scoot to the bedroom." He smacked her bottom. "I'll be right in. Prepare yourself."

She kissed the back of his neck. "Please don't make me wait too long."

Olivia barely made it to the bathroom before vomiting. Flat-out dread kept it quiet. The eggs Benedict and wine reappeared silently in one soft run. She swung open his medicine cabinet with fear ringing in her ears. Lots and lots of prescription bottles, but for who? Him or his trophies? She grabbed a tube of Crest 3D White, squeezed a line into her mouth and swallowed. She stared at her reflection, willing the toothpaste to stay down while she disrobed. Then she squirted another dab into her mouth and gulped some water directly from the faucet. She rinsed her mouth as quietly as possible. *Please, please, please.*

Olivia barely got to the bed in time, posed and ready. Mark studied her as he took off his shirt and placed it on his suit holder, then removed his pants. She could do this. He was physically perfect, after all. Besides, she had pleased him. She had been *such* a good girl. Surely it would be better.

It wasn't.

SUNDAY, MARCH 13

OLIVIA

1:47 P.M.

When it was over, Mark traced his work with his index finger. Tracing but not touching. He only touched the crenulated edges of his previous work. "You rule my heart, you and you only. You're exquisite, you know that, don't you?" Then he kissed her eyes. No one had ever done that before. No one would ever likely do it again. "You've surprised me, over and over again. I didn't expect that, Olivia." He rose. "And now I must feed my glorious sovereign. I heard your tummy rumbling. Can't have that." He winked at her as he got back into his clothes.

She had made him happy and there was no denying that it still gave her a thrill, gave her pleasure. That it did so made her sick.

"I shall return with a feast!" He actually blew her a kiss as he turned to leave.

Olivia knew she had to move as soon as she heard the door shut. But she couldn't. He had cut her again. There would be more scars. She started to gulp air. *Stop.* She and Kate had a plan. She couldn't let this, all this, have been for nothing. Olivia got up. She looked at the floor to avoid catching herself in the mirror. *It's okay. It'll all be okay. We will go to Rio.*

She stopped again.

She couldn't wear a bikini. The marks—all those marks—would show. She didn't look up. *You can do this. You are fierce. You are in a movie.* It was Kate's voice. She could do this. Olivia opened the closet door and carefully reached into the back left corner. *Please let it still be there, please.* Her hand reached under the wicker basket. There. It *was* a photo album! He actually kept an album. *She would buy a really cute one-piece, yeah, with adorable cutouts. Barneys had a bunch. She and Kate would go shopping together.*

She clutched it to her but couldn't will herself to open it. The album was edged in silver and covered in black crocodile. *Ever so tasteful, Mark.* It was smallish, maybe the size of an iPad mini. *Breathe. Breathe. Now!* Olivia opened the book and turned pages with fingers that were not complying. It was almost but not quite full. Her empty stomach threatened to rise again.

There were *so* many. Women, it was all women. Younger, slightly older. A lot of blondes. The photos seemed to go back years. The room spun. Olivia got to the bed before her legs gave out. Who were they? Why paper photos? Then she clutched her stomach. Of course. It was like Kate had said—he was so, so careful about his digital footprint, about his laptop, about his damn phone. All those convoluted rules about how to communicate with him. Digital doesn't die.

But if you burn a photo, it's gone forever.

Precious minutes slid by. *Have to move.* She knew this and yet still kept turning the pages, gazing at the beautiful faces—because, without exception, they *were* beautiful. Olivia paused just before she reached the end. It was as if she knew. Serena was not in there.

Even now, after everything, Olivia noted it with a small, sharp satisfaction. *Serena, was it because you got away? Or because you didn't matter enough?* And then she flipped the page.

No, Serena was not there.

But she was.

Her heart stopped. It was one of the shots that Halston took. A shot that Mark had asked him to take of her alone. Olivia's was the second-to-last photo. She remembered that he had asked Halston to take one other individual shot. She tried to turn the page, flipped too many by mistake and had to make her way back.

Kate.

Dread coursed through her. She had to get out of there now.

Get out!

No! Don't screw this up.

Olivia moved on unsteady legs and glanced at the clock. With fingers that still did not cooperate, she slid a few photos out of their sleeves. Sure enough, there in perfect script, on the back of each one, was a name. She tried to steady herself and focus enough to commit at least some of them to memory. Then she slipped them back in place and stumbled to the closet with her heart beating in her mouth. Was the binding facing her or the back wall or . . . ? Wait.

Their photos. They were in there.

Damn you to hell! No, you don't!

It was stupid. Crazy. Too big a risk.

But she had to.

Even with vibrating fingers, Olivia somehow managed to slide their two photos out of their cellophane sleeves. She raced to the living room and tucked them into the bottom of her Prada backpack, then staggered back into the bedroom. Her head was pounding and the names were already swirling. *Damn, damn!* She should have taken pictures with her phone. Too late now. *Damn!*

It seemed to take a long time to find the exact pose he had left her in. Where was her left arm supposed to be? The sheets? Olivia heard the door open. She heard his footsteps. Heard him coming to her.

You're watching a movie, you're watching a movie, you're . . .

WEDNESDAY, MARCH 16

KATE

It got so that I was talking to myself on the way to the office each morning. We were both a bit of a mess. I mean, she did it—pulled it off and everything—but the truth was that things were way, way scarier now. Olivia was unraveling. I could tell that guilt, shame and fear were having a party in her head. She felt gutted about retrieving only a couple of names.

"I know I should have got more. I should have got them all. I think I picked out at least three. Why can't I remember more?" She hit her forehead. "I can only see the album. You should've seen the album—black crocodile. How perfect is that? And I see blondes, Kate. A lot of blondes. I screwed up."

"Cut it out, will you?" I said for the three-hundredth time. "You walked buck naked into the jaws of hell. Two names are better than no names! And you got us—*our* photos—out of there. Clutch move!" I didn't tell her that the clutch move was what was keeping me up at night. What if that pervert liked to drool over his little book on a regular basis? We'd be dead, for sure. I managed to keep that to my-self. "So we're cool. I'll give the names to Johnny and then . . ." And then I was alarmingly fuzzy on the details, except that it couldn't in-volve the cops. The cops would bring the media maggots. No way, never again. I would figure out a plan, and a good one.

At some point.

I'd been staring at the same open file for what must have been twenty minutes when Ms. Goodlace and her shoes stopped by my desk, I mean Miss Shwepper's desk. It kind of freaked me out, but then again, everything was freaking me out. Goodlace stood there as if she was taking me in. I sat there taking her in—her and her ever-present two-inch-heeled Stuart Weitzmans—until I couldn't take it anymore.

"Ma'am?"

"I won't ask you how you are, Kate." It was said gently but also with authority. She couldn't help it. Her tone came with the posi-tion. "I know you'd just lie to me."

I started to protest, but she laid a hand on my shoulder.

"It's okay. I'm the head—everybody lies to me." She was trying not to smile.

And right then she reminded me of somebody, but just as I was closing in on who, it slid away.

"Ironically, being bombarded by lies and liars makes one espe-cially alert to the truth." She paused. "The truth is, Kate, you're the most gifted Waverly Scholar we've ever had. I'm in awe that you function so beautifully under the singular burden you carry. And that's only the burden I know about."

"Ma'am?"

She ignored me. "I also know you won't confide in me about whatever new burden you've taken on over the past few weeks." Again she stopped me from protesting. "You've been let down too

267

many times. But you made it here, Kate O'Brien—all the way to Waverly. And I'm here too. I need you to know that."

Sister Rose! That was it. Something about her tone, her touch reminded me of Sister Rose.

"My door is always open to you. Whenever you're ready. Always and for whatever reason. I'm here."

I finally looked right at her. "Thank you, ma'am."

She smiled a little but looked sad as she walked away. I felt bad about that. She'd never know how much those few words meant to me.

I *would* figure this out.

Olivia shivered through all our classes and laughed too loud at things that weren't that funny. Anka had been on high hover alert all week, so we couldn't really speak freely at home. By Wednesday, I couldn't stand it anymore. I had to do something.

I went to the market. I phoned ahead and thankfully got Mr. Chen, who always sounded happy to hear from me. I told him I was coming in for a shift after dinner. Of course he didn't understand a word I said, but I knew he would tell Mrs. Chen that the *gweilo* had called and she could take it from there. I also texted Johnny.

Mrs. Chen was on me like flies on fruit the moment I stepped in. "You sick? You too skinny. Big worry? Johnny no like skinny. You too skinny."

And this from someone who weighed maybe ninety-five pounds holding a bushel of potatoes.

"No, ma'am. Not sick."

"Ba!" she harrumphed.

"Little worried, though."

Mrs. Chen did not harrumph at that. She eyed me silently and then stomped away on her tiny slippered feet.

Okay . . .

I spent the whole time in the Apothecary section with Mr. Chen. Everyone had ailments on Wednesdays. It was like a thing. Mr. Chen was a calming presence, and I remained almost calm right up until Johnny came for me at nine thirty. As soon as he turned up, I started pulsing like a blender.

"Hey, Michelob, cappuccino time?"

"Isn't the bakery closed?"

"I know the owner. Come on!" He took my arm and waved to the Chens, who stood together in their matching aprons, looking for all the world like proud parents.

Johnny unlocked the storefront and then busied himself with their monster espresso machine. He'd changed quite a bit since we first met in the autumn. How had I not noticed before? Johnny was bigger, more filled out. It looked good on him. He offered me a perfect cappuccino with a heart design on the foam. "So what is it that you need, Kate?"

"Johnny!" My hand flew to my chest. "I am deeply insulted."

"Kate, you barely answer my texts all week, and now all of sudden you're batting your baby blues at me. Are you or are you not about to use me shamelessly?"

"Yeah." I shrugged. "I guess I am."

"I can live with that." He flipped the chair around and sat facing me with his arms draped around the back. "Exploit away. Sooner or later, you'll come to realize how irresistible I am."

Actually, I'd been realizing that for quite some time. To tell the truth, it made me deeply uncomfortable and kind of angry. "Thanks, Johnny. I have no idea where else to turn. I need you to run a couple of names against some dates and school locations. I know your college criminology search engines have got to be better than Google." Before he could ask, I said, "No, you don't want to know why, and no, I won't tell you why."

He gripped the back of the chair. "Are you in trouble?"

"Not yet."

"Would you tell me if you were?"

I took a gulp of cappuccino and almost spit it out. I'd forgotten to put sugar in it. "Not necessarily."

He growled a bit and then sighed. "Fine. I'll do it under one condition: a kiss."

"That's blackmail."

"No, it's not." He grinned as he crossed his arms. "It happens to be the price of this particular transaction. Well?"

Others had tried, of course—grabbed, groped, slobbered—but I'm stronger than I look and, well, *no one touches me.*

But Johnny?

"Fine," I heard myself say.

"Deal. What do you want?"

I reached into my purse for the lined yellow notepaper and flattened it on the table.

"I have two last names, Sanderson and Ulbrecht, and I have four possible schools, see?" Johnny leaned over. "There's the Pilot School in San Francisco, 2008 to 2010; the York School in Sydney, 2010 to 2012; St. Mary's School for Girls in Melbourne, 2012 to 2013; and the American School in Lucerne, 2013 to 2015. I'd like to know if those names come up in any database as missing or something."

"Kate, what the hell?!"

"I'm a very good liar, Johnny." I flashed back to Goodlace standing over me. "Exceptional, really. I don't want to lie to you, but I will. So don't ask."

He gripped his coffee cup so hard I thought it would shatter in his hand. But he nodded. "I'll run them after classes tomorrow."

"Don't text or email me. Call, okay?"

"Got it. So stand up, Michelob." He stood up.

"What, here?"

270

"Sure, unless you want me to kiss you in front of the Chens."

I stood up.

I was surprised by a thousand things.

That Johnny smelled like icing sugar and coffee surprised me but shouldn't have, I guess. It was a good smell. I didn't know what to expect. I'd never been kissed before, not really. Not since the third grade. No one got through my wall, ever. That I wanted him too surprised me the most. My heart was thudding, my breath was short and my feet were hot. Then he made all that go away when he cupped my face with both of his hands.

"It's okay," he whispered. "It's just a kiss."

Without letting go of me, Johnny leaned down and put his mouth on mine. He kissed me and I kissed him back, and we kept kissing until the world stopped and it was time to go.

He lied. It wasn't *just* a kiss.

I had no idea that *that* could be like that.

"Okay, then." He took my hand. "I'd better deliver you back to the Chens."

I didn't say anything, couldn't trust my voice. After he locked up, we walked through the crowds in silence. Except, of course, everyone in Chinatown kept calling out his name and greeting him. I kept my mouth shut. I was too busy sucking back tears. Because not for the first time, but with more fervor than I could ever remember, dear Jesus I wished that I was someone else.

If only, if only . . . I could be anyone but me.

THURSDAY, MARCH 17

OLIVIA

Olivia and Bruce headed for the park. The days were getting longer. It wasn't dark, even though it had to be almost seven. Bruce decided there were big dogs deep in the park that he had to get to. He pulled hard, crouched low for better purchase and strained so much against his leash that it looked like he was walking the wrong way into a gale force wind. It amused even the most hard-bitten Upper East Siders.

Olivia, for her part, felt energized, up to the task of reining in her dog. Up for anything. She was alert and totally present. She was even on board for the fear. Maybe it was because it was a shared fear. Maybe it was because underneath the fear was relief. Olivia would never again have to do what she had done.

The plan was good.

It would work.

And after, they would meet her dad in Rio.

And the scars would heal and disappear.

Mostly.

Olivia didn't feel like fighting Bruce's suicidal tendencies with the Rottweilers, so they just walked the length of the park on Fifth. Bruce's disappointment was epic. On their second pass, Olivia noticed a man slow as they neared him. He smiled at her, not the dog. This, of course, was grossly incorrect according to Upper East Side dog-walking etiquette. He didn't look homeless per se, but his long greasy hair hung about his face like seaweed. She wouldn't even have noticed him a week ago, but this was the new Olivia, the alert Olivia. She was quite pleased with herself.

"Time to go home, Bruce."

As soon as they got in, Bruce headed straight for Kate to complain. But Kate was on the phone and did her best to ignore him. Olivia zeroed in on her part of the conversation.

"Thanks again. I mean it."

"Yeah, no, I mean. It's cool. That's perfect. Nothing else."

"Yeah, I'm sure. I'm positive, Johnny."

"There's nothing to worry about." Kate eyeballed Olivia and nodded.

"Yeah, I promise. Thanks again, really."

She fell into the sofa. Olivia went over and put her arm around her.

"We got him," Kate whispered. "We got him. One of your names . . ."

"What?" Olivia's gut seized. But it was exactly what they wanted, what they needed.

We got him.

"The Sanderson girl went to the York School in Sydney when Mark was there." Kate clutched herself. "She went missing during his second year. She was a senior. Never found. No foul play suspected. The girl was a bit of a wing nut—wild, always in and out of trouble. She was actually suspended at the time. It was assumed that she ran off. But she was never heard from again."

"Oh, my God." Olivia gulped. "The other name?"

"Gretta Ulbrecht. She got married real young and is still in Switzerland."

"Okay, okay, so . . ." Olivia started and stopped.

"That still makes two! Remember Serena's cousin said that there was a suicide while Redkin was at her school? I think I assumed that she was South Asian too. Was that girl's photo in his little collector's album? That would make two girls gone at his schools *while* he was there."

"There *was* a pretty South Asian girl," Olivia said, nodding. "For a second I thought it was Serena, but she's definitely not there."

"So we hit a bull's eye. These are all small private schools, and you said there were a lot of photographs. It's not a coincidence. It's him."

They both sat back. "If only I'd got more names. There were so many pretty girls. What an idiot!" Bruce jumped up on them, half on her lap, half on Kate's. Bruce's idea of dog heaven.

"Leave it alone, you did great." Kate sat forward again. "Holy crap, it just hit me. All of them, of us—let alone the teachers, staff, etc.—but the girls, we're all seniors."

"Yeah, so?"

"Eighteen and over, Olivia! He can be accused of stuff *if* you catch him, maybe. But no matter where he goes, it's not going to be statutory rape. We're *all* seniors. It's genius."

For some reason that Olivia couldn't identify, this did not overwhelm her. It scared her, sure, but that was only sensible and sane. This was *it*. They had plenty. It was enough to blackmail him with. To get him out of the school and out of their lives. And they'd do it together.

Kate turned to her. "Okay, this is the time for me to suggest calling your dad and laying it all out. Put the whole mess in his hands. He's connected. Hell, he's an adult."

Olivia stiffened. "No." She shook her head. "My father is an officer of the court, and the law would have to get involved. Which means my stuff, Houston, your secrets would all come out. You'd kiss Yale good-bye for sure—too tawdry, too *New York Post* for an Ivy. And my . . . with Mark. I couldn't ever let my dad know about that." She shook her head again. "So, no. We stick to the plan."

"Sure?"

"Positive."

"All right, then." Kate exhaled. "It's just us. We do it ourselves. We *will* do it. Tell him to come over on Saturday night. He's got to have that open, since everybody's taking off for spring break tomorrow. Remember to say that you won't be here, that he and I will be alone."

"But I'll be in the kitchen. And we'll record everything." Olivia said this more to herself than to Kate. "Let's do this!"

Bruce licked both of them in an enthusiastic show of approval.

Olivia headed for the wine fridge after handing Kate a beer.

"A couple of girls are going to bring that monster down," Kate called after her.

Olivia poured some wine and tilted the glass toward her friend. "He'll have no choice. Two names and we'll toss in Serena for insurance, say she's willing to talk. He's trapped, Kate."

But a shadow had spread across Kate's face.

"What?" said Olivia. "This is perfect! He's out of here! After Saturday, gone baby gone!"

"Cool your jets." Kate hugged her knees, displacing Bruce in the process. "Guys like Mark don't spook easy. They're reptilian, methodical. He's not on drugs, doesn't drink. Redkin is under control at all times. And . . ."

"And what?" Olivia took a gulp and then another of her wine. "What?"

"*And* it's even worse if they do spook. That night? My mom threatened my father that night. He was crazy violent, smashing things, ripping into her. I was cowering, but she was never more courageous or strong than on that night. It shocked him, I think. My mom had this *moment*. She somehow got to his gun. She actually had *his* gun in her hand, but then, even when he went for me with the knife, my mother didn't . . ." Kate shook her head in disbelief. "She couldn't use it. She just couldn't. And, well, you know what happened. He was trapped too, Olivia. There's nothing more dangerous than an animal caught in a trap."

Olivia put down her glass and reached for her friend. "I'm not your mom, Kate." There was a sureness in her voice that Olivia didn't recognize, didn't know she possessed. "That bastard left scars all over my body. Trust me, if I had a gun in my hand, *I'd* use it."

SATURDAY, MARCH 19

KATE

7:56 P.M.

I wore Olivia's lace Chloé. She insisted. Mark hadn't seen it yet. The dress was white, "virginal," sweet but sexy.

"It'll put him at ease the moment he sees you in it. Trust me." She said this without making eye contact.

"You're sure he's absolutely clear on how to get in?"

"Take a breath, Kate. The man is highly, *highly* motivated not to be seen."

How did this happen? When did this happen? Olivia was the calm one and I was hyperventilating.

"He's coming by transit and he knows exactly how to get into the underground garage and take the freight elevator—the one *without* the camera—straight up to the penthouse."

"I wish Bruce were here," I moaned.

"Why?" she snapped. "So he could lick him to death?" Olivia had persuaded Anka to take Bruce over to her sister's for the first few days of spring break. "Go on," she'd said. "Your sister needs you both way more than Kate and I do. We promise not to have any wild and reckless parties while you're gone."

We resumed pacing. I checked Olivia's watch—eight o'clock. He was supposed to come at eight.

We looked at each other. She started backing away, heading for the kitchen pantry.

The doorbell chimed at 8:03. I turned to face her one more time. Olivia's eyes widened and she nodded. I watched her recede, taking my courage with her. I opened the door.

"Hi, Mark. Come on in."

He smiled. "I'm pleased to be here. You look particularly lovely."

"Thank you." I tried for a smile and hoped to hell that my face was cooperating. He looked good. How could someone without a soul look like that? Mark wore a tan linen blazer, a white shirt open at the collar and blue jeans. It was like he had just stepped off the set of a movie with Scarlett Johansson. It made everything worse. Especially since he loomed so large. I'd never really noticed it before, but Redkin was big. Bigger than Johnny. I was struck by the potential of his sheer physical power. Mark Redkin was a man, not a boy, and he was armed with a man's confidence and control.

Jesus, what were we doing?

"This way." I led him over to the windows and the art deco bar cart that we had stocked with every conceivable drink. It was also where we'd hid the phone we were recording on.

He whistled softly, taking in the expanse of the room. "Quite the place! I knew it would be something." He walked over to the window and surveyed the view. "Apparently it's been in Mrs. Sumner's family for over eighty years."

"Whoa," I whispered. "You are thorough."

He turned to me and smiled. "Yes, I am Kate." The smile was blinding and self-deprecating at the same time. "Information is my business, and I like to think that I'm good at my business. Hmm?"

"Yes, you . . . I've . . ." *Get a grip, get a grip.* "Well, what can I get you? Drinks are on the house."

"Just a Perrier for now," he said. "I want to be fully present."

I poured him his water and poured myself one as well. My hands did not shake. I'd gulped half of one of Olivia's Ativans before he came. The panic didn't lead, but it lurked. My tongue felt thick.

I imagined Olivia immobile in the pantry, straining to listen, afraid to breathe. Mark took his glass and strode over to the center window, the one that could open. He shook his head at the sight. It was, after all, one of the best views of the city.

"You've given me a merry little chase." He raised his glass to me. "It seems like I've waited for someone like you for a very long time, and once I found you, you made me wait even longer."

I opened my mouth to say something—God knows what—but he put his finger on my lips.

"But I believe you're worth it. I also believe I can help you with your aspirations. Yale, is it? Let's stop playing, shall we, Kate?"

Danger. Danger.

"Excuse me?" I stepped back. I knew it was exactly the wrong thing to do, but I couldn't help it.

Instead of answering, Mark twirled his finger, indicating that he wanted me to turn. I did so without exhaling. Now my back was to the windows. He paused as if he was considering his personal art project. Satisfied . . . no, *infinitely* satisfied with himself.

"Exquisite. You, the city . . . perfection." He shook his head. "We are actually alike, you know. This is a true thing." He held up his hand. "I know you don't see it, but you're very young. You're gifted and ambitious, and you've risen to heights against all odds, against all obstacles. I *have* been waiting for you, Kate. Think of the things we could share. We would understand each other completely. There would be no need to pretend."

His eyes were shiny. I looked away.

"Be honest, Kate, just for a minute. How ruthless did you have to be to survive what you had to survive and get yourself *all* the way here? I've done it. I know. Tell me, did you feel remorse for anything you had to do?" He brushed my arm with the back of his fingers.

No! That was different, not the same thing at all. I did what I had to do to survive. Survival of the fittest, baby. Beads of sweat pricked the back of my neck. He was twisting everything, confusing me, just like my father did, exactly like . . .

"A little honesty, that's all I ask. We can be honest with each other. I know you must feel alone. People like us do. But together, well . . . I know it all, Kate. Everything."

My stomach lurched. *How?* Then I realized he meant about my past, my father, my psych evals.

"You look afraid. Don't be. I'll take care of you. If it's Yale you want, Yale it will be. I'll get you that and more. Not only that, but if *he* ever gets out, I'll take care of him. And I would do that with pleasure. I would do that for you."

Twisting, twisting.

"But I'm not alone. Olivia is a good . . ."

"Be *honest,* Kate. Olivia is our tool. I saw your game from the beginning. Admired it." His expression softened. "Olivia is of no consequence to us. I've searched for *you.* And you need me. I think you know that now." He placed his drink on the side table. The table was a handcrafted Frank Pollaro that Mr. Sumner treasured. It was an expensive table. He should have used a coaster. I should get a coaster, he . . .

Panic foamed within me.

"I'll teach you how to nurture the gifts you have. I will teach you how to *be* Kate." He reached for me and took my arm.

Mistake.

He shouldn't have touched me.

I wrenched my arm away. "Your teaching days are over, Mark Redkin, right now."

"What?! What are you . . . ?" He was smiling through his confusion. "I haven't even begun to . . ."

"No. I . . . we know about the others." I gulped for air, got a small sip. "Julia Sanderson and the girl in Melbourne, and once the police start looking, there will be more, won't there? Many more."

"What is this?" He flexed his hand in slow motion. "They were two unfortunate young women who—"

"And Serena is willing to talk." Breathing was entirely optional. I went straight to script. "No one knows at this point. And we're willing to keep it that way. But there are conditions. You must leave the school during break—family crisis or something. You leave New York and we won't go to the police." I said it as practiced, but I could hear my tone—flat, fast, much, much too afraid.

He smiled. *"We?"* Jesus, he was amused.

"Olivia and me." Mark was not my father. He was not drunk. He did not explode.

This was worse.

"You're kids," he laughed. "Children should not play dangerous adult games. And need I remind you, you've both got skin in this particular game. If it becomes public—"

"It'll be your skin that will fry, *Mr.* Redkin. And you know it. Sure, we'll be humiliated, but you'll be locked up. They *will* connect the dots."

"What makes you think that I would allow either of you to

281

threaten me?" He faced me full-on and I stepped backward. "I am so very disappointed in you, my little *cockroach*."

If he meant to annihilate me by using that word, he made another mistake.

"You bottom-feeding deviant. You made my skin crawl right from the first time I saw you. I know what you are, you sick, twisted pervert, and lots more people will know unless—"

He was up and against me without having seemed to move. My back was right at the window. I saw him take in the handle, then smile a slow smile. He placed his left hand on my breast, pressed hard and then ran it slowly down my body.

I almost blacked out.

"You are such a tasty morsel. What a pity." He reached into his pocket with his right hand and flicked open a Swiss Army knife. He brought it to my face.

A knife.

Jesus. Again, a knife.

I froze. My brain froze. A knife.

He tilted his head. "You're going to jump, my crazy little virgin." He placed one hand up against the glass and the flat of the knife against my breast. He started to play with the tip. "It got to be too much for you, all that pressure. The past caught up to you, all those awful secrets. Maybe someone threatened you with exposure. You couldn't go through it all one more time. You've been increasingly worried that your father will find out where you are, even from prison. Dr. Kruger will vouch for the fact that your mental state has been deteriorating. The obsession with getting into Yale . . ."

My heart thudded against the knife, causing it to rise and fall in time with the beats—tha-thump, tha-thump. My thoughts scrambled. Olivia. How did he think he was going to deal with . . . oh, God, Olivia!

He'd kill her next. *Run, Olivia, run!*

"I can read your mind and your soul, Kate. It's why we would have been so perfect." He placed the point of the knife directly over the top of my breast. "I'll deal with your friend later; she's served her purpose. You know she's psychotic, don't you? Ah yes, on the school watch list. The administration knows. She actually thought she was pregnant last year. This year she thinks I'm a predator. And I'll let you in on another secret: Olivia hasn't been taking her meds." He leaned in and kissed my cheek. "I switched them out last week. She'll stay quiet once you're gone. I understand you have a little dog . . ."

Olivia.

He nicked the top of my left breast. Then Mark Redkin dabbed his middle finger into the wound and licked it. "Mmm." He pressed his body against mine. I was right up against the window. He put his tongue on me. My gorge rose, but I didn't wretch.

"You taste even better than I imagined." He kissed my cheek again, then my breast. "Such a pity," he groaned. "I'm going to open the window now."

Just as every single thing within me was shutting down, I caught sight of Olivia out of the corner of my eye. She was barefoot. *No! Hide! Run! Run, Olivia!*

She crept closer.

Closer . . .

"Mark, please!"

Closer . . .

"This is almost painful. We would have been perfect." He reached for the handle with his knife hand while gripping my throat with his left.

Olivia was hauling Anka's prized apple-green Le Creuset frying pan.

"Stop! Don't! Don't!"

"Shhh." He grabbed the handle.

And despite never holding a bat in her life, Olivia swung that skillet like she was the designated hitter for the Yankees, smashing it right into his head.

Mark went down like a slow-moving landslide, crumpling onto my feet.

Olivia stood motionless but panting. She was still clutching the Le Creuset. "I told you if I had a gun in my hand, I'd use it."

SATURDAY, MARCH 19

OLIVIA

8:27 P.M.

"Jesus, Olivia," Kate whispered. Why was she whispering? "I think you . . . I think we killed him!"

"Naw, he's not even bleeding." Olivia checked the back of the frying pan for traces of blood.

"I'm, uh, pretty sure you can bludgeon someone to death without making him bleed. This isn't a TV show." Kate was gasping for air. She hadn't moved. Her feet were still covered by a part of Mark's hip. "You saved my life! You . . ." Kate extricated her feet from under the body and leapt over to Olivia, who was still clutching the weapon with both hands, ready to spring into action. Actually, she was more than ready. She *wanted* to hit him again.

They stared at Mark for quite some time, trying to collect themselves. It didn't work.

Olivia looked blankly at Kate. "He was actually going to kill you."

Kate looked back at her just as blankly. "Yeah, he was. Yeah."

They continued to stare at each other.

"So, uh . . ." Olivia broke the spell first. "How do we know if he's alive or dead?" She was trembling now.

"I don't know, I don't know. How would I know? I don't know!" Kate shuddered in time with Olivia's tremors. She squinted at the body, which was on its side, as if he had decided to take a quick nap on the floor. "We could, uh, kneel down beside him and put an ear to his chest?"

Olivia shook her head. "That's not going to happen. He can't be dead."

"Well, whatever, it's hard to tell from this angle. We should roll him over."

"Ew, no."

"We'll push him over with our feet."

"Yeah, I guess, okay." They walked over to the window side of the body, giving it a wide berth as they did. Was this happening? Did this really happen? *What the hell had happened?*

"Ready? On three. One, two, three . . ."

Mark rolled onto his back. They grabbed each other and screamed.

His eyes were open.

"Oh, God!"

They jumped away from the inert body.

"He's alive!"

"No, he's not."

"Sure, he is! He's got to be. He can't be . . . We can't have . . ."

"Nothing's moving, Olivia."

They stared blankly at each other again. Shock? Was it shock? How long does shock last?

Kate swallowed. "I'll check for a pulse." But then she didn't move.

"Good plan," said Olivia, widening her stance and readying the skillet. "I'll be ready if . . ."

"Okay." ·

"Okay."

Minutes passed. Then finally, resignedly, Kate knelt down as far away from the body as she could while still being able to pick up his wrist. Now it seemed like hours had passed.

"Nothing," said Kate. "He's dead, Olivia. We killed him."

Olivia was actually ambivalent about the dead part. On the one hand, it was a problem for them, a nightmare mess. On the other, she was flooded with a righteous rage. For all that he had done to her, and all that he had made her do. *I was your tool? Of no consequence, am I?* She had to refrain from kicking the body. Instead, she waited for the fear to ricochet back in.

It did.

Olivia had killed somebody. Mark was dead. There was a dead body right there. Dead. What were they going to do? What could they do?

"What do we do now, Kate?"

"Well, uh . . ." Kate looked spacey. "I don't know. We should call someone. Yeah, get our stories straight and call. We have to call, I don't know, an ambulance. Yeah, or the cops . . . someone. We've got the tape. The tape will show—"

"What! Are you crazy? No way! It's got to be just us." Olivia looked at Kate in abject horror. "Get our *stories straight*? Kate, we couldn't straighten our stories with this guy to save our souls. Think about it! We'd be ruined. RUINED!"

Kate shook her head as she stared at the body. "Olivia, we have *killed* someone." Tears of fear or remorse slid down her face. Olivia couldn't tell which. "This is a dead body that used to be a human being!"

"Barely," Olivia spat. "Think! Cops? The papers? Try to wrap your head around the sexual scandal alone. Two Upper East Side girls. A predator infiltrating a top school. It'll get wall-to-wall-to-wall coverage. Olivia Sumner and her psychotic history. Kate O'Brien, aka Katie Medvev, aka the cockroach, and her tragic murderous past. Apples don't fall far from the trees when it comes to us and this!" She pointed to the body like it was a festering sore. "We'd kiss Yale and our lives good-bye for damn sure! Nu-uh-uh!"

Kate looked stunned. "But we can't—"

"The papers, the media! It would start all over again, the whole 3D nightmare. And there won't be anywhere on earth to hide after this one, baby. It would make what happened to you before look like a walk in the park. The locusts will descend and never let go. Your old man would know exactly where you are." Then she went for the jugular. "Think how pleased he'd be about this. Think, Kate, think! What the hell!"

"Hey!" Kate threw up her arms. "I was almost killed and a man is dead. I need a minute, okay?"

Olivia felt herself flush. "Okay, sorry. I'm not myself." She glared at the body. Yet . . . "But in a way I am, you know? I'm feeling weirdly clear. Look, what that jerk was saying about the risperidone was pure bull, Kate. They're never out of my sight, ever. He was scamming you. You've got to believe me. You just—"

"I believe you." Kate grabbed Olivia's hand. "S'okay, I believe you. You're no more nuts than I am."

And with that, and their front seats in the theater of the absurd, both girls burst out laughing. It was laced with hysteria and tears, but it was laughter.

Followed by silence.

"We're screwed, aren't we? There's no way out." Olivia felt the air and the fight leak out of her. It was hopeless. "We're finished."

"No, no. Not necessarily." Kate hugged herself. "Not if we can get rid of the body. We have to get it out of here. There's no blood, after all. No one saw him come in."

Okay, that was more like it. Olivia reverted to pacing, mindful of the body's position on the floor. "Okay, so I hit him on the side of his head with a flat object, right? That kind of injury might be consistent with a car accident. I've seen it on *CSI*. It's a blunt force trauma kind of deal."

"When the hell do you have the time to watch so much TV?" asked Kate.

"Hey, it's practically all I did in Houston."

Kate groaned.

"No, listen. Listen! A car accident is perfect! There's all sorts of really steep and weird places to go off on the Taconic. I know because Dad and I have almost done it in the winter on the way to the cabin."

"And what? We'll get your father's car service to spring into action?"

"Right, hmm." Olivia stroked the pan. "I don't drive—I'm a New Yorker. Do you drive?"

"Sort of, but not really. I passed my whatever thingy out west. The school let me use their SUV to train on and for the driving test. But I haven't sat behind the wheel since that day."

"But that's great! Like, we'll stage an accident and get ourselves back to the city. Wear sensible shoes. We can do this!"

"Olivia, a car. We need a car."

"Oh, right, yeah." She resumed pacing. Her mind was alternately racing and flooding.

"Wait!" said Kate before she ran off to her room. "Keep watching him."

There was zero chance of Olivia taking her eyes off the body.

Kate rushed back a minute later with her purse, furiously

searching though all the contents and secret pockets. She held up a small card triumphantly. "Found it!"

"Found what?"

"I found Kevin. Call Kevin for bad trouble, big trouble, she said."

"Who said?"

"Mrs. Chen. He's got to be part of the triads or some deep underworld stuff."

"And you accuse me of watching too much TV?"

"No, he's the real deal! Where's your phone?"

"My pocket." Olivia turned her back to Kate. She'd reverted to holding on to the skillet with both hands again.

"Kevin will get us a car. Are you sure there are no cameras in the parking garage?"

"Positive." Olivia nodded. "Aftab told me. It goes back to the hard-partying eighties, when there was a lot of stuff happening in this building that maybe shouldn't have been. It's how I knew to direct him." She gestured to the body. "What if . . . I mean, maybe your guy could just take care of him."

"That's probably a step too far. Someone else would know, you know? Someone we don't know. Potential blackmail. You're a big deal, Olivia. I mean I totally trust Mrs. Chen, but this guy?"

"No, you're right." Olivia shook her head. "It's the kind of thing that trips you up. One too many people, it's what screws up the killers on TV."

They snagged on the word killers. Kate's face clouded and she stopped breathing. But then, just as suddenly, she seemed to return to herself.

"No." Kate straightened. "We're not the bad guys here. You saved my life, Olivia. No one is going to suck us down a drain. I'm not going through that again. You and me, Olivia—together. Just us. This . . . he is not our fault! I know what I am. I'll do whatever it takes to survive, and I'm taking you with me."

You and me, Olivia—together. Just us. Kate was back and Olivia exhaled.

"I'll get us a car. Just a car. We'll be okay. You'll see—it will be okay." Kate dialed the number on the card. Her finger hovered over the call key. She nodded at Olivia, hit the button and closed her eyes. Waiting, waiting . . .

"Hello, is this Kevin?"

SATURDAY, MARCH 19

KATE

10:36 P.M.

None of us is prepared for tragedy. But let's face it, this wasn't my first time in a starring role. Turns out, experience doesn't help. I babbled like a lunatic on meth. Words spilled out in torrents all strung together and without pause.

Kevin was not a patient man.

I managed to impart our need for transportation. I also managed to avoid the word *body*.

"Weneedacar. Rightaway! Tonight! It'sanemergency!"

"Not traceable!" yelled Olivia.

"Nottraceable," I repeated. I didn't even know what that meant.

Eventually Kevin and I sorted it out. I think. From what I understood, the plan sounded solid. But then again, I wasn't sure what I understood.

Kevin was going to deliver a car, and not a stolen one. It would come from one of Chinatown's amenable Rent-A-Wreck establishments. The line—if needed—was that we had bribed some stranger to get it for us, since we were too young to legally rent.

He made me repeat this direction. He said that whatever happened, we would have to pay the manager of the Rent-A-Wreck for haulage and salvage compacting.

"It's standard," he said.

"But what if we don't need—"

"It's standard. No matter what happens, the vehicle will be hauled away and turned into a cube within a couple of days."

"Uh, okay, sure. How much, how do we . . . ?"

"Mrs. Chen will indicate the amount at some future date."

He said that he'd drive it into the garage and ring my cell once. I was not to answer. And then, he said several times, we were on our own. His debt to Mrs. Chen, whatever that was, was paid in full. The car would be there by midnight.

"I heard, I heard." Olivia was holding the skillet against her body. "It's good."

"Yeah." I had to sit for a minute. I kept running my hands down my dress. They were wet and sticky with sweat. "But we've still got to get Redkin to the car when it arrives." I pointed to the skillet. "Stick that thing in the dishwasher, and the knife too. Then we'll put it back in his pocket."

"Right," she agreed. "Your DNA." She looked at the dried blood on my chest. "We, uh, should . . . you should change, right?"

We were both tired. The shock was wearing off. The reality of what we had done was beginning to slither in.

And we still had a long, long way to go.

"Right." I had to get the knife. Did he move? Was that a twitch? How could he be dead? My mother was bathed in blood, but still she hung on for minutes. We talked. She made me promise. Yale. Was he looking at me? I couldn't close his eyes, so I closed mine as I extracted the knife. His hand was colder than the stone floor. Dead cold.

"Here, stick it, dishwasher." I gave the knife to Olivia. "I'll watch. When you get back, I'll change."

"Yeah." She nodded. "Yeah."

Olivia hadn't moved a muscle by the time I came back from changing into jeans and a sweatshirt. "Okay, so we have to figure out how to get him down to the car."

She nodded but didn't respond. It's like we took turns being stupid.

"Hey, I got it! Does this place have those pushcart thingies to move small bits of furniture and suitcases?"

"We do." She brightened. "They're in that little room off the garage but before the elevators. There's like three of them in there at all times."

"Okay, you watch him, and I'll go."

I took the freight elevator down. My future—hell, my life—was shredded. But I didn't cry. Instead, I saw myself walking through the Old Campus at Yale. I inhaled the crispness of October as I walked to one of my intro classes. Rustling leaves crunched under-foot. I waved at a couple of kids I knew from my dorm. We would meet later for study hall and then go for a coffee before my shift at the library.

I had pinned everything on Yale.

The sense of belonging and loss was unbearable.

I was in the storage room without knowing how I got there.

Sorry, Mom. I tried. I tried real hard. I swear to you and God, I tried. I failed.

I brought up the trolley. Neither of us wanted to touch the body. Hysteria was edging back in around us. We eventually decided to wear gloves.

Redkin was way heavier than he looked. It was awkward and awful, but we did it. We got the body all tucked in and then threw our coats overtop.

Somewhere in all of this, Olivia had poured herself a glass of wine. I went to take a sip from her glass and she shook her head. "If anything goes sideways, you have to blow zero for alcohol."

"Right," I said. Or I think I said. Because throughout all this, it was like I was watching myself from somewhere else. I was thirsty, but I couldn't have a drink. My cellphone rang once. We had to go, we had to go, we had to . . .

"Time to go," I said.

"Time to go," she whispered.

We wheeled Redkin into the elevator.

"We're going to take the Palisades on the way to Bear Mountain." Olivia said this with rather shaky authority. "I changed my mind about the Taconic. We need a river or at least an embankment to drive off."

"What?"

"Well, plan A was, like, off a cliff. This will be better." She was convincing herself, no doubt about it. "There's a spot to go off near Route 6 right before the Bear Mountain Bridge, I'm sure of it."

"What?!" I was yelling at this point.

"No, listen. The Dentons have a lodge at Bear Mountain. I know the route like the back of my hand. We went tons of times."

"When?"

"When I was a kid."

Oh, God.

The coast was clear when we arrived in the garage. We went to the appointed spot, and sure enough, there it was—a corpse of a car. It had to be at least thirty years old.

"It sure looks like something that would be untraceable," Olivia said, making a face.

We checked for other residents returning from a late dinner or whatever. It was as quiet as a tomb. All I could hear was my own breathing.

"He's got to go in the front with you, Kate."

"What? No! No way!"

"Yes, I've got it worked out!" She slapped the trunk of the car. "When we get to the bit off Route 6, we'll stop and you'll switch places with him. We can just slide him over and you can sort of drive from the passenger seat and jump out just before we hit the water."

"WHAT?! *Nooo!*" She was crazy, that was the only explanation. My life was in the hands of someone who was batshit crazy.

"It's the only way. Look, I'll be right in the car with you. We'll jump out together. He has a tragic accident and we make our way back to the city on foot, or catch the Woodbury bus, or, or . . . we'll figure it out."

What was I going to say? We'd passed through the "this is nuts" portal several hours ago. My mind emptied. "Yeah, okay."

She opened the squealing door with considerable difficulty. "A car accident just about always works. It'll look like he was on the run. It's foolproof!"

"Did you take too many pills?"

"Never been straighter or more scared in my life."

"Me too." But I couldn't come up with anything half as good while we stood there. "Fine, let's load him up." This was way harder than we had anticipated. Had he started to stiffen? Again, we were both caught off guard by how heavy the body was.

The car was so old it only had lap belts.

"Lean him over toward the door. I don't want him listing toward me," I directed. "Where are the keys?" Maybe there weren't any and we'd have to come up with plan C. I prayed hard for plan C.

"They're in the ignition," offered Olivia from the backseat, the natural seat for any born-and-bred New Yorker. "Plug 'Bear Mountain Bridge' into the GPS."

I wanted to hit her. "Olivia, there's no GPS on a car like this."

"Never mind, I'll Googlemap it."

I turned the key, and miraculously, the stupid car started. When I tried to hit the lights, the windshield wipers went off at hurricane speed. We both screamed. Three knobs later, I found the lights. "Okay, okay."

"So we'll take the George Washington and then—"

"Shut up! It'll be a miracle if we make it out of the garage. I'm pretty sure air bags weren't invented when this car took its first breath."

"That's good, though! The missing air bags, the seat belts—it'll all work great for us. You can do it, Kate. You can do anything. I knew that the moment we met. We'll get out of this, you just watch."

I slid the car into drive and held my breath. We lurched and braked and lurched and braked.

She leaned over the seat. "Maybe we should take a couple of laps around the garage before we hit the streets?"

We drove around in tight circles for almost twenty minutes. I would have kept driving for the rest of the night in the safety of the garage, but she wouldn't let me.

"Time's a-wastin'! You're good. Let's go!"

My heart was jack-hammering. I could barely hear her. My hands were sweating in my gloves. I gripped the steering wheel even tighter. At 12:57 a.m., we finally headed for the exit, and God knows where else, with our cargo.

SUNDAY, MARCH 20

KATE

1:03 A.M.

I can't begin to describe the mind-warping terror of turning left into actual traffic and onto Fifth. I swallowed hard, then harder. "Where am I going? Have you got it yet?"

Olivia leaned her elbows over the front seat, holding her phone with both hands. "So . . . okay, take a right onto Fifty-Seventh."

I hadn't exhaled since we left the garage. The nightmare of the streets momentarily displaced the nightmare of having a dead body beside me. There were so many lights—blinking, beckoning, strobing, changing—it was too much. We crawled across Fifty-Seventh. The car took it upon itself to shudder every so often. I took it upon myself to shudder right along with it. "Olivia, I'm seizing!"

"Okay, okay, here it is. Stay on Fifty-Seventh and then . . . hmm, it says take RT-9A north?"

"What the hell is RT-9A?"

"Don't know, but it says it's just past Twelfth, so I'm sure we'll see it."

"Jesus God."

"Then we take exit 14 onto the George Washington Bridge."

"What? No! We have to do the expressway *and* the bridge?"

"We'll be fine," she said, paying no attention to my panic. "*Then* we merge onto the I-95 S via the exit on the left toward the upper-level crossing into New Jersey."

"New Jersey! What the hell? New Jersey?!"

"Calm down. It's not like we're trying to sneak into Canada." She kept scrolling. "Then we take exit 74 and merge onto the Palisades Parkway North crossing into New York."

Cabbies were honking at us and passing me on both sides. The car groaned in a sulky protest every time I even thought about accelerating.

"Wait, wait. Where was that RT thing? We just passed Twelfth."

"Two blocks up."

The cabbies aside, I thought I was driving a bit better with less stop-and-go lurching.

"And near the end, we enter a roundabout and take the first exit, and then we'll find a likely embankment and—"

"Whoa! Did you say roundabout? What the *hell* is a round-about?"

"I don't know, but how tough can it be? People must drive through them every day."

I hate the GW. It looks like one of those Transformer monsters lying in wait for you. I wanted to jump off it as soon as I saw it. We made it over only because I had my eyes closed most of the way.

People honked at us less in New Jersey. Then people stopped honking altogether because it was very late and we were pretty much alone on the Palisades.

That was worse. It was easier to think about dark things in the dark. My hands hurt from gripping the steering wheel so tight.

What were we doing?

I kept glancing at Redkin. Neither of us had had the guts to close his eyes. He was freaking me out. It was like he was looking out into the middle distance. Like he was waiting. Like he was biding his time.

SUNDAY, MARCH 20

KATE

3:10 A.M.

It took us almost two hours to get to the roundabout. We circled it six times with Olivia yelling, "Take the first exit toward Bear Mountain Inn. The *first* exit!"

I was so fried that I didn't get it. It was a circle. The first from what?

"The first exit. The first—"

"Shut up! Shut up!" I hit the curve at too hard an angle and the body fell into me. "Jesus! Get him off, get him off, get him off!"

"Stop the car!"

I braked so hard that we lurched violently. Redkin's head hit the dashboard. The lap belts were next to useless. Olivia and I were fine except for the screaming. My foot was glued to the brake in the middle of the roundabout, in the middle of the dark and in the middle of God-knows-where.

"You okay?" she whispered.

"Yeah, sorry. I think I'm losing it."

"No, you're great. It's me. I'm wired. I'll shut up."

Olivia grabbed ahold of the body from behind and straightened him while I talked my heart into starting up again.

I finally got off at the first exit.

"We're almost there." She was still whispering. "Slow down. We've got to go over at the perfect spot to get him into the river."

Go over? It was three a.m. I could have sworn that Redkin was getting ready to stir. I felt his eyes on me. We crawled passed a traffic light and then an inn.

"Slow down more." Olivia rolled down her window and stuck her head out.

There was no moon and it had started to rain.

"Do you hear it?" she asked.

"What, the rain?"

"The river—the Hudson. It's churning. Must be all the spring runoff and the rain we've been having. It sounds like it's really moving. Slow down, slow down! That's it! Pull over just up there." She pointed to a small clearing within the trees, and somehow I steered the car to it. I turned off the engine and then silence.

"We made it," I said. No one was more surprised than me. "We made it."

Olivia reached over the seat to throw her arms around my neck. "You did great!"

"Yeah, well." I exhaled. "Let's get to it. We have to move the body to the driver's side."

"Right." The chirpy bravado in her voice was long gone. "Right. Then after that, you've, uh, got to drive from the passenger side down over the embankment toward the water. And when I yell, 'Jump,' we jump out of the car." She patted Mark's shoulder. "He continues crashing down into the water."

It was almost too stupid *not* to work.

We had trouble opening the doors. The rain must have made the hinges seize even more. It was pelting down hard. Olivia eventually gave up on the back passenger door and went out the left. We slid and shoved Mark over to the driver's side and belted him in as best we could. Then we rearranged ourselves into our new positions. Somewhere in all that commotion, it dawned on me that we were going to "walk back." Surely there were no buses out here. Walk back? To the city? In a downpour? On the highway?

I decided to table that piece of panic. *One clusterbomb at a time, Katie.*

It was disgusting having to lean closer to the rigid body to start the car. Chemical things were happening within the corpse—pooling, rigor. I swear he stank, but I needed to get real close. Once I got the car started, I stretched over with my left foot and placed it firmly on the brake. I would have to reach over the body to grab hold of the steering wheel. Who was I kidding? I was still afraid of him. I didn't think I could do it without puking.

But I did.

Just before I hit the gas, Olivia said, so softly that I almost didn't hear her, "After this, we'll join Daddy in Brazil. We'll go to Rio."

"Yeah, we'll go to Rio."

"Love you, Kate."

"Me too, you."

And then I stepped on the gas.

We started down, bumping, jolting, being tossed about. We hit air, landed.

I'd hit the gas too hard.

We were going too fast, even over the rough terrain. Way too fast. I couldn't reach the brake pedal, couldn't find it in the dark. Steep, Jesus. Too steep, too fast, too fast . . .

"OLIVIA!"

"Jump!"

"Can't!"

"Now!" she screamed.

"The door!"

Life changed.

"The door won't open!"

KATE and OLIVIA

The impact was bone-shattering. The car stopped its hurtling trajectory by crashing into a rock outcrop. But she'd gotten out before then. She was dazed and banged up but okay, mainly. She raced awkwardly down to the car, to her friend. It was bad, so bad. *No, no, no!* She opened the door. There was no problem opening it from the outside.

No! Stop! Think!

It would be dawn soon—cars, traffic, people. Even through the downpour, it was clear that the sky was lightening.

What should she do? What had to be done? What! What!

The body.

She had to get rid of the body. It had to be rolled out and down to the water. The Hudson raged as if it were on steroids. The river would take care of him and take care of them. She ran back around to the driver's side.

The lap belt was tricky. Her fingers were uncooperative. She did not once raise her head or glance at her friend, focusing totally on the task at hand. Mind-blinding terror did that. She inhaled, exhaled and then locked her arms under his and dragged him out of the car. Miraculously, the body wasn't as heavy as it had been in the penthouse. But she still had to stop, take a few breaths and reposition herself.

"Come on, come on, you can do this."

She was crying now. Her crying felt broken. But she wasn't. Far from it.

"Let's go, Mark."

She had to haul the body only a short distance before they got to a very steep pitch. She was breathing heavily but there was no fear. Not for this part.

"Screw you!" She placed her foot firmly against his hip and shoved, hard. "Go straight to hell!"

Redkin's body rolled and bounced, picking up speed the whole way. No rocks or bushes or tree roots slowed him down.

Straight in the water. First faceup, and then down as it was swept away. Gone, gone, gone. Man, that water was fast. She lost sight of him in seconds and then ran, slipping and sliding in the mud, all the way back to the car.

Oh, God, no. Oh, God. Oh, God. Was she breathing? Was she alive? What a mess.

"You were *supposed* to jump!" she yelled at her friend.

She stepped back just before throwing up. The rain was coming down in sheets now. As she turned back to the car she slipped and opened a wound on her knee that she did not feel.

You should never, ever move a body that has experienced trauma. Never. Everyone knew that. She knew that.

But she had to. She had to somehow get her behind the wheel, or they were finished. The car was supposed to have gone into the Hudson with Redkin in it. This was plan D. She had to . . .

Her body was as light as a broken branch. It was easy, except that she tried to take such care, and she was sobbing so hard that the snot and slobber were gumming up her gloves. "No, no, you don't." Now she was covered in blood as well. "You don't die on me! Not after all this. Don't you dare die!"

She belted in her friend and then took the belt off again. How to explain those injuries? She would say that they couldn't get the darn thing to click in.

She pulled out her phone and hit 911.

"Help! Please help, please! Hurry, hurry!" She pulled off both their gloves and shoved them into the back pocket of her jeans. "My friend . . , we had an accident. It's bad. It's so bad . . . I'm not sure she's breathing. Please . . . I don't know, past the roundabout just off Route 6 and . . . I don't know, I don't know." The trees started to sway. *Stop.* She couldn't pass out. They'd find the gloves on her. She had to tell the dispatcher where they were. She had to, she had to, she had to . . .

The ambulance came quickly. So did a fire truck staffed with softhearted volunteer firemen.

And so did the police.

KATE AND OLIVIA

6:30 A.M.

She remembered now that she had seen the detective before. Two days ago, when they'd been medevaced to Columbia Presbyterian. She remembered being struck by what a sharp dresser he was. It was a stupid thing to remember. What she did not remember, in the haze of all she had to remember, was what he had wanted to know and what she had already told him. Two uniformed officers ambled about the nurses station. Her stomach constricted. Thank God she'd had the presence of mind to ditch their gloves in a garbage cart during the commotion of their hospital arrival.

Except for the hospital gown that Maureen, the head nurse, had insisted she put on over her bloody clothes, she was still wearing the same things. She hadn't showered, brushed her teeth or combed her hair. The nurses kept slipping her juice boxes and sandwiches packaged in cellophane. They remained unopened. She was wild with exhaustion.

What must she look like?

What must she smell like?

She had to lie down. Instead, she gathered herself and leaned against the nurses station.

Detective Akimoto cleared his throat. "I'm sorry about the timing of this, but there is some urgency to this matter."

Urgency?

"The car?"

"No, I'm . . . no. The Rockland County sheriff made the appropriate calls to the city and the rental agency. Your story checked out. You're on the hook for haulage and damages, but the manager of Rent A Wreck is not going to press charges." He shook his head in disapproval. "It was a ridiculous thing to do."

She wondered, with not all that much interest, which part of the "ridiculous thing" he was referring to.

"There may be some insurance questions. And why two young ladies of means would decide on a whim to bribe a stranger to rent them an old heap is—"

"Crazy stupid," she finished for him. "I know, I know." She put her head in her hands. "At least I do now. But we honestly thought it would be the perfect practice car. Like, if we dinged it, it wouldn't matter, right? It was a wreck already. We needed to practice roundabouts." She wrapped her arms around herself. It all slipped out like butter. "See, we're going to England for a few days to surprise all our friends. They're there already. And Serena said that you can't spit without coming across a roundabout. What idiots, what . . ." She shook her head.

"Well, as I say, charges don't seem to be pending from either the rental car manager or the sheriff. You were on a dark, wet and unfamiliar road. The Rockland County officers said it happens to far more experienced drivers all the time."

Thank God for the rain. "Yeah, the rain came out of nowhere." She didn't recognize her voice. It was older.

He cleared his throat. "So I'm sure you'll be fine on that count, insurance issues aside. And I hope your friend will be fine too, of course."

But he looked doubtful. She wanted to slap him for that but didn't have the energy.

"My primary concern here is Mr. Mark Redkin."

Mark. Oh, God, oh, God. They found the body!

Where did they find the body?

The detective clicked his pen over and over again. The sound reverberated in her bone marrow.

The body. Did it wash up?

Was it close to the accident scene?

We're done. It's over. No, stop it. Concentrate. Keep it together. Keep it . . .

"I'm sorry, did you say Mr. Redkin?"

"Yes, Mr. Redkin seems to have disappeared, and we're very interested in locating him. Most of the staff and other students are away on spring break, but I understand that you girls knew him." The detective flipped through his little notepad. "That you were part of a fund-raising group he was in charge of."

"Mr. Redkin?" *They hadn't found him!* The room spun, but she stopped it through sheer force of will. "Well, I don't know. Like you said, it's spring break. He's probably gone off somewhere." She braced herself on the counter.

The detective seemed to consider something as he looked at her. "No. We've confirmed that he has not booked any trips, nor did he pack for such an occasion."

What? How would they know? They had to have been in his apartment. But why? When? What was happening?

"I'm sure he's fine." She feigned confusion. "I wouldn't worry—"

"It's a good deal more serious than that. There's a warrant out for his arrest. We received a credible tip several days ago that the man is likely a sexual predator. He's also being investigated for some disappearances."

Tip? What? Who would have . . . Johnny? Serena? One of the families making the connection? She needed to unfog. *Pay attention! What was he saying?*

"What? No way. Not Mr. Redkin."

"I'm afraid so. Apparently there has been an open Interpol file on him for years. We'll be speaking to everyone at the school. I understand that you and your friend were closer to him than most as part of"—he glanced at his notebook—"some fund-raising committee? We got that information confirmed with"—again he consulted his notebook—"your head, Ms. Goodlace. She was in fact very concerned about your safety. In your interactions with Mr. Redkin, has he ever approached you, either of you, in an unseemly or inappropriate manner? This is very important."

The detective didn't seem to care enough for her fragility, her well-being. She had to step it up a notch.

"No! Mr. Redkin? I won't believe it. He was nice to all of us." She swayed, then caught herself. "I-It's too much on top of . . . I don't . . ."

The detective reached over and steadied her. "Have you been attended to?"

She waved him off.

"It's not possible. Talk to the other girls, and you'll see. He was kind of flirty with all of us on the Waverly Wonders—that's our group—but nothing weird." *No way would Serena talk.* "I'd know about it. We had crushes on him, you know? Silly stuff. The whole school had a crush on him. This is crazy."

"I'm afraid it isn't. I need you to take it seriously. We need to find him and get him off the streets."

She kept shaking her head. "But one of us would have noticed something."

The detective stopped clicking his pen, sighed and seemed to come to a decision. "There was, in fact, irrefutable evidence in his apartment."

The album. They would have found the album.

It's okay. Their photos were gone.

"I need to press upon you why this is so urgent. We found a photo album full of pictures of young women, many of whom seem to be missing or have died in what can now only be called suspicious circumstances. You must remain alert. If you have any information whatsoever about his whereabouts, or if he tries to contact you—"

"What? Are any of us in that . . . ?"

"We don't believe so. Not from Waverly. But we suspect it was just a matter of time. It's a trophy album. He is a very dangerous predator. You must understand this. Is there anything you can remember that might be of help in locating him? Anything at all?"

"All I know is that he moved around a lot." She shrugged. "I mean, he was staff, you know? Maybe Claire or Morgan or . . ." She swayed again.

"You're exhausted. I can get one of the uniforms to take you home."

"No. I have to stay here. I need to be with . . ."

"I'm sure the doctors will keep you informed of any progress."

"Save your breath, Detective." It was Maureen. "She needs to stay here. Give me your card. If she remembers anything, the kid'll call. But I don't think either of them is going to be any use to you. They've got bigger fish to fry than catching your perp for you. Right now, she needs to be with her friend." Maureen shot the detective a look that would stop a bullet.

"Yes, well, certainly. I agree, but if"—he flipped out a card—"if anything comes to mind, or if he tries to contact—"

She started to tremble.

"Look, the kid's a wreck and you just gave her another shock. Get out of here. And take those uniforms out of my ICU. We'll keep an eye out for your predator. They're both safe here. Nobody gets by me."

And then Maureen, a warrior queen if there ever was one, practically carried her back into the room, sat her down and produced a pillow. "Don't you worry, honey. If that detective or the sicko comes anywhere near this floor, I'll stick him with a hypodermic."

OLIVIA

7:40 A.M.

Olivia tracked the green lines on the monitor. They were wavier now. That was good, she was sure of it. She reached for Kate's hand, careful of the wires.

"I told you, didn't I?" she leaned over to whisper. "The cops are gone, and so is Mark. God only knows where he'll wash up or when, but they're onto him. It's why that detective was here. Not for us! We did it Kate—we're bulletproof."

Olivia scanned the room as if checking for cameras or audio devices. She exhaled. "Can you hear me? You can hear me, right? I know you can hear me. Squeeze my hand."

Nothing.

"Kate, come on, come on . . ." Olivia would have cried, but she was running on empty. "Please squeeze my hand. I know you're in there. I know you can hear me. Squeeze, damn it, squeeze!"

And as if by magic, she did. Kate O'Brien squeezed Olivia's hand.

"That's it! That's my girl." The relief was dizzying. She should call in Maureen. No, that could wait.

"Don't worry about a thing, Kate. We're clear with the accident, the car and in Rockland. They're after Mark, *not* us. There's actually a warrant out for his arrest! They think he's done a runner. Ha!"

Another squeeze, a stronger one.

"Yes!" Olivia's heart was going to break out of her chest. "Daddy will be here in a couple of hours. *Our* dad—we're sisters under the skin, after all. Anyway, he'll take care of everything. He always does. You just get better, okay? You've got the ultimate in care here. My mom's people practically built this place, and I made sure they knew who I was. Maureen, she runs the ICU, well, she says that you'll be right back to normal . . . eventually."

She gripped Kate's hand tighter. "We pulled it off! Two kids!" Olivia laughed then. She still had laughter left. "That pervert will never scar anyone again. Who's of *no consequence now*, Mark? How dare he?"

Kate squeezed again.

"You're right, let's not dwell. On a brighter note . . ." With her free hand, Olivia reached into her pocket for Kate's phone and started scrolling. "So I checked, and your Johnny has been calling, texting, emailing, everything nonstop. I'd say he's got it bad." Olivia paused. "And I'll allow you that one. Maybe. What do you always say? We'll table that for later, shall we?"

She squeezed Kate's hand. There was no squeeze in response. Olivia glanced at the monitor. Kate must be tiring. That was it.

"I still have to figure out what to do with your phone. It's got the recording on it, of course. The phone either sinks us or saves us, doesn't it? Depends on the circumstance. But it is an *us* in either case. Us together, Kate. Forever."

Olivia stared at Kate's motionless body.

"I agree. I'll just hang on to it. I went through all your stuff, by the way. Got to change your password from 'Bruce123,'" she tsked. "I had no idea that you'd kept texting with Serena. S'okay." She patted Kate's hand. "Water under the bridge. But you won't ever keep things from me again, will you?"

Was Kate paler?

"Oh, and the most important thing of all! I was keeping this until I knew you could hear me, and I *know* you can hear me. I got into your Yale portal. It's official. You're in! We're both in! Yale, here we come! You made the cut. I *told* you. How could anyone turn you down? *Everyone* wants you, but you're only *my* Katie, right?"

Again, she didn't feel Kate squeeze. She should have—Yale was everything. So Olivia squeezed Kate's hand, hard. Then harder.

"That's right. We'll room together in a dorm for first year." Olivia began to smooth the sheets. She did so with great tenderness. "Then Daddy will get us a condo or we'll stay on campus. We'll see. It'll be better than ever. We'll dazzle them. I know you want that as much as I do."

Kate's hand went limp in hers.

"You *do* want that, don't you?"

Nothing.

"Look," Olivia flared, "it may be true that you can't kill a cockroach, but let's do remember that it was *me*. The only way you got to your damn prize was because of *me*, because of the kind of life *I* gave you." She brushed stray wisps of hair off Kate's bandaged forehead and whispered, "I own you."

Kate's eyes flicked open. They seemed to stare unseeing at Olivia and then shut. But for a second, maybe less than a second, she did see. Their eyes, blue on blue, locked and they saw. Olivia was sure of it.

"That's right," she sighed, "I knew we were alike from the first time we talked in English class, remember? I knew it deep in my bones. I'd already been watching you, of course. I guess all the girls had, but not like me, not the way I did." Olivia raised her feet and placed them at an angle on the bed. She did this cautiously, so as not to disturb her friend. "You'll realize that you don't need Serena or the Wonders, or Johnny. And certainly not that old bitch, Mrs. Chen. You just need me."

Kate's hand clenched and moved. Olivia took it as a sign of approval.

"Mark almost ruined it, almost stole you, but I showed him, didn't I? Still, I owe that deviant one thing. The meds, remember? Of course you do. He did switch them out, but that's okay! It's better, Katie. I'm much, much better. I don't need the risperidone. It ruins everything. I've never been clearer in my life. Don't you agree?" The green line was on the move. The waves broke deeper, climbed higher. "I knew you would." Olivia sighed deeply as she slid the phone back into her pocket. "I'm going to take care of you. I can do that. I'm the strong one now. And I'll hold your secrets too. *All* of them, all the dirty secrets."

Maureen popped her head in. "Any change?"

"No, but we're good. I'm right with her." And she squeezed Kate's hand.

When the door closed, Olivia crossed her arms and relaxed into the chair. Secrets can weigh you down. They crawl around your guts, demanding exposure to light and air. When they don't get it, they burrow in and change you. Olivia was a practiced secret keeper.

In fact, Olivia thrived on secrets.

ACKNOWLEDGMENTS

This novel spent much of its life as an amorphous thing, bristling with scattered ideas and a creepy spark of fear. Then Beverly Horowitz and Amy Black got ahold of it. Never was a writer better served. Amy held me steady throughout and gave me the courage to write what I needed to write. Then Beverly exploded my head with what was possible. I'm grateful beyond measure for their support, guidance and keen insights. My sincere thanks as well to Rebecca Gudelis, Janice Weaver and Melanie Flaherty for saving me from myself time and time again.

I can't begin to express enough gratitude to my family and critical first readers Nikki, Sasha and especially Ken Toten, who did some very heavy lifting this time around. Thank you, Marie Campbell, for tirelessly championing the work and the author. Thanks to Susan Adach, Nancy Hartry, Ann Goldring and Loris Lesynski for their patience and advice. Detective Darren Brennan was invaluable for all things criminal and police procedural. Any mistakes in either were mine alone.

This book and its theme represent a departure for me. Just over ten years ago, I wrote a short story for a collection titled *Secrets*. In my story, "Father's Day," a little girl tries to survive a visit from her father. For years, I wondered whatever happened to her. It nagged and clawed until I finally started to write. How could she have grown up to be anyone but my Katie in this story? Despite the darkness of the material, this novel has been an absolute joy from the first word to the last. A large measure of that is directly due to the inspiration and creativity of everyone who touched both it and this very grateful writer.

Turn the page for an excerpt from
Teresa Toten's award-winning novel:

HOW DO YOU FIND ORDER IN CHAOS?

THE UNLIKELY HERO

OF ROOM 13B

TERESA TOTEN

The boy inhaled as the door opened. It was as if he knew. The girl stepped into the room, and within the space of a heartbeat, he was lost.

The girl made her way toward the semicircle of chairs, not smiling exactly, but not hesitating either. She was older for sure. Probably. So it was hopeless, of course. She sat down directly across from him, at her end of the semicircle. Without looking up, she crossed her genius, perfect legs and flipped a long black braid behind her. By the time he exhaled, the boy was in love.

It was like he had drowned in a wave of *want*.

Without even knowing how he knew, he somehow did know that if *she* wanted, he would give the girl everything. Hers for the taking as of that moment were his iPad 3 (especially since he himself was no longer allowed to use it), his first-edition copy of J. D. Salinger's *Nine Stories,* his Xbox, his autographed Doc Halladay baseball *and* his most prized Orcs from the Warhammer Fantasy Battle game—the classic eighth edition, not the other poseur stuff. For *her* he would master his most troublesome rituals and offer up what was left of his sanity.

"Greetings, Robyn, and welcome!" said Dr. Chuck Mutinda, nodding first at her and then into a raggedy file folder. This simultaneously shattered and enhanced the moment. The boy now knew her name.

Robyn.

"Thank you," the girl said to her feet, and the boy stopped breathing altogether, so hypnotic was the sound of her voice.

The girl's eyes were blue. Up until that very second, the boy had never noticed the color of anyone's eyes, could not have told you the color of his mother's eyes. But Robyn's eyes . . . well, they were the shade of an angry sky rimmed by thick lashes the color of soot. Her beauty—which, shockingly, no one in the room felt compelled to jump up and comment on—was ravishing. Everything in him felt tossed and trampled.

He ached deep inside just looking at her, but he could not look away.

So *this* was what *that* was like?

"Robyn Plummer is a slightly late addition to our merry band, having recently completed the residential program at Rogers Memorial Hospital."

Residential. His heart stopped, then started up again. He focused on his breath the way Chuck had tried to teach him to do—except that he'd never really paid attention, so it didn't help. *Residential*. They were all freaked by the mere possibility of *residential*.

"Welcome, Robyn, to room 13B and the Young Adult OCD Support Group. Course," Chuck explained, "there is no room 13A, which makes a 13B a bit superfluous. And you will have no doubt also noticed that there is no thirteenth floor on the elevator. We have to get off on fourteen to get to this floor."

"Yeah, man, what's with that? I spent half an hour riding the damn elevator my first time here. I thought it was some psycho test," said Peter Kolchak, slouching into his chair. A couple of the kids snorted in agreement.

"So," continued Chuck, ignoring the interruption, "in some blessed existential way we, uh, don't exist." He said this as he said almost everything, with the faintest hint of a Jamaican lilt. He was long parted from that country, but not yet from the singsong rhythms of its language. He returned to the file. "Robyn is sixteen and . . ."

Sixteen! The boy seized on the number. Sixteen was bad. It was an even number, and therefore had to be sterilized. And it was very bad as an age. *Sixteen*—he repeated it fifteen times and tapped it out thirty-three times until it felt "just right." Okay, so it could have been worse. And then he realized it *was*. There was also the height thing. You could tell even when she was sitting. The height—*her* height—could be and certainly would be a barrier. Robyn was unusually tall for a sixteen-year-old goddess, and he, sadly, irrefutably, was quite short for a boy of almost fifteen. Too young, too short—definitely obstacles.